"Wolitzer has re-imagined the bitingly funny inner life of a female appendage to a Great Man.... When this man says, 'My wife is truly my better half,' we find out how true it is."

—*The Boston Globe*

"Meg Wolitzer has ripened into a chanteuse of a writer, a Dietrich of fiction; her smoky humor, her languid look at life, her breathless sentences are all let loose a little more than usual in *The Wife* ... ld is John Updike's world, but her w ... 's hard to tell how old she is becaus ... s. I hope that *The Wife* might appeal t ... en and women. It is as much about the male psyche as it is about the woman's."

—*Los Angeles Times*

"Here are three words that land with a thunk: *gender, writing,* and *identity.* Yet in *The Wife,* Meg Wolitzer has fashioned a light-stepping, streamlined novel from just these dolorous, bitter-sounding themes. Maybe that's because she's set them all smoldering: rage might be the signature emotion of the powerless, but in Wolitzer's hands, rage is also very funny.... Wolitzer deploys a calm, seamless humor not found in her previous novels. The jokes don't barge in and tap us on the shoulder. Instead, they gradually accumulate, creating a rueful, sardonic atmosphere.... The book represents a real step forward for Wolitzer."

—*The New York Times Book Review*

"*The Wife* isn't just women's lit with feminist issues. Deft and passionate, it raises questions about misguided aims and the deals we make with ourselves and others to reach them."

—*Newsday*

"There are women in New York City who would kill to be Joan Castleman, the narrator of Wolitzer's frothy new comic novel.... [Wolitzer] paints an urbane picture of the book world of the '50s and '60s, when male writers would put down their pens and use their fists. Her hilarious gripes about marriage make this tale a pleasure best indulged in away from your better half."

—*People*

"Meg Wolitzer's sixth novel, *The Wife,* may be her boldest yet—an exploration of the passionate highs and divorce-threatening lows of Joan and Joe Castleman's forty-year marriage, delivered with signature wit, warmth, and a wise, woman's-eye view."

—*Elle*

"*The Wife* speeds along, glittering all the way, equal parts Jane Austen and Fran Lebowitz: epigrammatic, perceptive, ironic, smart, and ringing with truth. . . . [It] crackles with such intensity that it's hard to put down even for a few hours. . . . [Wolitzer] grabs hold of that brass ring of universal experience and takes us all along for the carousel ride."
—*The Buffalo News*

"A delicious read. . . . Philip Roth and John Updike have written tales like this, only we never hear the wife's perspective. Wolitzer creates just the right voice for her overlooked heroine. She is at once witty and angry, bitter and tearful. . . . It is [Wolitzer's] understanding of marriage that makes this tale such a delicious pleasure."
—*The Cleveland Plain Dealer*

"*The Wife* is a difficult book to put down, written with Wolitzer's customary wit and verve."
—*The Raleigh News & Observer*

"Robustly satisfying . . . Wolitzer makes it easy and delicious to look, listen, and, ultimately, to judge. The vicarious experience is great fun. . . . Wolitzer is a fine writer who just keeps getting better. She takes her time, allowing her characters to develop real heft as she guides us through the world of New York literary life. . . .Wolitzer manages to modernize her novel in the timeless way she presents marriage itself."
—UPI (United Press International)

"The author's observations are sharp, true, and unsparing. . . . *The Wife* is surprisingly brief and easy to read but should be, perhaps not so surprisingly, long-lasting in its impact. Those echoes will continue off the page, raising again and again some profound old questions that still have all too few answers, for a long time to come."
—*The Dallas Morning News*

"Diabolically smart and funny . . . Wolitzer choreographs [Joan Castleman's] ire into kung fu–precision moves to zap our every notion about gender and status, creativity and fame, individuality and marriage, deftly exposing the injustice, sorrow, and sheer absurdity of it all."
—*Booklist*

"A tale of witty disillusionment . . . Wolitzer's crisp pacing and dry wit carry us headlong into a devastating message about the price of love and fame. If it's a story we've heard before, the tale is as resonant as ever in Wolitzer's hands."
—*Publishers Weekly*

"[*The Wife*] features amazingly crafted prose. . . . Complete with a staggering twist ending, this is not one to miss."

—*Library Journal*

"A triumph of tone and observation, *The Wife* is a blithe, brilliant take on sexual politics and literary vanity (as well as sexual vanity and literary politics). It is the most engaging, funny, and satisfying novel the witty Meg Wolitzer has yet written."

—Lorrie Moore

"Meg Wolitzer's sixth novel is her best—an astonishingly dry, funny, and gripping account of two writers trapped for life in an evermore bizarre marriage. Every detail she evokes about an era in American literary life, from college campuses to writers' parties, is persuasive, hilarious, and even frightening, while the indignation she registers about her heroine's predicaments is lightened and even liberated by her perfect comic timing. *The Wife* is a milestone in the career of one of her generation's truest novelists."

—Adam Gopnik

"The wife of *The Wife* is a brilliantly conceived character, smart and foolish, tough-minded and weak-willed, witty and profoundly sad. And Meg Wolitzer's observations about gender and creativity: They are not only pointed, but penetrating. She has written some fine novels, but this is her best yet!"

—Susan Isaacs

"How does Meg Wolitzer do it? Write those witty, deft, hilarious sentences that add up to so much tragic understanding of life? *The Wife* is a funny, sad, beautiful novel. Unforgettable."

—Katha Pollitt

"Unflinching and acute, *The Wife* packs a ferocious punch. And that is before Wolitzer's stunning twist of an ending. If you've ever wondered what a female Philip Roth would write, here is the answer."

—Stacy Schiff

"Funny, smart, sad, gripping, and utterly surprising. Meg Wolitzer's subjects are the yin and yang of love and hate, and the various strange and shadowy transactions at the heart of a marriage—specifically a marriage between members of that cohort too young to snuggle easily into the certainties of the Greatest Generation and too old to catch feminism's wave."

—Kurt Andersen

"A complex, compelling portrait of a marriage that raises painful issues, even as it has you howling with recognition."

—Allison Pearson

THE WIFE

A Novel

MEG WOLITZER

SCRIBNER

New York   London   Toronto   Sydney   New Delhi

SCRIBNER

An Imprint of Simon & Schuster, Inc.
1230 Avenue of the Americas
New York, NY 10020

This Scribner trade paperback edition July 2018

SCRIBNER and design are registered trademarks of The Gale Group, Inc., used under license by Simon & Schuster, Inc., the publisher of this work.

For information about special discounts for bulk purchases, please contact Simon & Schuster Special Sales at 1-866-506-1949 or business@simonandschuster.com.

The Simon & Schuster Speakers Bureau can bring authors to your live event. For more information or to book an event, contact the Simon & Schuster Speakers Bureau at 1-866-248-3049 or visit our website at www.simonspeakers.com.

Designed by Kyoko Watanabe
Text set in Aldus

Manufactured in the United States of America

1 3 5 7 9 10 8 6 4 2

The Library of Congress has cataloged the Scribner edition as follows:

Wolitzer, Meg.
The wife: a novel/Meg Wolitzer.
p. cm.
1. Authors' spouses—Fiction. 2. Authorship—Collaboration—Fiction. 3. Fiction—Authorship—Fiction. 4. Married women—Fiction. 5. Novelists—Fiction. I. Title.
PS3573.O564 W5 2003
813'.54—dc21   2002036660

ISBN 978-1-9821-0636-2
ISBN 978-1-4165-8488-9 (ebook)

For Ilene Young

Chapter One

THE MOMENT I decided to leave him, the moment I thought, *enough*, we were thirty-five thousand feet above the ocean, hurtling forward but giving the illusion of stillness and tranquility. *Just like our marriage*, I could have said, but why ruin everything right now? Here we were in first-class splendor, tentatively separated from anxiety; there was no turbulence and the sky was bright, and somewhere among us, possibly, sat an air marshal in dull traveler's disguise, perhaps picking at a little dish of oily nuts or captivated by the zombie prose of the in-flight magazine. Drinks had already been served before takeoff, and we were both frankly bombed, our mouths half open, our heads tipped back. Women in uniform carried baskets up and down the aisles like a sexualized fleet of Red Riding Hoods.

"Will you have some cookies, Mr. Castleman?" a brunette asked him, leaning over with a pair of tongs, and as her breasts slid forward and then withdrew, I could see the ancient mechanism of arousal start to whir like a knife sharpener inside him, a sight I've witnessed thousands of times over all these decades. "*Mrs.* Castleman?" the woman asked me then, in afterthought, but I declined. I didn't want her cookies, or anything else.

We were on our way to the end of the marriage, heading toward the moment when I would finally get to yank the two-pronged plug from its holes, to turn away from the husband I'd lived with year after year. We were on our way to Helsinki, Finland, a place no one ever thinks about unless they're listening to Sibelius, or lying on the hot, wet slats of a sauna, or eating a bowl of reindeer. Cookies had been distributed, drinks decanted, and all around me, video screens had been arched and tilted. No one on this plane was fixated on death right now, the way we'd all been earlier, when, wrapped in the trauma of the roar and the fuel-stink and the distant, braying chorus of Furies trapped inside the engines, an entire planeload of minds—Economy, Business Class, and The Chosen Few—came together as one and urged this plane into the air like an audience willing a psychic's spoon to bend.

Of course, that spoon bent every single time, its tip drooping down like some top-heavy tulip. And though airplanes didn't *lift* every single time, tonight this one did. Mothers handed out activity books and little plastic bags of Cheerios with dusty sediment at the bottom; businessmen opened laptops and waited for the stuttering screens to settle. If he was on board, the phantom air marshal ate and stretched and adjusted his gun beneath a staticky little square of Dynel blanket, and our plane rose in the sky until it hung suspended at the desired altitude, and finally I decided for certain that I would leave my husband. Definitely. For sure. One hundred percent. Our three children were gone, gone, gone, and there would be no changing my mind, no chickening out.

He looked over at me suddenly, watched my face, and said, "What's the matter? You look a little . . . something."

"No. It's nothing," I told him. "Nothing worth talking about now, anyway," and he accepted this as a good-enough answer, returning to his plate of Tollhouse cookies, a small belch puffing his cheeks out froglike, briefly. It was difficult to disturb this man; he had everything he could possibly ever need.

He was Joseph Castleman, one of those men who own the world. You know the type I mean: those advertisements for themselves, those sleepwalking giants, roaming the earth and knocking over other men, women, furniture, villages. Why should they care? They own everything, the seas and mountains, the quivering volcanoes, the dainty, ruffling rivers. There are many varieties of this kind of man: Joe was the writer version, a short, wound-up, slack-bellied novelist who almost never slept, who loved to consume runny cheeses and whiskey and wine, all of which he used as a vessel to carry the pills that kept his blood lipids from congealing like yesterday's pan drippings, who was as entertaining as anyone I have ever known, who had no idea of how to take care of himself or anyone else, and who derived much of his style from *The Dylan Thomas Handbook of Personal Hygiene and Etiquette.*

There he sat beside me on Finnair flight 702, and whenever the brunette brought him something, he took it from her, every single cookie and smokehouse-treated nut and pair of spongy, throwaway slippers and steaming washcloth rolled Torah-tight. If that luscious cookie-woman had stripped to her waist and offered him one of her breasts, mashing the nipple into his mouth with the assured authority of a La Leche commandant, he would have taken it, no questions asked.

As a rule, the men who own the world are hyperactively sexual, though not necessarily with their wives. Back in the 1960s, Joe and I leaped into beds all the time, occasionally even during a lull at cocktail parties, barricading someone's bedroom door and then climbing a mountain of coats. People would come banging, wanting their coats back, and we'd laugh and shush each other and try to zip up and tuck in before letting them enter.

We hadn't had that in a long time, though if you'd seen us here on this airplane heading for Finland, you'd have assumed we were content, that we still touched each other's sluggish body parts at night.

"Listen, you want an extra pillow?" he asked me.

"No, I hate those doll pillows," I said. "Oh, and don't forget to stretch your legs like Dr. Krentz said."

You'd look at us—Joan and Joe Castleman of Weathermill, New York, and, currently, seats 3A and 3B—and you'd know exactly *why* we were traveling to Finland. You might even envy us—him for all the power vacuum-packed within his bulky, shopworn body, and me for my twenty-four-hour access to it, as though a famous and brilliant writer-husband is a convenience store for his wife, a place she can dip into anytime for a Big Gulp of astonishing intellect and wit and excitement.

People usually thought we were a "good" couple, and I suppose that once, a long, long time ago, back when the cave paintings were first sketched on the rough walls at Lascaux, back when the earth was uncharted and everything seemed hopeful, this was true. But soon enough we moved from the glory and self-love of any young couple to the green-algae swamp of what is delicately known as "later life." Though I'm now sixty-four years old and mostly as invisible to men as a swirl of dust motes, I used to be a slender, big-titted blond girl with a certain shyness that drew Joe toward me like a hypnotized chicken.

I don't flatter myself; Joe was *always* drawn to women, all kinds of them, right from the moment he entered the world in 1930, via the wind tunnel of his mother's birth canal. Lorna Castleman, the mother-in-law I never met, was overweight, sentimentally poetic and possessive, loving her son with a lover's exclusivity. (Some of the men who own the world, on the other hand, were *ignored* throughout their childhoods—left sandwichless at lunchtime in bleak school yards.)

Lorna not only loved him, but so did her two sisters who shared their Brooklyn apartment, along with Joe's grandmother Mims, a woman built like a footstool, whose claim to fame was that she made "a mean brisket." His father, Martin, a perpetually sighing and ineffectual man, died of a heart attack at his shoe store when Joe was seven, leaving him a captive of this peculiar womanly civilization.

It was typical, the way they told him his father was dead. Joe had just come home from school and, finding the apartment unlocked, he let himself in. No one else was home, which was unusual for a household that always seemed to contain some woman or other, hunched and busy as a wood sprite. Joe sat down at the kitchen table and ate his afternoon snack of yellow sponge cake in the moony, stupefied way that children have, a constellation of crumbs on the lips and chin.

Soon the door to the apartment swung open again and the women piled in. Joe heard crying, the emphatic blowing of noses, and then they appeared in the kitchen, crowding around the table. Their faces were inflamed, their eyes bloodshot, their carefully constructed hairdos destroyed. Something big had happened, he knew, and a sense of drama rolled inside him, almost pleasurably at first, though that would immediately change.

Lorna Castleman knelt down beside her son's chair, as though about to propose. "Oh, my brave little fella," she said in a hoarse whisper, tapping her finger adhesively against his lips to remove crumbs, "it's just us now."

And it *was* just them, the women and the boy. He was completely on his own in this female world. Aunt Lois was a hypochondriac who spent her days in the company of a home medical encyclopedia, poring over the sensual names of diseases. Aunt Viv was perpetually man-obsessed and suggestive, forever turning around to display a white length of back revealed in an unclenched zipper's jaw. Tiny, ancient Grandmother Mims was in the middle of it all, commandeering the kitchen, triumphantly yanking a meat thermometer from a roast as though it were Excalibur.

Joe was left to wander the apartment like a survivor of a wreck he couldn't even remember, searching for other forgetful survivors. But there were none; he was *it*, the beloved boy who would eventually grow up and become one of those traitors, those cologne-doused rats. Lorna had been betrayed by her husband's early death, which had arrived with no preamble or warning. Aunt Lois had been betrayed by her own absence of sensation, by the fact that she'd never felt a thing for any man except, from afar, Clark Gable, with his broad shoulders and easy-grip-during-sex jug ears. Aunt Viv had been betrayed by legions of men—sleepy, sexy, toying men who telephoned the house at all hours, or wrote her letters from overseas, where they were stationed. The women who surrounded Joe were *furious* at men, they insisted, yet they also insisted that he was exempt from their fury. Him they loved. He was hardly a man yet, this small, bright boy with the genitals like marzipan fruit and the dark, girlish curls and the precocious reading skills and, since his father died, the sudden inability to sleep at night. He'd roll around in bed for a while trying to think soothing thoughts about baseball or the bright, welcoming pages of comic books, but always he ended up picturing his father, Martin, standing on a puff of cloud in heaven and sadly holding out a pair of saddle shoes still nestled in their box.

Finally, around midnight, Joe would give in to his insomnia, getting up and going into the dark living room, playing a game of jacks alone in the middle of the rag rug. During the day he sat on that same rug at the women's feet while they kicked off their pumps. As he listened to their unhappy, overlapping sagas, he knew that in some unstated way he ruled the roost and always would.

When Joe was finally sprung from the household, he found himself both enormously relieved and fully educated. He knew some things about women now: their sighs, their undergarments, their monthly miseries, their quest for chocolate, their cutting remarks, their spiny pink curlers, the time line of their bodies, which he'd viewed in unsparing detail. This was what would be in store for him if he fell for a woman one day. He'd be forced to watch her shift and change and collapse over time; he'd be helpless to stop it from happening. Sure, she might be desirable now, but one day she would be nothing but a giver of brisket. So he chose to *forget* what he knew, to pretend that the knowledge had never penetrated his small, perfect head, and he left this all-female revue and stepped onto the creaking train that sweeps people from their lesser boroughs into the thrilling chaos of the only borough that really counts: Staten Island.

Just a joke.

Manhattan, 1948. Joe rises from the fumes of the subway and enters the gates of Columbia University, meeting up with other brainy, soulful boys. Declaring himself an English major, he joins the staff of the undergraduate literary magazine and immediately publishes a story about an old woman who thinks back on her life in a Russian village (wormy potatoes, frozen toes, etc., etc.). The story is laughable and poorly written, as his critics will later point out while pawing through crates of his juvenilia. However, a few of them will insist that the *exuberance* of Joe Castleman's fiction is already in place. He trembles with excitement, loving his new life, enjoying the feverish pleasure of going with college friends to Ling Palace in Chinatown and ingesting his first prawns in black-bean sauce—his first prawns of any kind, in fact, for nothing that calls a shell its home has ever entered Joe Castleman's lips.

Those lips also receive the lips and tongue of his first female, and in short order his virginity is removed with the crack precision of a dental extraction. The remover is a needy but energetic girl named Bonnie Lamp who attends Barnard College, where, according to Joe and his friends, she has been given a merit scholarship in nymphomania. Joe is captivated by doe-eyed Bonnie Lamp, as well as by the amazing act of sexual intercourse. And, by association, he's captivated by himself. After all, why shouldn't he be? Everyone else is.

When he makes love to Bonnie, entering and slowly exiting, he's impressed by the way their interlocking parts emit little, rhythmic *clicks*, like a distant secretary's heels walking across linoleum. He's also fascinated by the other sounds Bonnie Lamp makes independently. In her sleep she seems to mew like a kitten, and he watches her with a strange mixture of tenderness and condescension, imagining that she's dreaming about a ball of yarn, a plate of milk.

A ball of yarn, a plate of milk, and thou, he thinks, in love with words, with women. Their pliant bodies fascinate him—all those swells and flourishes. His own body fascinates him equally, and when his roommate is elsewhere, Joe takes the mirror down from its nail on the wall and gets a long look at himself: his chest with its careless littering of dark hair, his torso, his surprisingly large penis for such a short and wiry person.

He imagines his own circumcision, so many years earlier, sees himself struggle in a strange bearded man's arms, accepting a thick pinkie finger dipped in kosher wine, then sucking wildly on that pinkie, mining it for nonexistent fluid, and instead finding only a whorled surface with no hidden pinhole source of milk. But in this image the painting of sweet wine down his gullet dazes him, makes a hash of all the proud faces around him. His eight-day-old eyes close, then open, then close again, and eighteen years later he awakens, a grown man.

Time passes for Joe Castleman, and he stays on at Columbia for graduate school, and during this period there's a shift in the environment. It's not just the change of seasons, or the continual bloom of new buildings with their crosshatches of scaffolding. Nor is it simply the small socialist gatherings Joe attends, though he hates to be a joiner, can't stand to be part of a group, even for a cause he believes in like this one, sitting earnest and cross-legged on someone's mildewed carpet and just listening, just taking information in, not offering anything of his own. And it's not only the increasing drumbeat of early 1950s bohemia, which leads Joe into a few narrow, underlit bongo clubs, where he develops an instant and lifelong taste for smoking grass. It's more that the world is truly opening up to him, oysterlike, and he walks inside it, tentatively touching the smooth ridges of its cavity, taking a dry bath in its silver light.

There were moments during our marriage when Joe seemed unaware of his power, and those were the moments when he was at his best. By the time he hit middle age, he was big and ambling and casual, walking around in a beige fisherman's sweater that never disguised his gut but merely cradled it indulgently, letting it swing when he walked, when he entered living rooms or restaurants or lecture halls, when he showed up at Schuyler's

General Store in our town of Weathermill, New York, purchasing a new supply of Hostess Sno-Balls, those pink, coconut-rolled, entirely unnatural marshmallow domes to which he was inexplicably addicted.

Picture Joe Castleman at Schuyler's on a Saturday afternoon, purchasing a fresh cellophane packet of his favorite treat and benignly patting the store's resident arthritic dog.

"Afternoon, Joe," Schuyler himself would say, an old stick of a man with a delft-blue, weepy eye. "How's the work?"

"Oh, I'm trying the best I can, Schuyler, for what it's worth," Joe would reply with a deep sigh. "Which isn't much."

Joe always did self-doubt very well. He appeared vulnerable and tormented throughout much of the fifties, sixties, seventies, eighties, and the first part of the nineties, whether he was drunk or not drunk, reviewed badly or favorably, shunned or loved. But what exactly was the source of his torment? Unlike his old friend the eminent novelist Lev Bresner, a Holocaust survivor and painstaking chronicler of an early childhood spent as a prisoner in a death camp, Joe had no one, specifically, to blame. Lev, with the gleaming, deep eyes, should have won the Nobel Prize for Sadness, instead of for Literature. (Though I've always admired Lev Bresner, I've never thought his novels were all they were cracked up to be. To admit this aloud, say, at dinner among friends, would be like standing up and declaring, "I like to suck on little boys.") It's Lev's subject, not his writing, that makes you flinch and tremble and dread turning the page.

Lev is authentically tortured; long ago, when Joe and I entertained regularly, he and his wife, Tosha, would come to our house for the weekend and he'd lie on our living room couch with an ice pack on his head and I would tell the kids *shush*, and they would drag their noisemaking toys out of the room, the doll that chattered its declarations of love, the little wooden spaniel that clacked when you pulled it on a string.

"Lev needs quiet," I would tell them. "Go upstairs, girls. Go on, David, you too." The children would stand for an extra moment at the foot of the stairs, unmoving, transfixed. *"Go,"* I would urge them, and finally, reluctantly, they would ascend.

"Tenk you, Joan," Lev would say in his heavy voice. "I am weary."

He would say it and it would be *allowed.* Anything would be allowed of Lev Bresner.

But Joe could never say he was weary; what did he have to be weary about? Unlike Lev, life had spared Joe the trauma of the Holocaust; he had bypassed it easily by being a charming little boy playing hearts with his mother and his aunts in Brooklyn while Hitler goose-stepped across another continent. And then, during the Korean War, Joe accidentally shot himself in the ankle with an M-1 during basic training, spending ten days being indulged by nurses and scraping the skin off tapioca pudding in the infirmary before being sent home.

No, he couldn't blame war for his unhappiness, so he blamed his mother, the woman I never met, but who has been described to me by Joe in detail over the years.

One thing I know about Lorna Castleman is that, unlike her two sisters or her mother, she was fat. When you're very young, a mother's fatness might make you feel safe, even proud. You flush hot with pride at the idea that your mother is the biggest mother you know; with haughty distaste you think of your friends' mothers, those unhuggable shrimps.

Later, according to Joe, you transfer this feeling onto your father. Your father should be big and fierce if possible, a wide-shouldered wonder taking you into his office or his store or wherever it is he spends his gloomy, manly days, lifting you into the air and letting the women who also work there fuss over you, giving you linty sourballs, probably the kind that no one likes: *pineapple.* Your father should be a powerhouse; you can ignore the shiny, rapidly enlarging spot on his skull, the grunts he makes when he eats his daily plate of pan-fried liver. He might be quiet and retiring, but still he's as strong as a draft animal, and when his urine hits the bowl it trembles the water, and the sound rings out like a brook that winds wondrously through all the streets of Brooklyn.

Meanwhile, you're suddenly *horrified* by your fat mother—this woman who can work her way through an entire Ebinger's Blackout Cake in its green windowed box—the thick spackled icing, the porous, pitch-dark interior—in ten minutes, *easy*, without feeling any shame. You're repelled by the mother with whom you used to stroll the neighborhood; she was always powdered and perfumed and large but noble: a sofa that walked.

You used to love her madly, wanted to marry her, tried to figure out whether or not that would be technically possible, and if it *were* possible that you might someday stand beside her and work a ring onto her finger, you wondered whether you could ever be worthy of her. Lorna, your mother, in her busy floral dresses bought at a store in Flatbush called the La Beauté House of Discount Fashions for Large Women, was everything to you.

But now life is different. Suddenly you want your mother to be small, constructed of wishbones only. Narrow, a size 2. Fragile but beautiful. Why can't she look more like Manny Gumpert's mother, a stylish woman whose body is as small and compressed as a hummingbird's? Why can't she just *go away*?

But she didn't, not for a long, long time. For years after poor Martin Castleman dropped dead in his shoe store, slumping down in his low vinyl seat with a girl's leg locked between his own, and a box of saddle shoes in his hands, Joe was left with his mother and the other women. She was there in his life until Joe was fully grown and had married his first wife, Carol, and only then, while circulating at Joe and Carol's wedding, did Lorna disappear. It was a heart attack that came out of the blue, just like her husband's had, leaving newlywed Joe orphaned and fully aware of his own inherited faulty pump. His mother's death was very upsetting, Joe said, though not as traumatic as his father's.

But I have to admit here that when he told me this story, my first, awful thought was: *good material*.

I pictured his big, flushed mother in high spirits; the aunts with their fancy dresses and clutch bags, the waiters circling with their trays of rainbow sherbet in frosted silver cups; I even heard the strands of sinuous klezmer music playing as he and his bride, Carol, danced.

"I don't really understand something," I once said, early on in our own marriage. "Why did you even *marry* Carol in the first place?"

"Because it was what you *did*," he told me.

But the thing was—or at least it was the thing that Joe would decide later—Carol was insane. Locked-ward certifiable, a classic lunatic. You can say this freely about a man's first wife, and the other men in the room will nod vigorously; they understand exactly what you're talking about. All first wives are crazy— violently and eye-rollingly so. They writhe, they moan, they snap into flame and crumple, they decompose before your eyes. Probably, Joe said, Carol was already crazy by the time he first met her at a lonesome coffee shop at 2 A.M., one of those Hopper's *Nighthawks* type of places where everyone who's slumped over the just-sponged counter looks like they might have a tragic life-story to tell if you make the mistake of agreeing to listen.

But Joe didn't understand this about Carol yet. He was back from basic training and his accidental self-injury. He was alone and open, and so when he first met her that night he let himself be charmed by the peculiar appeal of the childlike woman with the brown hair cut across the forehead in neat bangs and the feet that didn't even reach the floor. In her doll-hands she held a thick book: *The Collected Writings of Simone Weil.* Actually, it was the *Écrits* of Simone Weil, in the original French. He was immediately impressed, calling upon the one bit of obscure Simone Weil trivia that he knew—perhaps an apocryphal tidbit, but sworn to him by a college friend to be true.

"Did you know," he said to this girl Carol Welchak who happened to be sitting on the stool next to his, "that Simone Weil was afraid of fruit?"

She gave him a fishy look. "Oh, yeah, *right*."

"No, no, it's true," Joe insisted. "I swear to God. Simone Weil was afraid of fruit. I guess you could say she was a fructophobe."

Both of them began to laugh, and the girl picked up a slice of orange that was lying ignored on the edge of her plate of pancakes. "Come here, Simone, *ma chérie*," she said in a French accent. "Come and try my lovely orange!"

Joe was charmed. What a find! Apparently the world was full of girls like this, each of them simmering in her own stewpot, waiting to be savored by the men who would come by, lift their lids, and inhale.

"So what are you doing here by yourself in the middle of the night?" he asked. On Joe's other side, a longshoreman scratched at his rashy neck, making Joe recoil and try to move a little bit closer to the girl, although of course he couldn't, for the stool was bolted to the linoleum.

"I'm escaping from my roommate," said Carol. "She's a harpist, and she practices all night. Sometimes I wake up before morning and for a minute I think I'm dead, and that angels are flapping around playing music at the foot of my bed."

"That must be gratifying," Joe said. "Thinking that there *is* a heaven, and they've let you in."

"Believe me," said Carol, "I was a lot more gratified the day they let me into Sarah Lawrence."

"Ah, a Sarah Lawrence girl," he said with pleasure, deciding at that moment that she was a highly creative type, her hands damp with both acrylic paint from art class and ambrosia from some middle-of-the-night winter-solstice ritual. He also imagined her to be like one of those Mongolian sexual acrobats he'd read about, turning midair somersaults that would vault her directly and miraculously onto the pivot of his penis: *ka-ching!*

"Well, I used to be a Sarah Lawrence girl," she said. "I already graduated. So tell me, whoever you are," she went on, "what are *you* doing here in the middle of the night?"

It was clear that she didn't yet get it, didn't yet know that men like Joe—brash men who loved the free verse of their own voices and the smeared gleam of their reflections in their shoes—went to lonesome coffee shops in the middle of the night simply because they could. And New York City, at that particular moment in time, 1953, was a spectacular place in which to take a walk in the middle of the night if you were a young, ambitious, confident man. The city was constructed of neon lettering and bridge lights and subway steam huffing in checkerboard gusts up through vents into the street. Desperately kissing couples seemed to have been strategically stationed at every lamppost.

"What am I doing here?" Joe answered. "I'm an insomniac. I can't sleep at night, so I get up and go for a walk. What I do is pretend that the whole city is my apartment. Over there's the bathroom"—he pointed out the window. "And over in *that* direction is the closet where I keep my jackets."

"And this must be the kitchen, I guess," Carol said. "You just came in to get yourself a cup of coffee."

"Exactly," he said, smiling at her. "Let's see if there's anything in the fridge."

They swiveled their stools restlessly back and forth in a little mating dance. Then they got their checks and paid, each of them grabbing a handful of those chalk-dusted mint pillows that for some reason sit in a straw basket beside every coffee-shop cash register in the world, as though all the coffee-shop owners had gotten together and agreed on this protocol. And then he held open the door for her and together they headed out into the night. With Joe by her side, both of them sucking mint pillows and purifying their mouths for the kiss that was likely to come sooner or later, Carol could begin to enjoy the late-night wilds of the city in a way she never could when she was alone. What euphoria to know what it meant to relax and not worry, to be part of something enormous and vital. The night was cold, and the points of the buildings seemed to have been freshly sharpened. He held her tiny white hand, and together they made the grand tour through shuttered streets, because he was one of those men, and all of it was his.

* * *

"We'll be landing soon," the brunette flight attendant said almost apologetically as she strolled the aisle of our plane. By now, of course, nine hours into it, the entire experience of the flight had moved from the clean, expectant pleasure that was there at the outset to the cranky, restless filth that occurred when you stayed within a small space for too long. The air, once so antiseptic, was now home to a million farts and corn chips and moist towelettes. Clothes were crushed; people bore corrugations on their cheeks from where they had slept against the seat or on their own crumpled jackets. And even the brunette flight attendant, who had earlier seemed such a seduction to Joe, now looked like a tired hooker who wants to call it quits. She had no more cookies to offer; her basket was empty. Instead, she returned to her seat in the back, and I saw her strap herself in and squirt breath freshener into her mouth.

We were on our own again. Rows and rows behind us, separated by curtains, sat Joe's editor, Sylvie Blacker, and two young publicists, along with Joe's agent, Irwin Clay. Joe had no significant relationships with any of them. They were all of very recent vintage; his longtime editor, Hal, had died, and his former agent had retired, and he'd been passed on to other people, some of whom had already left their jobs, and these particular people were here not because they were close to Joe but because it was appropriate for them to come, to take partial credit by association. Joe's friends and the rest of our family had been left behind; he'd told them it wasn't necessary that they come to Finland, that there was really no point to it, that he'd be home soon enough and he'd tell them all about it, and so of course they'd had to listen to him. The airplane began to lower through a thatch of clouds, bringing Joe and me and everyone else down toward a small, beautiful, unfamiliar city in Scandinavia at the end of autumn.

"Are you okay?" I asked Joe, who always became frightened during the quiet anticlimax of a descent, when it seemed as though the engines were conking out and the plane was coasting like a child's balsa-wood flier.

He nodded and said, "Yeah, thanks, Joan, I'm fine."

I hadn't asked him the question out of actual concern; it was more of a marital reflex. All over the world, husbands and wives routinely and somewhat pointlessly ask one another: *Are you okay?* It's part of the contract; it's the thing to do, because it implies that you care, that you're paying attention, when in fact you might be deeply and relentlessly bored. Joe actually looked calm, I saw, though some of that was probably a side effect of sleep deprivation. I couldn't remember the last time he had gotten a decent night's sleep. I'd always known him to be an insomniac, but every year his sleeplessness inevitably reached a kind of crisis right before the winner of the Helsinki Prize was announced.

Always, each year, you hear stories about how some winner or other assumed the call was a prank. There are legendary tales of writers being shaken from sleep by a ringing telephone and cursing the man with the accent on the phone, telling him, "Do you know what time it is?" Only then, lifting to the surface of consciousness, did they realize what the call was about, that it was genuine, and that it meant that their life would change shape forever.

This wasn't the Nobel prize, of course; it was a few steps down, a defiant stepchild that had enhanced its reputation over time by the sheer power of its prize money, which this year was the equivalent of $525,000. It wasn't the Nobel, just as Finland wasn't Sweden. But still the prize was an extravagant honor and thrill. It elevated you—if not to Stockholm heights, then at least partway up.

All of them, the novelists, the story writers, the poets, desperately long to win. If there is a prize, then there is someone somewhere on earth who desires it. Grown men pace their homes and scheme about ways to win things, and small children hyperventilate over the prospect of gold-plated trophies for penmanship, for swimming, for just being cheerful. Maybe other life-forms give out awards, too, and we just don't know it: Best All-Round Flatworm; Most Helpful Crow.

Several of Joe's friends had been talking to him about the Helsinki Prize for months. "This year," said his friend Harry Jacklin, "you're going to get it. You're getting old, Joe. You shall wear the bottoms of your trousers rolled. They don't want to overlook you; it would be egg on their faces."

"You mean egg on *my* face," said Joe.

"No, *theirs*," insisted Harry, whose own field was poetry, which pretty much guaranteed that he would remain entirely unknown and broke forever. Even so, he was deeply competitive; a mean vein of spite ran through him, as it did through all of the poets Joe knew. It always seemed that the smaller the pie, the greater the need to have more of it.

"I'm not going to win," Joe said to Harry. "You've told me I would win for three years straight. You're like the boy who cried wolf."

"It needed time," said Harry. "Now I get their strategy. See, they were sitting there in Helsinki, eating their smoked fish and waiting. Their plan was that if you were still alive by now, they'd give it to you. You're politically correct, and that really counts these days, at least as far as the Helsinki is concerned. You've got that extra gene, that sensitivity toward women. That unwillingness to objectify the opposite sex, isn't that what they say about you? That you invent a female character and put her in a marriage, a family, a king-sized bed in the suburbs, and yet you don't feel the need to describe . . . I don't know, her *pubic hair* in literary terms: 'a burnt-sienna nimbus,' or whatever, like the rest of your crowd would."

"I don't have a 'crowd,' " said Joe.

"You know what I'm saying," Harry went on. "You mix in all this *feminism*, if you want to call it that—even though it always makes me think of dykes with chain saws. You're an original, Joe! A great writer who isn't a total prick. You, you're fifty percent prick, fifty percent pussy."

"Ha!" said Joe. "That's so kind of you to say. And lyrical, too."

But other friends agreed with the poet's logic, pointing out that this year there weren't too many obvious contenders for the Helsinki Prize anywhere in the world. In America, it had been a year of literary deaths, one after the other, men whom Joe had known since the fifties, when they used to gather sometimes for socialist meetings. A decade later they gathered at marathon, all-night readings whose purpose was to protest the war in Vietnam and suck all the energy out of the audience. And then they gathered again in the early eighties after they had all sheepishly agreed to pose for ads for a fearfully expensive wristwatch manufactured by an old, elegant German company with an unsavory Nazi history. And then, finally, they began to gather for one another's funerals. Every single one of those writers, Joe noticed at the service for playwright Don Lofting, still wore the German wristwatches they'd been given.

Harry Jacklin was right that there were few of Joe's peers left standing who deserved the prize, few writers whose body of work was such a marbled block of muscle. Lev Bresner's Helsinki moment had come seven years earlier—no surprise at all, it had been expected for a long time—but even so, that news had sent Joe to bed in a darkened room for days, subsisting mostly on barbiturates and scotch. Then, three years later, Lev had miraculously gone on to win the Nobel prize, and to this day Joe could hardly bear to talk about it.

The Nobel prize was well beyond Joe; we both knew that, and somehow we'd both accepted it. Though he was popular in Europe, his work didn't traverse the globe in the important way it would have needed to. He was American and introspective and always taking his own pulse on the page. As Harry had said, he was politically correct, yet somehow he wasn't at all political. Even the Helsinki Prize was a reach. Yet critics had always admired Joe's vision of contemporary American marriage, which seemed to plumb the female sensibility as thoroughly as it did the male, but amazingly without venom, without blame. And early on in his career, his novels had made the leap into Europe, where he was considered even more important than in the States. Joe's work was from the old, postwar, "marital" school—husbands and wives stranded in tiny apartments or boxy, drafty colonials on suburban streets with names like Bethany Court or Yellow Swallow Drive. The men were deep but sour, the women sad and lovely, the children disaffected. The families were crumbling, full of factions, American. Joe included his own life, using details from his childhood and his early adulthood and then his two marriages.

His novels were translated into dozens of languages, and the shelf in his study was lined with these books in translation. There was his first novel, *The Walnut*, that slender book from a much more innocent time, about a married professor and his best student who fall in love, leading to an event that causes the professor to hurriedly abandon his wife and child, flee to New York City with the student, and eventually marry her. This book is pure autobiography—the story of the two of us and Joe's first wife, Carol.

Beside it on the shelf were the foreign versions of *The Walnut*, variously called *La Noix, Die Walnuß, La Noce, La Nuez,* and *Valnot.* And then there was his Pulitzer prize–winning book *Overtime,* also called *Heures Supplémentaires, Überstunden, Horas Adicionales,* and *Overtid.* The Pulitzer prize had been restorative, a bracing snootful of pleasure, but it was so many years ago that even that dose of gratification was by now forgotten.

In the author photograph on the back of *Overtime,* Joe still had his thick head of floppy black hair, which sometimes, to my surprise, I still grieve for. It long ago thinned out and went white, but back then it used to fall across his face, and I would push it away so I could see his eyes. He was attractive and thin as a greyhound in the early years, his stomach hard and concave. His erections were endless, held aloft by some woman's invisible hand (not necessarily mine), a muse who whispered into his hot ear, *You're brilliant.* Decades have elapsed since the Pulitzer, though there have been other American awards, too, prizes that took Joe to chicken-breast luncheons in the bland banquet rooms of New York hotels to claim his loot and give a speech, while I sat quietly watching with the other wives and the occasional husband. But now it was time for another prize, a big one. He needed the fuel it would provide, the sumptuous, caloric pleasure and the accompanying delirium.

On the night before the call from Helsinki would come, *if* it was going to come, I went to bed early. Joe, of course, was still prowling the house. It is an old house, painted white and well kept, standing behind a low stone wall tufted with moss, and it dates back to 1790. There are many rooms for a sleepless man to walk through. I knew that if I were a better person, I would have stayed up with him, the way I used to do each year. But I was tired, and longed for sleep the way I used to long for the press of our two bodies. And besides, I didn't want to go through this yet again. I could hear him scrabble around downstairs like a hamster, opening drawers in the kitchen and taking things out, banging together what sounded like a cheese grater and a spoon, in an obvious, pathetic attempt to wake me up.

I knew how he operated; I knew everything about him, the way wives do. I even knew the inside of him, having been there that day in Dr. Ruffner's office to review the footage of Joe's colon. We sat and watched light travel through his most intimate inner tubing, and after that we were really bound together for life. When you watch your husband's colon at work, at play, see the shy, starburst retraction of his sphincter, the amble of barium through an endless human hose, then you know that he is truly yours, and you are his.

And then, years later, in the company of a small, elegant, Brahmin cardiologist named Dr. Vikram, I had the chance to see sonograms of Joe's heart, that defective, overachieving fist, its mitral valve closing sloppily, almost drunkenly.

And I knew him again tonight, could see the way his mind was forming ideas, hunches.

"I might actually have won this time," Joe had said to me at dinner. We were eating Cornish game hens, I remember, with their pileup of tiny bones on the plate afterward. "Harry thinks so. Louise does too."

"Oh, they always think so," I said.

"Don't you think it even *might* be the case, Joan?" he asked.

"I don't know."

"Just give me a percentage," he said.

"You want me to give you a percentage of your chances of winning the Helsinki Prize?" Joe nodded. On the table stood a milk container, and at that moment my eye happened to leap to it and so I said, "Two percent."

"You think I have a *two percent* chance of winning?" he asked glumly.

"Yes."

"Oh, fuck it," he said, and then I shrugged and said I was sorry, and told him I was going to bed.

So there I lay, knowing I had extraordinary power in this moment of withholding, knowing that I ought to go to him, to keep him company as he kept vigil. But instead I just lay there, fully awake, and a very long time passed, and finally I heard his footsteps on the old, narrow stairs. If I wouldn't come to him, then he would come to me. Wives are meant to be sources of comfort, showering it like wedding rice. I used to do this superbly for him and for all three of our children, and mostly I enjoyed the job.

I always sat up with Joe when he agonized, and with the kids during their various bad dreams, and even during a mescaline trip our daughter Alice once took, in which all of her childhood stuffed animals came to life and mocked her. She was so frightened that night, and she clung to me like a marsupial, or like a much younger child, saying, "Mom, Mom, help me, *please*, help me!"

Her cry was plaintive and almost unbearable, but like all mothers, I held on tight with racing heart and poker face, babbling an endless cycle of motherly white noise at her, and eventually she came down from the trip and was able to sleep.

And I did this kind of thing again and again during our son David's explosive outbursts, which have taken place periodically over the years. In school, where they told us he was brilliant but emotionally troubled, he lashed out at other kids. In his twenties and thirties there have been bar brawls and street fights, and once he repeatedly hit his recovering-heroin-addict girlfriend with a heavy loaf of bread. This is our heartbreak: David is a rangy man in his late thirties now, alternately indifferent and angry, a handsome nighttime word processor at a New York law firm who has no other ambitions, no hopes for happiness or glory. But he is one of *my* children; Joe and I made him. And so when, in moments of repentance, he has come to me, I've negated his claims of worthlessness, countering them not with any hard evidence, but simply with my quiet, effective presence in a nightgown, and the compassion that rolls out easily in the face of the suffering of one's own child.

I always made myself available, both to David and to his sisters, Susannah and Alice, and I was good at it. I spoke softly to them, and when the situation called for it I would stroke their hair and bring them cups of midnight water.

Now, late at night in the house, waiting and anxious, Joe wanted me to stroke *his* hair, to push it away from his eyes the way I used to do. He reached the landing and came into the bedroom, lying down and putting his arms around me while I pretended to be asleep. I could tell, instinctively, that he didn't really want this touch to spread out into sex, but that he was running out of alternatives. Sex used to be a good idea, one we both liked equally, the coats on somebody's bed spilling to the floor, a mouth on a breast, a mouth on a penis. Occasionally, afterward, we would discuss the high hilarity of all these objectified pornographic images, their primitive quality, the way they equalized us, smacked and flattened our entire species into one pancake of desires and fluids and predictable outlets for similar urges.

Urges. We both had them, Joe and I, and usually we weren't embarrassed by them, though once, long ago, he'd said to me,

"You could kill a crocodile with those thighs, Joan," so severe was my grip on him, and I was embarrassed. Women don't want to have the tungsten strength of their sexual desire pointed out to them; it's supposed to go unnoticed, like the passing of gas. For a long time I was as strongly sexual as he was, and then suddenly, somewhere in my forties, I realized that I *wasn't* anymore, that it had simply gone away, taking with it my happiness, my willingness, my sense of being Joe Castleman's other half.

But on this night of anticipation, though we'd barely touched each other in ages—had it been a whole year?—Joe suddenly seemed to find a hidden stash of longing and nostalgia inside himself, and so he slid a hand to my breast, and I felt the nipple collect itself into an obedient knot.

"Don't do this," I said, no longer pretending to be asleep.

"Don't do what?" He knew what.

"Use me because you can't sleep," I said.

"I'm not *using* you, Joan," he said, but he dropped his hand. "You're so inflammatory. I just wanted to touch you."

"You wanted to find something to do with yourself," I said, sitting up in bed. "You are completely nuts and climbing the walls."

"All right, fine, maybe I am, but I don't understand why you're *not*," he said. "This is one of those nights when we find out if the world has passed me by."

"You know it hasn't," I said. "There's so much proof of that; how much do you need? You own the entire world, Joe. You're still up there. You still matter."

But he shook his head. "Nah," he said. "I don't feel it at all."

I looked at him, realizing I was still able to extract some tenderness toward him from inside myself. Here was a moment of it, a core sample lifted from me in the middle of the night. I could be furious at him, could dislike him and think of devious psychological ways to punish him, could go to bed early and leave him to wander our big old house forlornly, but despite my better instincts, here I was.

"Do you know that you're a totally pathetic person?" I said.

"I trust you mean 'pathetic' in the best sense of the word," said Joe with a slight smile.

"Oh yes," I assured him. "Absolutely."

Joe lay with his head against my shoulder, and we settled in for what remained of the night. If the sun rose in the morning and we were still lying here like this, the telephone having stayed silent, he would know that another year had passed and he hadn't won the Helsinki Prize, and that most likely he never would. But still, somehow, everything would be all right, because he had a wife, which is something that everyone needs.

Joe once told me he felt a little sorry for women, who only got husbands. Husbands tried to help by giving answers, being logical, stubbornly applying force as though it were a glue gun. Or else they didn't try to help at all, for they were somewhere else entirely, out walking in the world by themselves. But wives, oh wives, when they weren't being bitter or melancholy or counting the beads on their abacus of disappointment, they could take care of you with delicate and effortless ease.

At five-twenty in the morning, my sleep was very deep, occasionally punctuated by the usual barnyard assortment of snorts and sighs that most people my age begin to make. But Joe was lying wide awake beside me then, when the telephone rang.

Later, when telling the story to friends, he would revise the events of the night, putting himself in the role of an innocent sleeper startled awake by the phone. In this idealized version, the phone rang and he sat up in bed, disoriented ("Wha . . . ? Wha . . . ?"), and his hand reached out and grabbed for the phone, knocking over a glass of water. When he eventually spoke into the receiver, it was in a mush-mouthed, unprepared voice. And I, beside him, was supposed to have gasped and embraced him when I heard the news ("Oh Joe, Joe, you've worked so hard for this. . . ."), and then we both began to cry.

He had to tell it this way, otherwise he would have seemed too eager, like someone who had been confident that the call from Finland really *would* arrive this time.

The truth was that Joe reached for the phone in one swift movement, knocking over nothing. His voice was strong when he said hello. The connection was infused with a crackle and the slightest quality that suggested both voices were trapped in a time-delay tunnel.

A foreign man spoke, his tone both meek and hearty at once. He asked for Mr. Castleman, "Mr. *Yoseph* Castleman," he specified, and then he told him the news. Joe swallowed, felt his chest expand with an aching pride that seemed a troubling, distant relative of heart attacks; he pressed his palm flat against his heart, shushing it.

"Can my wife, Joan, get on the extension?" Joe asked Teuvo Halonen, the acting president of the Finnish Academy of Letters. "I think she should hear this too."

"Of course," the Finn said.

By this time, I was sitting up in bed and staring at Joe with wild eyes, my own heart going nuts, chemicals flooding into me from every port, and I scuttled down the hall in my nightgown to pick up the phone in what used to be Susannah's room.

"Hello," I said into my daughter's pink Princess phone. "This is Joan Castleman." I sat on her bed beneath the bookshelf with its ancient, pristine sets of Nancy Drews and Trixie Beldens.

"Hello, *Yoan*—that is, Mrs. Castleman. I am hearing that you wish to be part of this conversation," said Mr. Halonen. "Well, your husband is our choice for this year's prize."

I gasped. "Whoa!" I said. "Oh! Oh my God!"

"He is a wonderful writer," continued Halonen calmly, "who deserves these accolades. We are honored to have had the opportunity to choose this gentleman, for we find his work to have been heartbreakingly beautiful and important over the years. His career has a great span to it; he has grown in stature, and it has been a pleasure to observe. Each book is increasingly mature. I must say, my personal favorite is *Pantomime*, for in many ways the characters of Louis and Margaret Strickler remind me of myself and my wife, Pippa. So fallible! So human! You should know," he went on, "that later today, Mrs. Castleman, you shall be fending off the press."

"I'm not a movie star, Mr. Halonen," said Joe from the other extension. "I'm a fiction writer, and that's not very big in the States anymore. People have much bigger things to worry about now."

"But the Helsinki Prize is important," Halonen said. "We know it's not the Nobel, of course," he added obligatorily with a self-conscious and revealing laugh, "but still everyone gets excited. You will see." He went on to explain more details, including the breathtaking prize money and the visit to Helsinki that Joe would be making. "We expect you to come, too, Mrs. Castleman, of course," he added quickly. This week there would be an official interview done at the house, and next week a photographer would do a formal sitting with Joe, in preparation for our trip to Finland. "But I recognize that we have awakened you," Halonen continued, "and I shall let you get back to sleep now. The undersecretary from our offices shall be in contact with you later today." He must have known, of course, that no one ever went back to sleep after receiving this call.

We all said good-bye like old friends, and when we had hung up I ran into our bedroom, throwing myself down beside Joe on the bed.

"Oh my God, this is it now," I said. "You were right. You were *right*. I feel like fainting, like vomiting."

"I didn't know I'd be right." Joe leaned against me. "This is the beginning of a new phase, Joan."

"Yes, the insufferable phase," I said.

He was silent, ignoring that. "What should I do?" he asked after a moment.

"What do you mean, what should you do?"

"What should I *do*?" he repeated, childlike.

"Call Lev," I said. "He'll tell you what he did. He'll give you tips on everything. He'll walk you through it step by step, how you deal with it. But basically, I think you do what you've always done. It'll be the same, but bigger."

"Thank you, Joan," he said to me quietly.

"No, don't say that. Don't start. I don't think I could take it."

"But I have to say something," he said.

"There's nothing new to say," I told him. "And please, no matter what happens, don't even think about thanking me when you get up on that stage in that gigantic hall, or whatever it is, in Helsinki."

"But I *have* to," he said. "It's what everyone does."

"I don't want to be the long-suffering wife," I said sharply. "You can understand that, can't you? I mean, come on, Joe, think about how *you'd* feel."

"Can we worry about that later?" he asked.

"Yeah," I said. "I suppose we can."

He kissed me hard on the mouth, and we both tasted the vinegar of sleep. Then he did the strangest thing: he slowly got up and stood on the bed, towering unsteadily in the room, looking down from this new angle. The room was tilted but still ordinary. Joe Castleman knew he was special, though not so special that he could avoid the things of everyday life. They surrounded him, as they always had. Yet now, he knew, he could pay less attention to them; he could let himself exist in another world, a parallel dimension where big-time prizewinners lay on chaises eating figs in the sun and thinking of nothing but themselves. He would have to fight that impulse, keep himself from getting soft. He'd have to keep publishing, keep his output strong and constant.

"What are you doing up there?" I asked now, peering up at him as he stood on the bed.

"I want to jump," he said. "Like the kids used to."

I thought of David and Susannah and Alice, and the way their small bodies had shot up into the air, pajamas flapping, shrieks of pleasure accompanying each jump. Why did children love to jump? Was there actual *pleasure* to be found in the up-and-down of childhood: the bed, the playground swing, the seesaw, as opposed to the blindly determined in-and-out of adulthood?

"Come on," he said. "Jump with me."

"For joy?" I asked, not smiling.

"Maybe," Joe said, though he must have known that joy was not exactly here right now in this bedroom at dawn, with the sun discreetly poking into the windows, illuminating both our faces, pointing out the similarities between men and women that age creates, the androgynous tempering and etching.

What *was* here was something else, something exciting but maybe a little bit too exciting, too stimulating, so that it blurred the sensations, reducing the possibility of joy until it dwindled down to nothing.

"Jump with me," he said again.

"No," I said. "I don't want to."

"Oh, come on, Joanie."

It was a name he hadn't called me in a very long time, and he understood that the siren call of it would have an effect. It did. Despite myself, it roused something in me. I was an idiot to be taken in again and again by him, wasn't I? To celebrate him, to sing him, but I couldn't find it in me to be any other way. It took a moment, but finally I brought myself to a wobbly standing position on the bed.

"This is extremely weird," I warned.

We faced each other, bouncing lightly. We certainly didn't feel the kind of freedom our kids had once felt, the simplicity of bodies inhabiting undefined space, and I reflexively crossed my arms over my chest so my breasts didn't swing up from under my nightgown and sock me in the chin. I tested the mattress, getting used to the give of it, its trampoline possibilities. Despite everything, there *was* some pleasure here, no matter how self-conscious; it lightly stirred the air as we started to jump.

Soon the telephone would be ringing all the time, and it would always be for him, or about him. So what else was new? I was used to that by now; Joe had been famous for a very long time, and there's an inevitable uniformity to fame, regardless of its level or quality, whether it's the TV kind with its feral, laser-bleached teeth or the political kind with its puffed hair and cuff links, or Joe's kind: the rumpled sweater and the perennial drink gripped in a fat hand.

Soon the round of interviews and congratulations would start. Soon it would be too much for me to bear—as the days passed I began to see that. I wasn't going to handle this well; it would inflame me with the worst kind of envy. It would leave me all alone in my unadorned, wifely state. Soon he would gloat and preen and discuss his triumph nonstop, inflated with ecstasy and self-importance. Soon it would be intolerable. And soon, too, we'd be on an airplane—this airplane, now—lowering slowly through the clouds into an unlikely pocket of Scandinavia and into the end of everything between us. But for one moment on the bed, Joe and I were fine, entirely the same, our ridiculous late-life selves in crumpled pajamas, briefly lifting off above the earth, before finally settling back down.

Chapter Two

IT KILLS ME to say it, but I was his student when we met. There we were in 1956, a typical couple, Joe intense and focused and tweedy, me a fluttering budgie circling him again and again. Even our clothing is an embarrassment, at least seen from the Olympian vantage point that time provides: his suede elbow patches that attempted to transform a Brooklyn Jew into Mr. Chips, and my long plaid skirts and flats, which I wore because he was short and I was tall, and the last thing I wanted to do was scare him away.

There was no danger of that; he wasn't scared of me, he was extraordinarily confident and dedicated. He pursued me and I responded, just the way other students and their professors were doing all around the country, engaging in steamy little couplings that were pleasurable and infuriating and grossly imbalanced. I felt honored to have been chosen by him, and relieved, too, for it lifted me out of the prolonged stupor that seemed to have infected the entire student body of Smith College in 1956. This wasn't strictly our fault. Though many of the girls in my dormitory chattered like castanets about getting married right after college and buying homes in places like Old Lyme, Connecticut (Chancey

Foster had already decided which one she wanted: a sprawling Tudor with a goldfish-stocked pond, though she had not yet selected a husband), we were not all silly, or empty, or unaware. There was an intense knot of imperious, political girls in my dormitory, and while I liked them and felt excited when they got fired up at dinner, I wasn't one of them. Though filled with my own opinions and information, I was too soft-spoken, too mild. I was an English major with a side interest in Socialism, though on a campus comprised of vines and porch swings and dinner rolls, this interest was almost impossible to sustain, for everything here was washed in a golden, female light.

None of us was in the *thick* of anything; in 1956 we understood that we were being kept separate from the world that mattered, the world of single-minded, odious men on Senate subcommittees with their big microphones and their slicked-back hair, and men in hotel rooms with their pressing needs. We were being preserved for some other purpose, willingly suspending ourselves like specimens in agar for four years.

When Joe first arrived at Smith that fall, he was stunned by the sheer volume of femaleness, something he hadn't experienced since he'd lived among women in Brooklyn. But this, of course, was different: this was young and freshly showered, this was dewy and waiting and extremely responsive. This was the female equivalent of a prison full of men, all of whom would *know it* the moment a woman entered the prison gates. She would be palpably sensed, she would be felt through some kind of bloodhound radar; as she swished on through, the entire prison population would tremble as one. Which is exactly what *we* did when Joe walked into the classroom in Seelye Hall, seventeen minutes late, on the first day of classes that September.

Girls were everywhere in his view, of course; he could just as easily have plucked another one from a life of term papers, field hockey, and Saturday-night mixers, but instead he plucked me, and up I went—*whoosh*—without any resistance at all. The other girls were ubiquitous, chattering, equally pluckable, though they were also more patient, taking their sweet time at everything they did. A bathroom door in my dormitory would swing open to reveal a girl with a naked leg up on the sink, a razor traveling leisurely up a field of foam. They crossed the Smith campus in clusters, these girls, as though they might simply tip over if forced to stand alone. The air was congested with the scents of three dominant perfumes that joined together like distinct strains of pollen, giving the whole place the quality of some sort of nectar bar.

The men we usually had access to weren't men at all, really; I understood that they were a rehearsal version, a softer, less demanding breed than what we'd eventually have to contend with. And they, too, were hidden far away on their own gated campuses until the weekends, when they would suddenly burst into town with their baby faces and thick necks, leaping out of their cars like soldiers on leave, following the zigzag trail of pollen and carrying some of us off to local bars, or dances, or beds.

At age nineteen, I wanted nothing to do with these boyish, slightly illegitimate men. After a couple of evenings spent in their company, drinking foamy tropical drinks shaded by tiny umbrellas, eating steak and foil-wrapped potatoes and talking dully about our postcollege plans, or about Army-McCarthy, or about whether Judge Kaufman had been too tough on those poor, sallow-faced Rosenbergs (*absolutely not*, the date usually said with a fist down on the tabletop and the grim, sorrowful conviction he'd probably picked up from his father), I'd decided: *enough*. No more drinks. No more putting on pearls, or fluffy cardigans, no more staring O-mouthed into a mirror as I applied Taste of Xanadu lip color, no more being met in the parlor of my dormitory by a galumphing boy with an outsized Adam's apple. No more grasping, no more breasts perennially being popped from the shells of brassiere cups in the darkness of that same boy's car, no more letting his wet and hopeful doglike face land on those breasts. For if I kept doing those things, I knew, then I would become tinier and less substantial, of no real interest to anyone, male or female, and when I finally had access to the world, it wouldn't want me.

I've always had a fear of being small and ordinary. "How can I just have this one life?" I used to ask my mother incredulously when I was twelve and sat at the dining room table in our apartment in New York after school, eating a cruller. I'd delicately chew the whorls of fried dough and try to look into the windows of other apartments across the double width of Park Avenue.

My mother, an angular, worried woman whose life was spent serving on committees to organize charity dinner-dances at the Pierre and the Waldorf, didn't really know what I was talking about, and my sudden spasms of nascent existentialism always made her anxious.

"Joan, why do you say such things?" she usually said before drifting into another room.

By the time I was in college, I was desperate to have a big effect, to tower over people, to loom, which seemed a completely unlikely possibility in the occasional moments when I saw what I'd become: a slender, hygienic Smith girl who didn't know much about anything, and had no idea of how to learn.

English 202—Elements of Creative Writing—was held in the late afternoon on Mondays and Wednesdays. I'd heard that the class had previously been taught by a Mrs. Dymphna Worrell, who'd published flower poems ("One Sprig of Freesia," "The Bud That Wouldn't Bloom") in a publication put out by the New England Horticultural Society, and who sat sucking lozenges and praising everyone's work in the same sweeping way: "Expressive use of language!" But now Mrs. Worrell had retired to a rest home in nearby Chicopee, and none of us knew anything about her replacement except his name, which the course catalog listed as Mr. J. Castleman, M.A.

I enrolled in the class not because I imagined I was talented, but because I *wished* I was, though really I'd never tested it out, for fear I would be told I was average. There were twelve students in English 202, and after we'd arrived at the seminar room in Seelye Hall on the first day of class and chatted blandly for several minutes while opening our notebooks to fresh, hopeful pages, the entire classroom fell into a worried silence. Whoever J. Castleman, M.A., was, he was late.

But when he swung into the classroom at seventeen minutes past the hour, I wasn't prepared for him; none of us was. He was in his mid-twenties and skinny, with uncombed black hair and high color stippling his cheeks. He was definitely handsome, but seemed to have been constructed in a slapdash manner, and his books were loosely held together by a strap, giving him the appearance of a frantic schoolboy. Professor Castleman walked with a slight limp, a hesitant scraping of one foot before it lifted off the floor.

"Sorry," he said to the class, popping open the clip that held everything together, and releasing a burst of his belongings onto the surface of the wide, glossy table. He took from his coat pockets two handfuls of walnuts in their shell. Then he looked up and said, "But I sort of have a good excuse. My wife had a baby last night."

I didn't say a word, but several of the other girls began to murmur their congratulations; one said "*Awww,*" and another one said, "Boy or girl, Professor?"

"A girl," he said. "Fanny. After Fanny Price."

"The Jewish vaudeville entertainer?" someone tentatively asked.

"No, Fanny *Price,* from *Mansfield Park,*" I corrected quietly.

"Yes," said the professor. "That's right. Extra credit to the girl in blue."

He looked at me gratefully, and I glanced slightly to the side, uneasy at having singled myself out. *The girl in blue.* My remark suddenly seemed so obviously vain and self-serving, and I could have slapped myself on the side of the head. But I had always been the kind of reader who marked up books and lent them out indiscriminately, knowing I'd never see them again but wanting friends to read them and be as thrilled by them as I was. I'd owned three copies of *Mansfield Park* at one time or another. For some reason, I wanted him to know all of this about me.

J. Castleman, M.A., brought from his pocket a small silver nutcracker, and then picked up a walnut. As quietly as possible he began cracking nuts and eating them. Almost reflexively, he offered them to the class, but we all shook our heads and murmured "No thanks." He simply ate for a few moments, then closed his eyes and ran his hands through his hair.

"The thing is," Castleman finally said, "I always knew that when I had a baby it would have to have a literary name. I want my children to know how important books are. And I want all of you to know that, too," he said. "Because as you get older, life sort of eats away at you like battery acid, and all the things you once loved are suddenly harder to find. And when you do find them, you don't have time to enjoy them anymore, you know?" We didn't know, but we nodded somberly. "So I named my baby Fanny," he went on. "And when you girls start to become baby machines in a few years, I expect all of you to name your little girls Fanny, too."

There was uncomfortable laughter; none of us had any idea of what to make of him, though we knew we liked him. He stopped talking for a moment, taking time to crack a few more walnuts, and then, in a softer voice, he spoke a little about the writers he particularly loved: Dickens, Flaubert, Tolstoy, Chekhov, Joyce.

"Joyce is *it* for me," he said. "I bow down before the genius-shrine of *Ulysses*, of course, though I have to admit my heart really belongs to *Dubliners*. It doesn't get any better than 'The Dead.' "

Then Castleman said he was going to read to us from the final passages of "The Dead." He produced a sea-green paperback copy of *Dubliners*, and as he read aloud we stopped twiddling our pencils and rotating the rings on our fingers and yawning silently in

that sluggish, late-afternoon way. Parts of the novella, particularly near the end, were stunning, and the room became absorbed
and silent. His voice, as he read, was reverential. When he was
done, he spoke for a few minutes about the meaning of the death
of poor, doomed Michael Furey, who had stood lovesick in the
frozen night in James Joyce's story, and died.

"I would kill to write a story half as good. Literally kill," the
professor said. "Well, okay, figuratively kill." He shook his head.
"Because when I really face the facts, girls, I remember that I'll
never even come *close* to doing what that man did." He paused,
looking away self-consciously, then he said, "Now comes the
moment in which I have to confess that I'm trying to be a writer
myself. I've written a few stories here and there. But for now," he
went on quickly, "we're not supposed to be talking about me;
we're supposed to be talking about *literature!*" He pronounced
the word archly, with humor, then looked around the room.
"Who knows?" he said. "Maybe one of you will write something
truly great one day. The verdict isn't in yet."

I understood that he was implying that for him the verdict
was in, and it wasn't good. He continued to speak for a while
longer, and the most diligent girls in the class took notes. I peered
sidelong at Susan Whittle, the redheaded, blush-prone girl in
mohair beside me. On a page of her binder, in perfectly formed
letters, she had written:

> Fiction = ART MIXED WITH EMOTION! i.e., the novels of
> Virginia Wolfe (sp?), James Joyce, etc., etc. Experience should
> be undiluted. *Similes!!* Note: MUST pick up streamers & keg
> TODAY for soph. mixer.

Outside the tall windows of Seelye Hall, the light was being
wiped from the sky; I saw a few girls walking along the paths, but
I didn't register them particularly; they were people walking,
nothing more. I looked back at Professor Castleman. He was a
new father with a wife and a baby lying in the warmth of the

nursery of the local hospital. He was a sensitive, intelligent man with a suggestion of a limp; he'd most likely gotten it in Korea, I guessed, or else as a child, having survived polio.

I imagined him ten years old, trapped inside the cylinder of an iron lung, lying with only his head sticking out, while a kindly nurse read to him from *Oliver Twist*. The image was pitiful, made me almost want to cry for the poor boy whom I was starting to confuse, in my mind, with the character of Oliver Twist himself. I felt an uncomplicated love for Professor Castleman, and even a kind of love for his wife and tiny baby, the three points that made up this delicate Castleman constellation.

When class ended, many of the girls tried to establish personal contact with the professor, as though to say: *Yoo-hoo, over here!* It wasn't that they necessarily imagined him as their lover—he was already taken, after all—but even something about his *being taken* made the situation so much more exquisite.

"Write what you know," he advised as he sent us off to complete our first writing assignment.

That night after dinner (shepherd's pie, I remember, for I sat there looking at it and trying to describe it to myself in a writerly fashion, though the best I could come up with was, pathetically, "a roof of mashed potato spread thickly atop a squat house of meat"), I climbed to the upper reaches of the Neilson Library. On tall steel shelves all around me were ancient bound volumes of scientific abstracts: *Annals of Phytochemistry, Sept.–Nov. 1922; International Journal of Haematology, Jan.–Mar. 1931.* I wondered if anyone would ever open any of these books again, or whether they'd remain shut for eternity, like some spell-fastened door in a fairy tale.

Should I be the one to open them, to plant kisses on their frail, crisp pages and break the spell? Did it make any sense to try and write? What if no one ever read what I wrote, what if it languished untouched on the chilled shelf of a college library forever? I sat down at a carrel, looking around at the ignored spines of books, the lightbulbs suspended in their little cages, and I listened to the distant scrapes of chair legs and the rumble of a lone book cart being rolled along one of the levels of stacks.

For a while I stayed there and tried to imagine what it was I actually *knew*. I'd seen almost nothing of the world; a trip to Rome and Florence with my parents when I was fifteen had been spent in the protection of good hotels and pinned behind the green-glass windows of tour buses, looking at stone fountains in piazzas from an unreal remove. The level of my experience and knowledge had remained the same, hadn't risen, hadn't over-flowed. I'd stood with other Americans, all of us huddled together, heads back and mouths dropped open as we peered up at painted ceilings. I thought now about how I'd never been entirely naked in front of a man, had never been in love, had never gone to a political meeting in someone's basement, had never really done anything that could be considered independent or particularly insightful or daring. At Smith, girls surrounded me, the equiva-lent of those American tourists. Girls in groups were safe as shep-herd's pie.

Now I sat in the upper part of the library, freezing cold but not minding, and finally I made myself begin to write something. Without censoring it or condemning it for being trivial or narrow or simply poorly constructed, I wrote about the impenetrable wall of femaleness that formed my life. *This,* apparently, was what I knew. I wrote about the three different perfumes—Chanel No. 5, White Shoulders, and Joy—that could be smelled everywhere on campus, and about the sound of six hundred female voices rising up together at convocation to sing "Gaudeamus Igatur."

When I was done, I sat for a long time at that carrel, thinking of Professor J. Castleman and how he'd looked in class with his eyes closed. His eyelids had had a purplish, nearly translucent quality, making them appear inadequate to the task of keeping the world out. Maybe that was what it was like to be a writer: Even with the eyes closed, you could see.

* * *

During his office hours the following week, sitting on the bench in the hallway, I waited with nearly rabid anticipation. Someone was already in there; I could hear the dueling murmurs of a male voice and a female one, punctuated by an occasional shriek of female hilarity, all of which increased my annoyance. Was there a cocktail party going on? Were drinks being served, and damp little sandwiches? Finally the door opened and Abigail Brenner, one of the other students from the class, emerged, holding her tedious story about her grandmother's recent death from double pneumonia, which she had been reworking pointlessly since the first day of class. From within the office, I could see Castleman at his desk; his jacket was off, and he was in his shirtsleeves and tie.

"Well, hello there, Miss Ames," he said, finally realizing I was there.

"Hello, Professor Castleman," I said, and I sat across from him on a wooden chair. He held my new story in his hand, the one I'd left in his department mailbox.

"So. Your story." He looked at it serenely. There were almost no markings on it, no red-pen hieroglyphics. "I've read this twice," he said, "and frankly, both times I've found it to be wonderful."

Did he say this about everyone's story? Had he even said it about Abigail Brenner's dumb story about her grandmother? I didn't think so. It was *my* story that was good. I had written it for *him*, specifically wanting to please him, and apparently I'd succeeded.

"Thank you," I said quietly, not meeting his eyes.

"You barely know what I'm talking about now, am I right?" he asked me. "You have no conception of how good you are. I love that about you, Miss Ames; it's a very touching quality. Please don't change."

I nodded, embarrassed, and I understood that this was how he wanted to see me: unusual but innocent, and I found that I didn't mind appearing this way. Maybe, I thought, it was even true.

"Miss Ames, Miss Ames," he said, smiling. "What am I going to do with you?"

I smiled back, beginning to feel at ease in this strange new role. "As my friend Laura would say," I told him, "maybe you should pickle me."

Castleman folded his hands behind his head. "Well," he said slowly, "maybe your friend Laura has a point." Then the playful moment passed and we got to work, leaning together over my story. There was walnut on his breath, I noticed. " 'The trees bent back, as if in apprehension,' " he read aloud. He made a bunched-up face, as though he'd eaten a bad nut. "I don't think so. Kind of phony, don't you think? You're better than that."

"Well, yeah, I wasn't sure about that line," I said, and all of a sudden I knew it to be the worst line ever written in the history of student assignments.

"You got carried away with your own voice there," Castleman said. "I did that myself when I was an undergraduate. Of course, unlike you, I had no reason to get carried away."

"Oh, I'm sure you're a good writer," I assured him.

"I don't know what I am, but I'm certainly not one of the naturals," he said. "I'm the type that sits there slaving away all day and thinking someone will give me credit for effort. But here's an important thing to remember, Miss Ames: In life, *no one* gives you credit for effort."

There was a knock on the door, and Castleman quickly closed my short story, then said, "So when you're sitting up late at night agonizing over your work, just know that you have an admirer."

"Thank you," I said.

"And for God's sake," he said, "get rid of those apprehensive trees."

I laughed in what I hoped was a knowing way, and then stood, taking the story from him. Our hands briefly touched, knuckle to knuckle.

"Come in!" he called out, and the door swung open and Susan Whittle, the redheaded girl from class, entered. Her skin, I'd noticed before, was so sensitive that all her reactions expressed themselves plainly on its surface. She seemed in a constant state of mortification; even now, a doily of pink spread down her neck. I, however, was entirely calm, as though I'd been given a horse tranquilizer. I glided from the office, past the other offices where students and professors bent solemnly together, past the bulletin boards with their flyers about summer programs in Rome and at Oxford, past the elderly English department secretary with her glass jar of hard candies.

After that day, I felt peaceful in class, as if the imaginary horse tranquilizer had a long half-life. I was totally absorbed whenever Castleman spoke about literature or the craft of writing. He sat with his scatter of walnuts on the table, and he kept cracking the shells, picking the meat from the pried-open lips and chewing while he spoke.

One day he told the class that a "talented lady writer" would be giving a reading at the college the following week, and we were all required to attend.

"They say she's very good," he said. "I've only read the first chapter of her novel; it's kind of bleak and disturbing for someone of the female persuasion, but I think she's terribly smart, and you all have to go. I'll be there with my attendance book, checking off names, so don't even think about skipping it." A few of the girls glanced at each other uneasily, actually seeming to believe his threat.

The following Wednesday evening I went to the Reading Room of the Neilson Library to listen to Elaine Mozell. This was the first reading I'd ever attended, and the chairs were arranged informally. Someone from the English department gave a brief introduction, and then the writer, a big and blowsy fair-haired woman with a purple scarf at her throat, stood at the podium.

"This is from my novel, *Sleeping Dogs*," she said in one of those voices that seemed to have been extensively primed by alcohol and cigarettes. I recognized the timbre and admired it; nobody I knew really talked like that. "I know most of you haven't read it," she went on, "because it's only sold 1,503 copies, despite so-called rave reviews. And most of those 1,503 copies," she went on, "were bought by my relatives. Who were paid hand-somely by me."

There were a few uncertain laughs, including mine. Whatever her book was like, I wanted to admire it. This suddenly seemed to be an important goal, and when she began to read I was relieved that in fact I *could* admire it. It was the story of a girl's sexual initiation on a farm in Iowa, and Elaine Mozell used graphic language about the way the new farmhand pushed himself into the girl as they lay together in the hayloft, with the animals grunting their approval below. The girl's point of view was represented, as well as the farmhand's. This wasn't a domestic novel by any means; it jumped outside the world of the girl's farm life and even graduated into some actual detailed facts about corn and soybeans, and, very briefly, about the history of the John Deere Company.

Contemporary novels by men often seemed to include Homeric catalogs of information, moving from the costs of things to what they felt like and tasted like. Land, sea, the difference between wheat and chaff. Elaine Mozell's novel was similar; her carefully chosen words rolled out in that nicotined voice, and as she read aloud she seemed to wake up the entire dreary room. She finished reading to great applause a solid hour later, and her face was flushed. Then she chugalugged the glass of water on the podium, her lipstick scalloping its edge.

Afterward, at the small reception, she stood in a corner of the room with its thin carpets and its old rust-and-sepia-colored globes, flanked by two faculty members, a man and a woman, and all three were talking in loud voices, though Elaine Mozell was the loudest of all, her voice rising up every so often in laughter and relief. She didn't have to perform anymore tonight; she didn't have to stand there in front of us, talking about sex and irrigation. She didn't have to use the word "thresher" anymore. She was free again, and it showed in her bright eyes and now frankly red face. She was knocking back some whiskey, and while the other faculty members seemed to grow subtly drunk, Elaine Mozell became obviously so.

I stood in a gawking cluster of girls from my creative writing class, all of us watching the novelist and the animated satellites around her. Professor Castleman had now become one of those satellites, and I saw him angle for a place at Elaine Mozell's elbow. She turned to him, they briskly shook hands, he whispered something into her hair, and then she laughed appreciatively and whispered something right back at him. I felt ridiculous standing at the side in my cardigan and tartan skirt. My skirt had one of those oversized gold safety pins stuck in it, and I suddenly wished I could pluck it out and jab myself in the eye with it.

I wouldn't have approached her on my own, but now Professor Castleman saw me and beckoned, and soon he was introducing me to Elaine Mozell, telling her that I was "an extremely promising young writer." She looked me over; I felt convinced that her eye went right to my stupid safety pin. *I'm better than I look*, I wanted to say, cringing as I shook her big, hot hand. I told her how much I'd loved her reading, and that I planned to read the rest of her novel on my own.

"Good for you, if you can find it," she said. "I'm afraid you'll have to dig through lots of piles of loud male songs of innocence and experience. And then maybe you'll get to my little tale, buried at the bottom."

All around me, Castleman and the others protested, telling her how that wasn't true, that her novel was powerful in its own right, and blah blah blah.

Suddenly my professor said, "Oh, come on, Miss Mozell, it can't be as bad as all that."

"And how exactly would you know?" she asked him.

"Well," he said, "there are quite a few female novelists out there whom I admire greatly. Like those Southerners, that quilting bee made up of Flannery O'Connor and those others. Women whose work is inseparable from the region they inhabit."

As he spoke to her I saw the looks exchanged, the dot-dash code between them, the cocking of her head, the way he leaned his elbow against a wall to appear casual, the way both of them were interested in each other, and the rest of the faculty members and students stood in a docile ring around them like people singing the parts of villagers in an opera and stepping back to let the two principal players have their moment. She was bitter and difficult, a once-good-looking woman who had gotten a little too heavy and shouldered too much resentment to attract many people anymore, and yet Professor Castleman was taken with her. Maybe he was repelled by her, too, but still he was attracted. She was gifted; her gifts were strange and discomforting and sort of *male*. She was one of those angry women, this Elaine Mozell, angry because her novel had sold 1,503 copies and because she understood how talented she really was, but that it might never really matter.

"Listen," she was saying now, "Flannery O'Connor *is* a genius, and I mean no disrespect to her, but she's also something of a freak of nature, so visionary and devoutly Catholic and *stern*."

"She's an important writer," one of the other men insisted. "I teach her every year in my course on the grotesque. She's the only woman on the list; there's really no one like her."

"But Miss Flannery O'Connor has something going for her that I don't," Elaine continued. "Her Southernness gives her this ready-made, colorful region to write about, and for some reason it always seems so incredibly exotic to people." She paused and let one of the men fill her glass again. "The public likes to hear about the crazy old South, and they certainly may admire Southern women writers," she continued, "but they don't want to *know* them, you know? Because they're strange creatures, O'Connor and that squirrelly little androgyne Carson McCullers. I don't want to be a strange creature. I guess I just want to be loved." She took a deep drink and then added, "You know, I wish I was a lesbian, I really do."

There were murmurs of protest again. "You don't mean that," I heard a timid female dean say, but Elaine Mozell overrode her.

"Oh, in a way I do," she said. "The problem is that I love men passionately, even though they don't deserve it. But if I happened to be one of those *literary* lesbians, I wouldn't give a goddamn about what the rest of the world thought of me, or *whether* it even thought of me at all."

There was more response, more talk, and eventually the others turned away; the night was growing late and I could see the janitors waiting outside the room with their mops, and I stood crumpling a Smith-crested paper cocktail napkin in my hand, also waiting, though what I was waiting for was obscure to me. Elaine Mozell saw me waiting, and suddenly she took me by my arm, pulling me aside into a small alcove so quickly I couldn't even express surprise.

"You're talented, I hear," she said.

"Well, maybe," I began.

"Don't do it," she said. No one else heard this; we were surrounded only by marble busts of commendable, long-dead women.

"Don't do what?"

"Don't think you can get their attention," she said.

"*Whose?*"

She looked at me sadly, impatiently, as if I were an idiot. An idiot with a safety pin plunged into her skirt. "The *men*," she said. "The men who write the reviews, who run the publishing houses, who edit the papers, the magazines, who decide who gets to be taken seriously, who gets put up on a pedestal for the rest of their lives. Who gets to be King Shit."

"So you're saying it's a conspiracy?" I asked gently.

"If you use that word it makes me appear envious and insane," Elaine Mozell went on. "Which I'm not. Yet. But yes, I guess you could call it a conspiracy to keep the women's voices hushed and tiny and the men's voices *loud*." She raised up her own voice on this last word.

"Oh, I see" was all I could say, vaguely.

"Don't do it," she said again. "Find some other way. There's only a handful of women who get anywhere. Short story writers, mostly, as if maybe women are somehow more acceptable in miniature."

"Maybe," I tried, "women are *different* from men. Maybe they try to do different things when they write."

"Yes," said Elaine, "that could be true. But the men with their big canvases, their big books that try to include *everything* in them, their big suits, their big voices, are always rewarded more. They're the important ones. And you want to know why?" She leaned closer and said, *"Because they say so."*

Then she abruptly left me, and I walked back to my dormitory, but all night I felt sickish, restless. As it would turn out, Elaine Mozell's writing wouldn't last. Her novel would go out of print and would never be reprinted; it would disappear, becoming a curiosity, the sort of moldy, obscure title that people buy for twenty-five cents at a tag sale on the side of a road in Vermont, and then put on the shelf of their guest room, but no guest ever actually takes it down to read.

I've occasionally wondered what became of Elaine Mozell, because after *Sleeping Dogs*, I don't believe she ever published another novel. Maybe it was too hard for her; maybe she got married and had children and life intruded and there was simply no time for her work; maybe she became an alcoholic; maybe every publisher turned down her manuscripts; maybe she had "no more books left inside her," as people often sorrowfully say about writers, envisioning the imagination as a big pantry, either well stocked with goods or else wartime-empty.

Maybe she died. I never found out, for her novel joined the vast, rolling graveyard of unloved books, and perhaps she threw herself on top of the grave, inconsolable.

One day, a month into the semester, having had three conferences with Professor Castleman during office hours, each one held aloft by his elaborate praise, he called my name at the end of class and I walked up to him, brimming, steadying myself.

"Miss Ames, I wanted to ask you something," he said. "Would you walk out with me and we can talk?"

I nodded, seeing the way the others took note of this moment. One of them, Rochelle Darnton, whose short stories featured inevitable surprise endings—"Just like O. Henry!" Rochelle had explained in her own defense—sighed as she shrugged into her coat, watching student and teacher lingering together, as though she knew that she would never be asked to walk out with Professor Castleman, that she would never be asked to linger, to loiter, to give more of herself than she already did.

I thought Castleman might be about to tell me that he was nominating me for a $100 college literary prize. Or maybe, I thought, he wanted to ask me to have dinner with him, to go out on a clandestine date, the way a girl who lived on my hall had done with her chemistry professor. I wasn't sure which it would be: art or love. But with someone like J. Castleman, love of art could transform quickly into human love, couldn't it? I hoped this was true, but was immediately mortified by my own thoughts, which seemed both delusional and deeply corrupt.

We'd arrived at the middle of the campus when he said to me, "I was wondering, Miss Ames, whether by any chance you're free Saturday night."

I told him I was. All around us, girls trudged past.

"Good," he said. "Would you be interested in baby-sitting? My wife and I haven't gotten out since Fanny was born."

"Sure," I said flatly. "I love children."

Which wasn't even true. I felt a flush of humiliation about what I'd imagined, and how different the truth was, but still this was better than nothing, better than being ignored by him. So on Saturday night I declined to attend Northrop House's big band party, walking away from the sounds of "String of Pearls" cranked loud on a phonograph, and the parry of male voices in the snapping air, and instead headed along Elm Street until it shook off its collegiate feel and became simply part of a neighborhood where families lived.

Bancroft Road was dark, with no streetlamps, and I could see into front windows where faculty members and their wives and children shuffled around living rooms. Was this the epiphany of adult life, that it actually *wasn't* exciting and vast in possibilities, but was in fact as enclosed and proscribed as childhood? What a disappointment, for I'd been looking forward to the open field, the imagined release. Or maybe, I thought as I watched a young mother stride across her living room, then suddenly stoop down to pick something up (A shoe? A squeak toy?), only men ever felt that release. For women in 1956 were always confronting boundaries, negotiations: where they could walk at night, how far they could let a man go when the two of them were alone. Men hardly seemed troubled by these things; they walked everywhere in cold, dark cities and pin-drop empty streets, and they let their hands go walking, too, and they opened their belts and then their trousers, and they never thought to themselves: *I must stop this right now. I must not go any further.*

Here on Bancroft Road, it appeared that I was in a land in which everyone seemed to have stopped themselves from going too far. This was Smith, not Harvard; prestigious but not of high academic voltage. The men who held these faculty positions would initially feel relief at being here, and would settle in for the long run, but something would probably steal over them eventually, a desire to move on, to burst out into bigger cities, to not waste their Ph.D.'s and carefully composed lectures on girls who would dutifully absorb everything and then immediately go get married and reproduce, inevitably beginning the long process of forgetting.

The Castleman house was a gray saltbox, set back from the street behind a bumpy lawn. The bell on the front porch made a halfhearted *blat* when I pressed it. In a moment Professor Castleman himself was at the door, lit from behind by a yellow bulb.

"You must be freezing," he said as he let me in. He wore a half-opened dress shirt, an unknotted tie draped around his neck. "I'm warning you, it's chaos here," he said. He smelled of some sort of shaving balm, and a spot of blood was on his chin. The record album from *South Pacific* was playing distantly, and from somewhere behind him a baby rhythmically cried, and then a woman's voice called out, "Joe? Joe? Could you come up?"

His name was Joe. I hadn't known this, and I'd been afraid to attach a specific first name to him. His wife descended, carrying the baby over her shoulder. I lifted my eyes to look. The baby was quiet now, though bright red in the face. Mrs. Castleman wasn't beautiful; she was a small, frazzled woman in her middle twenties, with boyish brown hair and darting eyes. What did he see in her? I imagined my professor in bed with this unglamorous little woman. Mrs. Castleman was so different from the Smith girls who grazed all around the campus like gazelles nibbling foliage. She stood with her hand reaching up the back of the baby's outfit to check the status of a diaper, and she gave the appearance of a puppeteer in that moment, the hand inside the cloth, the baby entirely under her power, at least for now.

"Hello," Castleman's wife said without much interest. "I'm Carol Castleman. Nice to meet you."

I tried to appear neutral, cheerful, a Smithie straight out of a college brochure. Autumn leaves should have been falling all around me as I stood at the foot of the uncarpeted staircase. "You, too," I said. "Hello, honey," I forced myself to say in the general direction of the baby. "Aren't you adorable."

"We haven't left her with a sitter before," Mrs. Castleman explained. "But she's still so young, I can't imagine it'll scar her for life, regardless of what I've been trained to think." The professor's wife shifted the baby to her other arm and explained, "I'm studying to be a psychoanalyst." Then she added, "Let me show you around."

The rooms of the house were disorganized, with piles of books and toys and tilting lamp shades. Carol Castleman didn't seem to care, or to feel the need to apologize. The baby slept in her parents' room, and I was taken up there, knowing that I was about to enter the place where Castleman lay each night with his wife. The bed was made, though clearly in a hurry, and beside it was a white wicker bassinet. On one of the night tables was a scattering of walnuts. Joe came out of the bathroom and stood in the doorway, now fully dressed. His hair was wet and pushed back off his face, and his tie was knotted. From the record player, a dreamy, tropical female voice sang, *"Here am I, your special island, come away, come away...."*

"Carol," he said. "Is the tour over? We should get going."

His wife took his arm, and in that frozen pose they appeared to be a clean, presentable young faculty couple going out for the night. They clearly received something from each other, a reciprocity that was founded on things I couldn't even imagine, for he was so handsome and she so shrunken and ordinary. I thought of my own parents, who were as remote as two stalactites hanging side by side in the same cave, never touching in public, my father in his dark suits that smelled leafy and masculine, my mother in her dresses with patterns that gave them the appearance of tablecloths. My parents had separate beds made of dark, shellacked wood, and once, after she'd had a lot to drink at a dinner party, my charity-addled mother swept into my room late at night and confided that my father had recently been "rough" with her "in a marital way." I only understood this much later, though simply the idea of it was awful: my big, impersonal, corporate father roughing up my slender, tablecloth-wearing mother as he mounted her in one of their high twin beds. Here in the presence of this husband and wife who were *not* my parents, and who lived in a world much more complicated than mine, I felt retarded and slack-jawed. I'd called Fanny "honey," but I hadn't meant it at all. The nucleus of attraction was the baby's father, a man who ate walnuts and read James Joyce aloud to his students.

"Good-bye now!" the Castlemans called as they left, leaving telephone numbers and bottles and clean diapers behind. "Good-bye!" they sang as they headed into the night air to a faculty dinner party.

When they were gone, I gathered up the loose sack of baby and explored the bedroom in depth. Here were the clues to this man, all the evidence I'd ever need. Here in the closet were his shoes, lined up and worn, and here on the dresser was a bottle of his aftershave. Then, on a table, I saw a copy of Rilke's *Letters to a Young Poet*, with my professor's name on the flyleaf. "Joseph Castleman," he'd written with big flourishes, "Columbia University, 1948," as though he was guaranteed to be famous some day, and to excite someone who would eventually open this book and come upon his name. By 1956, of course, he still wasn't famous, but the signature excited me anyway, and I ran a finger along it, tracing the curlicues. Then I put the book down and sat on his side of the bed, laying the baby beside me. I picked up some walnut shells, letting them sift through my fingers, and for a moment Fanny and I regarded each other coolly.

"Hello, you," I said. "I'm falling in love with your daddy. And I'd really like to go to bed with him."

In a final burst of nerve, I sprang up and opened the night table drawer. It was as though I needed to find out what it meant to be a wife, to have a life spent beside a man. And sure enough, I found something: a white plastic diaphragm case nestled against a tube of the cream that had to be squirted in along with it, as well as an applicator, all of it making me uneasy, forcing me to imagine the wife of my professor sliding plastic and potions into a deep slot in her body, preparing herself for him. There was a dental pick with a rubber tip in the drawer, too, and a single walnut. I picked up the walnut and looked at it; a red heart had been painted on it, and beneath it were the words: *C., I love you true.—J.*

The walnut was more disturbing than the diaphragm. A diaphragm was a necessary, impersonal device, the sort of thing that Smith girls obtained by taking the bus to Springfield and visiting an old female gynecologist from Vilna who barely spoke English and asked few questions. But the inscribed walnut was much more intimate, and therefore somehow perverse. It even looked female, I thought, observing the lips of the nut and the grooves in the shell and the cold silk of the bumpy surface with its red-painted heart. I placed the nut back in the drawer and turned my attention to Fanny, who was suddenly crying and in need of something: A bottle? A change? Who the hell knew? Her crying was an irritant, sand in the pants, and I couldn't understand the universal fetish surrounding babies, why they were the prize I would supposedly desire in a couple of years.

I picked the baby up and held her, ineffectually shushing and rocking her. I had no power here, no authority, not even the secret kind like that of a newly sexual girl with a diaphragm buried deep inside her.

Still, though, when the Castlemans returned later, I pathetically tried to make Joe more aware of me. He thanked me and paid me and even offered to give me a lift back to Northrop House, but when I said that I'd be fine on my own, he didn't insist. Instead, he seemed relieved to return to the quiet disorder of his dim house and the now-unconscious baby in the bassinet, and I was relieved, too, for what would we have talked about? How would we have survived the awkwardness as we sat on the cold, bouncy front seat of his car, heading for my dormitory, a place that I didn't want to be? Where *did* I want to be? Not there, but not here, either, living life as a sleep-starved faculty wife and envious of the way my husband simply wandered in and out of our house whenever he chose. So I wandered out of their house on my own, too, trying to give the appearance of independence instead of loneliness.

The next morning, returning to my library carrel, I wrote about a small, furtive faculty wife about to go out with her husband for the evening, walking down a flight of stairs with her baby over her shoulder, the woman's hand inside the baby's sleeper like a puppeteer at work, imagining that she might be able to control her child for years to come. The mother trades the shadows and smells of her faculty house for the cold night air and a brisk walk with her husband toward another house, where all the lights are on, and music is playing, and faculty couples stand in hopeful clusters.

When I was done, I tried to write from the point of view of the husband, including his thoughts as he stood beside his wife, his hand on her elbow as though women might need help navigating any new living room they entered. But something stopped me. I didn't really know what men thought, or *how* they thought, couldn't imagine what powered them, what steered them, and so I decided not to try.

Several days later, after I'd handed in my writing exercise, Castleman asked me to come see him during office hours. I climbed the wide stairs of Seelye Hall knowing that he'd either praise me as he usually did or else tell me I'd invaded his privacy by writing this piece, which the class would read. When he ushered another girl out and let me in, he sat holding my story in his hand.

Finally he leaned forward and said, "Miss Ames, I want you to listen to me. I've already told you that your work is good. But I'm not sure that I got through to you. The way you probably see it, my class is just like any of the others: French, or Renaissance art, or whatever it is you're taking this semester. You'll be very happy to get an *A*, and that will be that. But I guess I feel it's important for you to understand that you can really *do* something with this, if you choose to."

"What do you mean?" I asked.

"Well, you could probably expand it and sell it as a short story, for instance. And then keep writing more of them, and sell those, too. Maybe not to the very top places—God knows how they decide who to let in—but certainly to some of the better small literary magazines. And you might even decide to write a novel," he went on.

"Why?" I said.

"*Why?*"

"Why would I want to do that? What's the point?" I thought of Elaine Mozell pulling me aside in the alcove.

Castleman looked at me. "I don't know," he said, shrugging. "Because you're good. Because you have something to say. Plenty of writers have only one or the other, but not both. And it's always interesting when the world gets to see things from a woman's perspective. We're so accustomed to getting the man's view; whenever we get a chance to see through the eyes of a female, it's *refreshing.*"

Elaine Mozell didn't write like a woman usually did; she wrote with big, sweeping arcs and lists and the assumption of authority, and because of all this she also seemed greedy, inappropriate, not female at all. All of my characters so far had been girls or women, and the tone of my writing was quiet and observant, almost catlike. Women would want to read my writing, I thought, not men.

Maybe Castleman was right; in several years I could publish a perfectly decent first novel, a coming-of-age story with a title like *Summer at the Shore,* and I might be asked to give an alumnae reading at Smith. The girls in the audience would nod in recognition, while the few men present would drum their fingers and wish they were somewhere else. The men would long for armored writing, protected writing, writing that was musclebound and never ceased flexing itself. Writing that chose to take in the entire world, including the hundred-year wars as well as the ten-minute arguments in some suburban couple's avocado-hued kitchen.

But Professor Castleman was a man and he liked *my* fiction. "Personally, I have trouble writing about women authentically," he admitted. "It all comes out sounding like men talking. A bad ventriloquist's act, where you see the guy's mouth moving the whole time. I still can't connect to the hearts of women, to all that feminine mystery, and those secrets they keep. Sometimes I just want to shake it out of them." He stopped. "It's extremely frustrating to me as a writer," he said. "The wall that separates the sexes, that keeps us from getting to know each other's experience. Everyone has to face this, more or less, though some of the best writers seem to find a clever way around it. As for me, I'm afraid I'm extremely limited."

"Oh, but you aren't," I said quickly.

"You've never read my work," he said. "I've had two stories published in my life; you don't know them."

"I'd like to," I said.

"You would?"

"Yes, definitely."

Castleman moved some papers and books and walnuts around on his desk until he fished up a slim literary magazine called *Caryatid: A Journal of Art and Criticism.* I'd never heard of it, and probably almost no one else had either, and Castleman seemed both proud and embarrassed as he handed it over to me.

"You can borrow it if you'd like," he said. "Let me know what you think."

I nodded and said I was flattered, and that I was sure I'd love it. Then I looked down the table of contents to find the name of his story. There it was, "No Milk on Sunday," by J. Castleman— and as I read the name he slid his chair forward until our knees were touching. I looked up, shocked that he was so close.

"Maybe," he said, "you could tell me how to make it better." It was the first contact between two sets of blind knees, signifying something not quite decided, something still up for grabs. Was this a conversation about writing? He took an index finger and slowly moved it to my lips. Then Castleman's face came forward, and suddenly he was kissing me in this plain little office where piles of ordinary student stories lay unloved. He kissed and kissed me, and though he seemed to want to lick and swallow my talent, my perceptiveness, whatever it was he thought I had, I still felt that of the two of us he was the important one, and I was unfinished. He could finish me, I thought; he could provide the things I needed to actually become a whole person.

He kept kissing me, but did nothing more; his hands braced my shoulders, not shifting from their mooring. Even untouched, I nearly had an orgasm, and was surprised and then embarrassed by my exaggerated responsiveness. *The girl was embarrassed,* I thought, a story opening before me, and I felt relieved to be at a literary distance from myself and this man who was holding my shoulders and kissing me until I felt sure that even if I hadn't been a writer before, I was one now.

I told no one in Northrop House, not even my friend Laura, who suspected something was up but didn't push me for specifics. "This has got to be good, am I right?" she said, and I simply smiled, preferring to keep the moment to myself, unwrapping it and reimagining it during a history lecture, or when taking a shower in the tin stall with the green rubber curtain, listening to the waterfall of other showers all around me. On the first night that I knew I'd have uninterrupted reading time, I sat in my bed with *Caryatid* open in my lap. Delicately, carefully, I turned to his story and began to read. I was excited, anticipating something that would only enhance what I already felt about him. My lips moved along with the story as I read, but soon it became apparent that the story was no good. I was confused; *how could this story be no good?* Yet in the universe of "No Milk on Sunday," the women characters spoke in stilted sentences, and the men were clichés of uneducated men, all glowers and stoic, unspoken pain. The story was like an imitation of something literary, made by someone who hadn't developed a distinctive voice of his own.

Elaine Mozell's farm story had been more authentic, more believably male. Castleman was an actual man; why couldn't he write like that? What was wrong with him that he couldn't? I closed the journal and put it aside, upset and sorry I'd read it, not having any idea of what to tell him. Maybe, I thought, he would forget he'd given it to me and would never mention it again, and I wouldn't have to go through the unpleasantness of talking to him about it. Maybe, I hoped, it would simply never come up.

Wednesday at noon, a note came to me through intercampus mail in an English department envelope, and I snapped it up quickly, moving away from the other girls who were milling around opening letters and Bundt cakes sent from home.

Dear Miss Ames,
My colleague, Professor Tanaka, who teaches Eastern
religions here, has asked me if I would recommend a
student who might come in and feed and walk his dog
once a week on Friday afternoons. Would you be
interested in the job?

Sincerely,
J. Castleman

The letter, it seemed, was in code, so I immediately wrote back and agreed to walk and feed Professor Tanaka's dog, though I doubted the dog existed. The following day, a key and an address appeared in my mailbox, and on Friday I walked down a sloping street called Crafts Avenue and let myself into an apartment building with a bakery downstairs. The building smelled of yeast, and when I entered the third-floor apartment with the nameplate that read "H. Tanaka," an actual dog began a frenzy of yipping from somewhere inside. It was a dachshund, old, gray-haired, and desperate for company, its spine curving in discrete ridges like a dinosaur's.

"Here, boy," I said as I walked through the barely furnished living room, and even in his arthritic state the dog began to mount my leg, as though he, too, knew why I had come here.

In the kitchen I found a can of Beef-o for Small to Medium Dogs, poured it into a tin bowl, keeping my head averted from the stink, and watched dispassionately as the dog ate like a wolf. After I took him for a short walk, I went back inside and sat on the rug. The nameless dachshund, sated and happy, lay on his back and exposed his graying stomach to me, his penis sliding from its casing, then retracting. There were a few Japanese prints on the walls above us: women in kimonos serving thimbles of tea, and a series of scenes involving rock pools and nesting cranes. I was sitting in this unfamiliar, calm room, looking around me, waiting, when the bell rang.

"Who is it?" I asked through the intercom.

"Joe," he said.

So he was Joe now; that was new. I let him in quickly.

"Hello," he said, and he walked past me, putting down his books and papers and folding his coat over the back of a chair. "Is the dog behaving himself?" he asked.

"The dog is fine," I said. "I wasn't even sure he was real."

"Oh, he's definitely real," Joe said.

"I know. He mated with my leg."

Joe smiled. "So pretty soon we should be seeing little half-dog, half-leg creatures running around the apartment, am I right?"

"Right," I said.

Now he stood still and looked at me. "Miss Ames. I mean, Joan. What should we do with you?"

"Pickle me?" I said.

He stepped forward and then he held me in his arms, kissing my hair and neck. "So can we go to bed, please?" he asked.

Professor H. Tanaka's bedroom was much like the living room, with just a few prints on the walls and a simple bed. A gray light filtered in through the paper shade, enough to reveal the basic image of Joe as he stripped off his clothes. He was good-looking, tightly muscular. There was a scar on his foot, pink and shiny, the tissue pulled tight. A bullet hole, I assumed, the source of his slight limp, and I imagined him as a Korean War hero, though later, of course, I'd learn how he'd accidentally shot himself in training camp. When he touched me, his skin was cold as a seal's. In bed, with my own clothes gone, my nipples seemed to turn and tighten, and I resisted the impulse to cross my arms and cover myself. My breasts felt excessive, a detail that men generally liked, though it embarrassed me. I saw him look at my breasts and at that seemingly arbitrary patch of pubic hair, but I tried to imagine I was with him by the side of a Japanese rock pool, and that what we were about to do now would be as gracefully executed as a tea ceremony. I held his penis in my hand, observing it for an uninterrupted moment. It was my first penis, and it seemed so optimistic in a way, much more so than he was. It was agreeable, ready, unconscious of the possibility of failure. I lay back against the pillow and watched him snap on a Trojan, which made a single *twang* like a banjo string, and then I let him push into me, hoping that in some larger way my presence here helped him. I knew I was certainly helping myself, lifting above the flocks of girls with their long plaid skirts swishing. Joe was quickly breaking a sweat, and his ice-cold feet curled around mine, holding on like those of some primitive tree-dweller. The way he shoved into me was very painful, and this surprised me, as though his sensitivity and love of books might have some bearing on the level of pain he would inflict when he deflowered a Smith girl. I thought again of his knees in gray wool trousers, and now his bare knees, those dusty, exposed knobs where the skin was pulled tight, the calves below flexing and releasing. I wrapped my legs around him, and I seemed to be holding him by mechanical means; I'd never known my legs were this strong. A while later, I wanted to sleep, but Joe didn't, or couldn't.

"Oh, don't worry about me, I never sleep," he told me. "It's one of the most basic facts about me."

"One of the only facts I know," I said.

"I'll tell you anything you want," he said, and waited for me to ask.

I had no idea of what I wanted, and so I posed some simple questions about his upbringing (Brooklyn, Jewish, fatherless), his education (Columbia University, B.A., M.A.), his military history (Korean War, briefly; self-inflicted shrapnel sending him home before combat), his marriage (bad, to a woman grown shrill, whose most significant crime was that, since the baby was born, she no longer wanted to have sex. She *refused* him, he said, turning away from him again and again. "Do you have any idea of what that does to a man?" he asked me, and I had to say that no, I didn't), his politics (unoriginal: thrilled when Welch stuck it to McCarthy, stirred by *Brown* v. *Board of Ed.*, especially as he had a couple of close Negro friends in the city), his favorite moments (listening to Mark Van Doren lecture at Columbia), and his out-look on life (melancholic, like most writers).

After I had exhausted the interview, we were silent for a while, until suddenly he said, "Oh, now I want to ask you something."

"Go ahead," I said, thinking that he was going to ask me all about myself, and that I'd have to tell him the mundane details of being a privileged girl growing up in New York City: the Brearley School, my formal-dance class, my parents' puzzling coldness, the money that was scattered around me like an uninteresting gar-nish. And I'd also have to tell him of my insecurities, my perco-lating political sympathies, my desire not to be insubstantial. I dreaded having to talk to him about myself, and yet I was also relieved. So this was what it meant to be with a man: he told you things that he cared about, then you told him things you cared about, and you each responded with outrage or sympathy at appropriate points in the other person's story. It was like having a friend, a strange mirror version of yourself—though with an entirely different anatomy and set of memories. When you were both done talking you felt as though you'd been given extraordi-nary access into each other's inner workings and storehouses of experience.

But instead, he asked me, "So what did you think of my story?"

His story; *oh God.* For a moment I had no idea what to say. I was confused, and flustered, and said nothing at all.

"Did you read it yet?" he persisted.

I nodded, trying to form some sort of emergency response as quickly as I could. "Yes," I said brightly. "Just last night. I was going to tell you." Then I waited a second. "I loved it," I told him. It was easy to say that.

"You did?" he said. He propped his head up on one elbow. "You didn't think the ending was too abrupt? The part where he gives her the scarf and then walks away?"

"No," I said. "Not at all. It was the *gesture* of the scarf that counted, wasn't it? I thought it was perfect." But I knew it wasn't perfect; it was all wrong, it was forced.

"You really mean it?" he asked me.

"Of course. I was going to tell you, but you got there first."

"Well, that's just wonderful," he said, smiling. "Now you've really made my day, Joanie."

I let out a quiet breath; the praise had made him happy and peaceful, the way sex was supposed to do. Eventually he said it was time to go; he had to stop off at the State Street Market to bring home a sack of flour his wife had requested, and he also had to pick up some baby formula for his daughter. Flour and formula; these were the paraphernalia of a life that had nothing in common with mine.

We stood and dressed, turned shyly away from each other. "Joe," I said, trying out the plain, single syllable. He looked at me. "What do you think is going to happen?" I asked him.

He didn't answer for a second, and then he said, "How can I possibly know? We'll have to wait and see, I guess."

A little while later, as I walked by myself back to campus in the deepening afternoon, past the hardware store and the second-hand bookshop and the grand facade of the Academy of Music, I wondered whether he might ever love me, and how I might rush that love into existence.

As it would turn out, we soon developed a routine, meeting once a week when I walked and fed Professor Tanaka's dachshund. "Walking the dog" became a euphemism. *The dog is very hungry today,* he would tell me as he flipped up the hem of my dress and touched me with the tip of a finger. I had myself fitted for a diaphragm in the dim office of the Lithuanian female doctor in Springfield.

One day when we lay in Professor Tanaka's bed, Joe handed me something wrapped in tissue paper and a ribbon. I opened it and saw that it was a walnut, and that on the side he had written something in red paint with a fine brush. *To J.,* it read. *In awe. J.*

I held it for a moment, trying to rearrange my disappointment into something else. Of course he had no way of knowing that I'd gone through his wife's drawer and seen the almost identical walnut he had given to her. I didn't like eating walnuts; sometimes you got some shell with the meat, and you ended up trying to pull flecks of it off your tongue like tobacco leaves. And the taste was too dark and somehow wrong, as though you were eating bits of cork floating in a glass of wine. Joe had said he liked walnuts for all of these reasons; they were a complicated nut, with all those knobs and curves in them. A walnut left an oily trail behind after you had eaten it, an aftertaste that Joe also liked. He liked the taste of women, too, he had said once in Professor Tanaka's bed; he liked the first moment when he could dip down and taste me, even though I was embarrassed in the beginning and unable to relax with his head clenched in the grasp of my legs. All I could think about was what he was tasting, the mix of salt and talc and who knew what else. Nothing could hide a woman's taste, thank God, he'd said. A walnut, too, could always be detected when it was baked into a cookie, or when its oil was used in a salad. There was a sweet, dark taste released, with the hint of decomposition, like something found on the floor of a forest.

I put the walnut on the bureau in my room in Northrop House, leaving it there among the crisscross spray of bobby pins and the jumbo tub of cold cream. Weeks passed and his walnut stayed on the bureau. I had almost forgotten it was there until the day when I came home from my art history class on Holbein and Dürer and opened the door of my room to find Joe's wife sitting on the bed, waiting for me. Carol Castleman stood up when I came in.

"Can I help you?" I asked, and I thought for an insane moment that Joe was dead, and that his wife had come here to break it to me, as though I would be the truly bereaved one, not her.

"Can you *help* me? You know why I'm here," Mrs. Castleman said. She wore a camel-hair jacket and a creased skirt; she was small, frantic, unspooling. "I let you into my house," she continued, her body starting to fibrillate. "I trusted you with my baby, okay? And this is what you do. You act so young and adorable, but you have a lot of nerve."

"Who told you this?" I asked miserably.

Carol Castleman didn't say anything. She just held up her hand and opened it slightly. Inside was the walnut, the one that Joe had given to me. Proof. Elsewhere in Northrop House, girls were getting ready for dinner; from downstairs, the smell of Yorkshire pudding was lifting through the building, eggy and thick and nourishing, an imitation of a previous life at home, a life in the womb, a life in which people took care of us, and we didn't have to do a thing for ourselves. I wanted to eat that consoling food right now, to dig into a plate pooled with roast beef juices while hearing dinner-table stories about comically bad dates with Yale men. But instead I was here, facing Joe's furious wife, who was holding a walnut in her hand.

"So tell me about it," Carol Castleman said.

"I can't," I said, starting to cry.

She let me cry for a little while, watching me the whole time, irritated, and then finally, when she couldn't take it any longer, she said, *"Tell me."*

"I'm not a bad person, Mrs. Castleman," I tried, and what I really meant was: You see, I'm not actually much of a person yet at all.

"You little bitch," said Carol Castleman. "You Smithie bitch with your stories. I've read those stories, and you want to know something? They're not so terrific. I don't know what the hell he goes on and on about them for; you'd think they were written by James Fucking Joyce."

And then Joe's wife drew back her hand and hurled the walnut. It shot straight at me, but there was no time to shout or move out of the way. When it struck me, it was with a hard shock, one solid *bop* in the middle of my forehead, making a sound like a cobbler's hammer, and for a suspended moment I wobbled before falling to the floor.

I was vaguely aware of the sound of feet galloping toward me down the hall, and then the appearance of a ring of girls' faces suspended above me, each one wearing an openmouthed expression, like a group of carolers in action. Someone had curlers on, another one had a pencil behind her ear. Everyone began speaking in overlapping voices, yet no one seemed to know what to do. Somewhere in the background Carol Castleman was weeping and telling the roomful of girls that her life had been destroyed. But all I could think about now, as I lay on the rug with a lump rising in the center of my forehead, was the fact that my own life had finally begun.

Chapter Three

THE HELSINKI-VANTAA Airport is like every other airport in the world, only a little blonder. Not blond like Sweden or Norway, those cool albino hotbeds, but blond enough in patches to make any American take notice. The Finns have a Slavic darkness running right through them, but still there are plenty of fair heads bobbing in this tiny, lovely northern country. I couldn't help but think this as Joe and I and the rest of our party moved through the airport in a whirl of Finns, some of them taking pictures, some asking questions, all of them wanting something from him, a touch, a word, a gently tired smile, as though his talent might rub off in these casual moments, imparting a little bit of a glow to them, which they would return by giving him a touch of their own brand of Scandinavian goldenness.

They were blond and attractive, so many of these Finns, and the rest of them were simply noble- and heroic-looking, like heads carved on Viking ships, and he was a small, seventy-one-year-old, formerly handsome and dark-haired Jewish man from Brooklyn. But somehow, the lovefest between him and them was boundless, continuing all the way through the airport corridor, which struck me as being as long as a smorgasbord table. *Love me*, he seemed to say to them through his glazed and flight-worn eyes.

Yes, we will love you, Mr. Yoseph Castleman, the Finnish people seemed to reply, *if you will love us back.*

And what was not to love? They had chosen him, hadn't they—the elderly men who comprised the Finnish Academy of Letters, and the younger ones, too, the hipsters who were probably only in their sixties. Joe seemed not to notice anything, so much was he getting a kick out of the pomp of his arrival; this was what he had been waiting for, always: to step off an airplane and be met like the Beatles landing in America. It would have been even better for him if, like the Beatles, he could have descended one of those shaky tin stairways onto an airstrip, his thin hair whipping around his head, waving his arm to the adoring people below. But instead we had stepped from the plane into one of those carpeted accordion tunnels and then wound up in the early-morning terminal outside the city limits, a clean, white space with eerie, department-store chimes playing and an amplified, soothingly generic female Euro-voice speaking incomprehensibly about departing and arriving flights, and then, inexplicably in English, asking would Mr. Kyosti Hynninen please meet his party at the baggage carousel.

Going past the duty-free shops and kiosks and backlit wall photos of the splendors of Finland, Joe was friendly and charming to the members of the press who approached him and the handful of government representatives with their official clip-on badges that featured tiny images of their own Scandinavian selves, but I knew he was barely listening to anything they said in their careful English. He was high right now; he was ecstatic.

I thought of Joe's beginnings spent in the female universe of that Brooklyn apartment, his first, bad marriage and its noisy end, his second, long marriage and Joe's professional ascendance during it. Then the kids, oh the kids! I hadn't known what it would be like to have a household populated by children. I'd had stirrings toward babies, but fear as well. My desire to have a baby was swaddled in the need to make Joe happy. I couldn't separate them; I peered into an imaginary carriage and saw Joe's oversized head poking out from beneath the blanket.

But when they were born, they became themselves, not him. Each child revealed his or her own specifics. Susannah, our first, was given extra attention, like all firstborns. She would come into the kitchen, where I'd be frying a lamb chop in a pan, and she'd announce, "Me help," knowing that the food was for Joe, who was busy in the bedroom.

"All right, my girl, you help," I'd say, and Susannah would spear the chop in the hot pan and plunk it down on a plate, adorning it with crumpled pieces of paper meant to look like flowers. Then she'd carry it carefully down the hall and kick Joe's door a few times in lieu of knocking. I'd hear murmuring between them: a father's distracted words, a daughter's quivering entreaties to "look at the plate, Daddy, *look*," and then a father's quick change of gears, his voice raising up in praise and saving the day.

Me she loved; him she adored. I never minded this, and when she and I were together I felt completely relaxed, gratified by her smell, her smooth skin, her feverish excitement at all new things. If she'd had a tail it would have been continually thumping. When I was unavailable to her—when I was otherwise engaged, which was often, and had to leave her with a baby-sitter—her face would take on a tragic cast, and it would almost kill me.

Her sister, Alice, wound up sturdy and athletic and more independent. She wasn't good-looking like her sister, merely *healthy*-looking, her body small and tight like Joe's had once been, her hair light brown and cut close to the head in Roman-boy fashion. When Alice became a teenager, her lesbianism finally presented itself, after many telegraphic years of crushes on favorite young ingenue–type teachers and a bedroom papered over with the witchy-haired women of rock, and tennis Amazons with hard brown thighs packed incongruously into little white dresses. And when it did present itself, I was relieved to hear it said aloud, though Joe seemed startled and personally hurt.

"I like girls," she burst out to us one night, out of nowhere, in the kitchen.

"What?" said Joe, who'd been at the table, deep in the newspaper.

"I like girls," Alice continued bravely. "*That* way. You know." The refrigerator suddenly stirred and clicked and began to manufacture ice cubes, as if to fill the awful silence.

"Oh," said Joe, staying pinned to his chair. My heart was immediately racing, but I walked over to Alice and hugged her. I told her I was glad she'd said something, and I asked her if there was someone in particular she liked. Yes, she said, but the girl had been horrible to her. We talked politely about it for a minute or two, and then she slipped off to her bedroom.

"It's not about *you*," I'd said to Joe that night in bed, as we furiously whispered back and forth. This would be a theme of our conversations about the children.

"Yes, I'm aware of that," Joe said. "That's my point."

"So what are you saying, you *want* to be the centerpiece of your daughter's sexuality?"

"No," he'd said. "Not at all. You're a mother. You can't understand what I might feel about this."

"Oh, that's a good one," I'd said, wanting him to believe that mothers knew everything, that we were the omniscient narrators of our families' lives.

David, the youngest, the troubled one, seemed incapable of finding a life for himself. Joe and I were always holding our breath and hoping everything would work out for him, but this was magical thinking. Very little would work out for David; that had become increasingly clear, and his life was up for grabs.

But still we loved him. We loved them all, Joe and I, though not quite together. The children received two separate channels of love, one from me, a reasonably steady flow, and one from their father whenever he thought of it, whenever he could manage to turn away from himself. He was distracted so much of the time, caught up in the details of his professional life and all the accolades that kept accumulating like inches of snowfall. The children and I simply watched as Joe's career grew and grew.

And now, finally, he had made it all the way to Finland. The country was bafflingly sweet and bracing and fresh. Once a year, it was roughly roused from its slumber: *Wake up! Wake up! An important person is a'comin'!* As we kept walking through the airport with our publishing entourage, I realized that if I wanted to, I could easily disappear into the wilds of this country and never return. I wouldn't stand out in Finland, with my fair hair and pale skin. I would fit right in, and they would think I was one of them. How wonderful to be able to begin a bewildering new life here, instead of returning in a week to the house in Weathermill, New York, with my giant baby of a husband, my genius, my very own winner of the Helsinki Prize.

"Joe," I said, "look to the left. They're trying to take your picture."

He turned obediently, and there was a rapid flutter of stutter-whirring, and he held himself a little more stiffly and grandly. Tomorrow the photographs would appear in newspapers, showing this old American Jewish man squinting into the lights, revealing his awkward humanness, his exhaustion from air travel mixed with the vanity that had long propelled him through airports and the world.

Outside the terminal, a limousine waited for us, as dark as its driver was fair, and the first strike of frozen air made me feel as though my lungs would collapse as we quickly slipped from building to car. It was the beautiful fall-foliage time of year here that the Finns called *ruska*, with its changing flip-book of brooding colors. Only late autumn, and yet Joe and I were both shocked by the cold. It was unmanageable, I thought, and I imagined a society in which people went skittering from house to car to office and back to car to house, and then the day was done. There wasn't much sunlight left in this day, though right now the sky seemed hugely bright and endless. The sunlight in Finland tricked you into believing it would last; you couldn't imagine that it would shut itself off with such grim finality even before the enzymes in your stomach had barely started to break down the components of your lunch.

The car ferried us gently past the waterfront and the glass fronts of shops on the boulevard called Mannerheim that sold delicate things wrapped in foil and crinkled paper, and past sudden, long stretches of bridge rail. We'd been to Finland once before over the course of our marriage, back in the 1980s, when Joe had been invited to give a reading as part of the five-hundredth-anniversary celebration of the Finnish book, and it had seemed to me at the time that the entire country was shot through with ice.

I liked Finland for its absence of overt rage or street crime. This wasn't the United States, this wasn't Spain. It was calm here, and moody, a gorgeous, elegant place with slightly off-kilter serotonin levels. A depressed country: this was an easy diagnosis to make, given the suicide statistics, which Scandinavia sometimes tries to deny, just the way Cornell University tries to allay the fears of incoming students' parents about the famous Ithaca gorge, which, like a harvest ritual each fall, claims the life of a few more hopeless freshmen. *Don't worry,* the college brochure should say. *Though some students do in fact leap to their deaths, most prefer keg parties and studying.*

All of Scandinavia was alluring, with its ice fishing and snowcaps, but everyone knew about the legend of ingrained unhappiness among Finns, Norwegians, and Swedes: their drinking, their mournful, baying songs, their muffled darkness smack in the middle of the day.

"And here is the Helsinki Opera House, Mr. Castleman," the driver said as our car smoothly went past an enormous building that appeared capable of containing an entire kingdom within its thick walls. "It is where you will go, sir, to receive your award and be feted."

"Yes, Joe, you will be fetid," I murmured, but he didn't hear.

I envisioned us in the Opera House, with Joe being honored for a body of work that surely must have puzzled the Finnish

people, though apparently they read it anyway. They were a profoundly literate people. The winter was nearly endless; what else
could they do but read? *The novels puzzle me, too,* he probably
wished he could say to them in shaky Finnish, painstakingly
accenting every word on the first syllable like the Finns do. His
books were populated by unhappy, unfaithful American husbands and their complicated wives. Maybe it would have done
Joe's characters some good to have *their* days shortened, to force
the sun to set a little sooner on their miserable marital and extra-
marital shenanigans.

And then, after the ceremony, we'd be eating dinner at a long
table in an enormous, chilly marble hall. Members of the Finnish
Parliament would murmur in his ear, but he wouldn't be intimi-
dated by them, for they weren't royalty. The Nobel prize, on the
other hand, gives you a hefty shot of royalty, seating you beside
King Gustav for an evening of awkward conversation.

What had the King of Sweden and Lev Bresner talked about
that night in Stockholm, the king sitting beside our friend,
swathed in robes like a herring in cream? I didn't have a clue. Joe
would never have to make such a conversation. He wasn't big
enough in scope or darkness. Already it was killing me to be in
Helsinki, to watch him encircled by people, to listen to their
gravely earnest questions, to hear his answers, to watch them
anoint him with essential oils and declare him the best.

I hadn't known for certain, before I'd gotten on the airplane in
New York, that I would leave him. I'd had fantasies over the
years, little scenarios in which I said, "Joe, it's over." Or else, simply, "Well, guess what, you're on your own now." But none of
these had been translated into *action;* instead, like most wives I'd
hung on for dear life, but in the past few weeks it had become too
much, it was more than I'd bargained for, and I wouldn't stay
much longer.

I kept looking at him, absorbing the familiar bump in his nose,
the purpled skin of his eyelids, the thin white hair, and recalling
that he had once been an angelic young boy, and then an ambi-

tious and handsome young writing instructor, and then a nervy, celebrated novelist who stayed awake all night and wanted to suck up the entire world and hold it in his lungs for a moment before letting it out. And now he was old, with a humbling bio-prosthetic heterograft porcine valve (however you slice it, it's just pig meat) stuck like a clove into his heart, and pig memories somehow looped into his brain: happy images of rooting around among old nectarines and tennis shoes. His energies had been funneled in a thousand directions and were now becoming depleted, and wherever he went, there were laurels crunching and rustling beneath him, and twining vines and leaves he could lounge upon, contented.

Before long our car pulled in front of Helsinki's Strand Inter-Continental Hotel. Men in uniforms leaped from the hotel in synchrony, appearing untouched by the cold, yanking open the frozen doors of our car, and soon we were inside, our luggage trailing us, the owner and his ecstatic wife springing forward to say hello and to offer Joe their congratulations. Opulent warmth immediately replaced the startle of cold, and the interior smelled to me like the deepest part of a forest in some Scandinavian folk-tale, perhaps a tale called "Young Paavo and the Five Wishes."

Light seemed to slant into the lobby, as if through a break in the overarching branches of some enormous trees. Improbably, I smelled pine, and sap, and all at once, demented from jet lag, I felt like lying down right here on the dense carpet of the Inter-Continental Hotel, proving myself to be the sad, unbalanced wife of the newest winner of the Helsinki Prize.

But still we had to keep going. We traversed the spongy forest floor, going past mahogany walls and long golden hallways, fol-lowing the spanking-clean bellman and his two assistants, all of whom could easily have been brothers in a family in which the children were bred exclusively to service the Finnish hotel industry.

Joe was confident now, walking quickly. He was easy in his skin, gliding smoothly by. The fact that he was the outsider, the

Brooklyn boy, only added to the peculiar cachet he enjoyed in this alien country. Other than a small cluster of reporters and photographers and his nominal editor, Sylvie Blacker, the rest of the publishing people and Irwin, Joe's sleepy agent of recent years, there didn't seem to be any other Americans in sight. Whenever we were in Europe, we could usually recognize them by their slouch and smile, the way they clutched their beloved copies of the *Herald Tribune*, or by their too-bright clothing, their eagerness to be talked to by other Americans, as though without the familiar, rounded syllables of the heartland, they would become as frightened as lost children.

Both of our daughters had offered to accompany us to Finland, but Joe didn't seem to want them there, so they stopped asking. They were used to this by now.

"The thing is," Joe said to Susannah, "if you come, I'll feel so guilty about having no time for you. I'll worry about it. It'll distract me. Instead, why don't you and Mark and the boys plan on coming to Weathermill when I get back? We can spend a long weekend here. I'll be a hundred percent available. I'll give myself over to all of you. I'll be your love slave."

He had an impish look in his eye, that old-man whimsy he'd learned to do well ever since age had caught him and slowed him and damaged his heart. I felt that he *would* be distracted having the kids there, but that really his concerns were for himself, not them. He'd won the Helsinki Prize. He took it seriously. He wanted to savor it slowly, carefully, and not have to be distracted by making sure that everyone around him was happy, which in any family is an impossible task.

Over the years, when he'd won lesser prizes, there they'd been at the banquets and dinners and cocktail parties, his scrubbed children at various stages of childhood and adolescence. I wasn't sure how he felt about their presence, but me, I'd loved having them around me. I'd clung to them when it all got to be too much. To be honest, I'd used them as human shields. There they'd been in their pretty little dresses, and David in his monkey suit, strangling under the knot of some green and gold slippery tie from The Boys' Shoppe.

I'd always had a lot to drink at these celebrations, guzzling down the white wine they offered me, and the champagne, and anything else. My children could always see it, could tell the moment when my eyes became swimmy.

"Mom," Susannah once whispered as we stood under a tent at the Academy of Arts and Letters, to which Joe had just been inducted. The wet mouthfuls of poached salmon I'd eaten at the lunch hadn't been enough to absorb the full force of the spirits I'd consumed. I was pickled. I rocked lightly back and forth on my feet, and Susannah, age thirteen, steadied me with her hand.

"*Mom,*" she said a little louder, scandalized. "You're *drunk.*"

"A little, honey," I whispered back. "I'm sorry. I mean, I'm sorry if I'm embarrassing you."

"You're not. But let's go somewhere," she said, and I let her steer me away from the Big Top for a while. We walked down to the street there in uppermost Manhattan, where a few taxis loitered and a man stood smoking outside a bodega. We sat on the stoop of a building in our formal clothes and I drank a bottle of guava nectar that she bought me at the bodega, and tried to sift through the fog so I could return to the festivities.

"If you're so miserable," my daughter said delicately, "then why don't you leave him, Mom?"

Oh, my darling girl, I might have said, *what a good question.* In her worldview, bad marriages were simply terminated, like unwanted pregnancies. She knew nothing about this subculture of women who stayed, women who couldn't logically explain their allegiances, who held tight because it was the thing they felt most comfortable doing, the thing they actually liked. She didn't understand the luxury of the familiar, the known: the same hump of back poking up under the cover in bed, the hair tufting in the ear. *The husband.* A figure you never strove toward, never worked yourself up over, but simply lived beside season upon season, which started piling up like bricks spread thick with sloppy mortar. A marriage wall would rise up between the two of you, a marriage bed, and you would lie in it gratefully.

What I actually said to Susannah was "Who said I'm miserable?"

She looked at me pointedly, silent. "When I get married, I want it to be so easy that everyone will look at us and understand exactly why we ended up with each other," she said.

So she married a man who was different, but not, as it would turn out, satisfying. Mark was attractive, built like a whippet with a runner's body, golden filings of hair on long tan wrists. But the man never read a book unless it was a biography of Jefferson or Franklin or a true story of an Arctic expedition; fiction was outside his realm, and so in fact was art of any kind.

Susannah was lonely; I knew that about her, could see it among all the other small trophies of unhappiness that she lined up on triumphant display for me, the way children often do, providing an entire museum of disappointments and inviting the parents in, as if to say: *You see? You see how you fucked me up and what it led to? It led to this!*

My daughter was a woman whose father had disappointed her. She'd made Joe clay pots over the years in art class, an endless ceramics shower in a prolonged effort to win his attention. She already had his love; love was easy. Attention was something else entirely, and how could she ever get that? She wasn't a sex partner. She wasn't a colleague. She wasn't a *book*. She was a girl at a potter's wheel, furiously spinning cups and bowls and plates for a father who would never drink out of them, never eat off them, but would occasionally stuff a clump of pencils in one of the mugs or shove one of the plates to the back of his desk.

Eventually Susannah stopped the pottery altogether, said it was too time-consuming, though by that point she'd quit Stengel, Mathers & Broad and was home with her boys—my adorable grandchildren—Ethan and Daniel all day.

Alice had never really tried to win Joe over in the ways that her sister had. It was as though she'd sized him up early on and realized it was impossible to capture the heart of such an egotist. Other women liked Alice, were charmed by her. She looked good, in a bracing, freshly laundered way. As an adult, she tolerated Joe, gave him hard, affectionate hugs, and was slightly more loving to me. Pam, whom she lived with now in Colorado, was perplexing to me as a life choice for Alice because she seemed so *literal*. She was pretty in a flattened and poreless way; her eyes were small and light. She practiced Pilates, and her cooking was superb, if you could open yourself to the wonders of all the different members of the root-vegetable family.

But of course I really did understand what Alice got from this marriage: Pam was the wife, and that was what my daughter wanted, perhaps without even knowing it.

Both our daughters were home with their families right now—one with real longing and regret, wishing she could be here with us, with him, the other not really caring all that much. David, of course, didn't offer to come. He almost never went anywhere, but kept to a simple path each day, like a monorail: his neighborhood coffee shop, a used comic book store, a Chinese take-out place, his job, and then home again. He had no curiosity about this trip we were on; he'd asked nothing, offered no congratulations, made no inquiries. While Joe and I traveled the length of a hotel lobby in Finland, David was in his basement apartment reading one of those graphic novels he loved, with their pen-and-ink depictions of a bleak futuristic life. He'd have a white carton of Chinese food open on his lap, depositing noodles everywhere. I saw him filling himself up with oily take-out food and reading about fantastical lives and hidden postapocalyptic worlds, and occasionally confronting a strand of memory about a life that he hadn't lived in a long time. *Childhood.*

I walked beside Joe now, our bodies moving together through space, neither of us looking at the other. No pure tenderness existed here; whatever we had was threaded with familiarity. As we headed with the bellmen toward a bank of dimpled-glass elevators that led to a private VIP floor, I noticed a young woman glancing at Joe with an expression of interest. She appeared nervous and tentative as she stepped forward and blurted something out in his direction.

"Mr. Yoseph Castleman, you are a wonderful writer!" she said. "My felicitations to you."

She wasn't beautiful, exactly, though she wore an expression of Scandinavian grace. Her hair was the color of a manila envelope.

"Thank you," said Joe, smiling and stopping briefly. "That's very kind."

He extended a hand and she shook it; her hand held on, clutching his for just a little too long. Vaguely, it occurred to me that she might be a stalker, but then I remembered that I had never heard of a Finnish stalker. Stalkers often seemed to come from the Midwest, though occasionally they rose up like swamp creatures from the wetlands of Florida. Over the years Joe had received letters from some of them, and though the men tended to be more overtly threatening, it was the women he feared most. Men were so obvious with their hostility, and if you were in danger you'd know it. Joe had been in danger more than once, and the person who had been most hostile to him was our son.

David wasn't insane, he wasn't psychotic, only "marginal," only "borderline," those catchwords for all unpredictable outsiders. And David was fragile, which meant that it was easy to knock him over, to make him lose his way.

The night that David threatened Joe, I wasn't home; instead, I was out at Lois Ackerman's house for a meeting of my longstanding women's book group, which that month was reading *The Golden Bowl*. Joe and David were alone in the house together. It was a freezing night in upstate New York. David, in his twenties at the time, was staying in our house because his apartment had flooded and he had nowhere else to go.

To say that he was a stellar child at the beginning is to make light of his intellect, the somber way he approached everything big or small. When he was born, Joe had been thrilled to be the father of a boy, at last; a boy would save the day, would give back something of what Joe had lost when his own father had dropped dead so long ago, changing the future.

Joe often turned his attention to David in a way I'd never seen him do with the girls. They went fishing together, they played pool, they hiked Mount Cardigan in New Hampshire in heavy boots, carrying knapsacks I'd stuffed with foods they liked. Most of these activities were done in the presence of other men, usually writers. Joe rarely took David off alone; what would they have talked about, hour after hour? As a boy, David liked to pummel you with questions, one after the other, like one of those fact-crammed children's books: Do insects have eyelids? How come you can't tickle yourself? Why are people interested in the smell of their own farts? Joe became weary quickly, and when he returned from an outing he would hand David off to me and disappear for hours.

I'd go and visit with David in his room, sit on the side of the bed as he removed his muddy boots. "Did you guys have fun?" I'd ask, touching his head. One day, I knew, I wouldn't be able to touch his head; one day he would flinch as though my hand were burning hot. So I'd better do all the touching I could while he was still young. He tolerated my touches but never basked in them the way the girls did. This was a boy thing, I decided. A necessary part of manhood. He just sat there patiently, waiting until I'd finished.

Like Joe, David was handsome, dark, big-headed, with black curls. Joe was thrilled by our son's intellect, by the fact that the school had said he was a genius. When David was little, Joe often took him to bars, though I didn't know it at the time, and our little boy played with his Hot Wheels cars in the sawdust at his father's feet. Other famous writers and groupie types reached down and absently ruffled David's hair; he barely seemed to register their touch, or if he did, he never felt it as affection, and he was rarely affectionate back. He lived in our midst, he did his schoolwork with alarming speed, making very few mistakes, and he went off on hiking trips with Joe and Joe's friends, but there was no real warmth emanating from him. His sisters had always been puppyish, wanting to please, confiding in me about friends and working for hours on Valentine's Day cards for their father, but David was cooler, more remote, less rewarding.

A psychiatrist we consulted long ago told us we were making something out of nothing. "He's a brilliant boy," the man said, for apparently he'd never tested a child who scored as high as David, and the Salinger's Glass Family level of his IQ simply canceled out any possibility of his being defective. He wasn't autistic, like the son of a poet we knew who walked around repeating fragments of phrases from TV commercials. "Rice-a-Roni, the San Francisco treat . . ." that boy would sing, his voice high and ethereal.

David was extraordinary, we were told by everyone, and we should just leave him alone. Joe in particular was insistent that we give David enough "latitude," as he put it, imagining, I suppose, that David would use all that space to invent, to cure, to compose, to dream. But instead he kicked another kid at school in the groin, and he upturned a cafeteria table. And once he taunted a teacher, saying she had a mustache like Hitler and that no man would ever love her. She feared it was true and called in sick every day for a week.

Off to a residential school for troubled but intelligent kids— one of those places with beanbag chairs everywhere, and "circle time," and a full staff of therapists—David kept to himself, then graduated first in his class and miraculously was accepted to Wesleyan, thanks to some string-pulling and heavy bartering on Joe's part. But David lasted less than four semesters; in New York City over sophomore spring break, he threatened a man with a box cutter in an East Village bar, and wound up in jail. When we went to see him, talking to him from the other side of a Plexiglas wall, David was agitated and restless, mortified to be confronted in prison by his parents. Joe kept asking how in the world David could have done this, and David understood that the subtext was "How could you have done this to *me*?"

"How could I *do* this?" David said. "What kind of a question is that?"

"It's a reasonable question," Joe said. "So answer it."

"We're concerned," I added.

"I know you're concerned, Mom," David said finally, addressing me only, as if Joe weren't there. "I fucked up, okay? I have anger issues."

"*Issues,*" said Joe acidly.

"Yeah, *issues,*" said David.

"You don't just have issues, you have a whole subscription," said Joe.

David turned and walked away, facing the corner, and it wasn't until we got him out of there that he spoke to us again. We took him back to our house that night, and he said very little over the next few days. We tried to talk about the legal situation, but he appeared mostly uninterested. When we drove him back to Middleton, Connecticut, David was eager for us to go.

"Okay," he said, after we came inside with him. "Well, thanks for the ride. Do you need anything? Because I really should get back to things. . . ." We didn't know it yet, but he would quit school abruptly, permanently, a few weeks later, without explanation.

That night, he wanted us to leave right away and not bother him. He was dismissing us. I was briefly insulted, but I got over it. Joe didn't. He stood in his coat with his hands jammed into his pockets. And when we did leave, a few minutes later, David hugged me, surprising me by the sudden gesture. Joe he simply nodded to. He didn't like his father, and maybe never had. But now the shape of the dislike seemed to be changing. I didn't pick up on the extent of it, and neither did Joe.

Over the years, David, after he left school and moved to New York, got into occasional bar fights and confrontations with women. He would describe these scenes to me in mortified detail, as though talking about someone else entirely. He never spoke specifically about his anger at Joe. I knew that sons often raged at their father. I'd read Arthur Miller, and the usual body of Greek drama. I could picture the classic distant, towering father, and the son with the primal, unmet needs. I could imagine the passage of years, and the slow freeze on the part of the son, met eventually by the slow thaw of the father, by which point it's far too late. Damage has been done, and the son turns away, saying "Sorry, Pop," and leaves the old man hunched and weeping in his BarcaLounger. But I never really saw any of that in our family.

For a long time David and Joe stayed at a certain level of uneasy, mutual dislike, maybe contempt. But finally it was ratcheted up much higher. This was the night that David's apartment became flooded, the entire place suddenly ankle deep in murky New York water. His books and newspapers were sent floating, and because he had nowhere else to go, I insisted he come stay with us.

"It's just for a while," I said. And so he came.

At first the living situation went surprisingly well. The house in Weathermill is big, and David kept to himself except during meals, fixing himself fried-egg sandwiches for snacks and then going out for the night, visiting the local bars to drink and shoot pool. Old high school friends who still lived in the area would call—friends who worked at the Rexall drugstore, or for their father's exterminating business—their voices low and hangdog on the telephone. Who were they, really? Pornographers? Drug dealers? I had no idea. My son's world was closed to me.

The night David turned on Joe seemed peaceful enough at the start. We had dinner together, the three of us. Joe and I did most of the talking, while David offered a few monosyllables between forkfuls of steak. Nothing seemed unusual to me. When I went off to Lois Ackerman's house for my book group, I remember feeling grateful to be going, to have a reason to get out. David was oppressive. It was a sad thing when you wanted to be away from your son, but it wasn't a tragedy. After the drive along winding roads, when I sat down in Lois's living room surrounded by these kind and intelligent women who shared a common interest in closely reading the books we'd forgotten all about since college, I wished I could stay there, move into Lois's spare room. She was divorced, and clearly lonely; when she kissed everyone hello, she hugged too hard, lingered too long. She was tall, lantern-jawed, dressing in heavy turquoise jewelry she'd acquired on her solo trips to the Southwest. Lois was always solo. Her isolation was painful to her, yet very appealing at times to me. Her house seemed to be an oasis, the big bed covered in a pristine duvet, the night table with its box of French caramels, bottle of Nivea lotion, and pile of old Merchant-Ivory videos. The place was man-free. Quiet. Right now it chimed with the sounds of women's voices. Individual words and phrases rose up from the conversation: *modernity; narrative structure; Princess Casamassima.*

The food was good, too, the coffee table strewn with dips and small, marinated things. I was relaxed, drinking and eating and joining in the spiraling discussion of betrayal within a marriage. I didn't know if it was paranoia, but it seemed as though, whenever I made a comment, everyone listened more keenly, because they knew I had firsthand knowledge of betrayal. Still, I wasn't feeling particularly betrayed at that moment.

And Joe, meanwhile, was sitting in our living room at home with a swirling, clinking bourbon, appreciatively listening to Herbie Hancock on the new Bose sound system he'd just bought. (The men who own the world are obsessed with sound systems; don't ask me why.) He was nested in his maroon chair reading the paper and drinking and listening. David was upstairs in our house, burrowing in his childhood bedroom.

I thought the evening would go on like that; I thought everyone was doing what they ought to be doing. Then the telephone rang at Lois's. She answered, then came and got me. "It's Joe," she mouthed silently, as Sylvia Brumman continued an overexcited, stuttering comparison of early versus late Henry James.

I picked up the telephone in Lois's kitchen and spoke, alarmed to hear Joe's strained voice saying, "Hello, Joan, sorry to disturb you, but things are a bit difficult here at the moment."

"What does that mean?" I asked.

"David," he said.

"David? What's the matter?"

"Yes, he's right here," said Joe.

"You can't talk?" I said.

"No," he said. "I can't. But maybe you should come home. I could use you here."

And then Lois popped her head into the kitchen to make sure everything was okay, which of course it wasn't. I made my excuses, then left immediately and roared home. One thing led to another, and that night I convinced David to let me drive him to a small psychiatric hospital in Westchester for an evaluation. He ended up staying there for two weeks, sleeping a lot, adjusting to the antidepressant medication they'd put him on. When a couple of the women from my book group called me to find out what had happened, I vaguely told them there had been a "scene" between Joe and David, and I left it at that. I didn't want to discuss it. No one asked for details. They knew I had a troubled son, and how painful that was to me.

Though David still takes medication, or at least he's supposed to, he's never had to be hospitalized again. For the past couple of years he's managed to keep working at the same law firm, appearing there late at night, often looking ragged, but his typing skills are intact. There have still been occasional fights, dustups, nothing too serious.

The tension between David and Joe never really went away, though I guess we all grew used to it. But potential violence came from elsewhere, too, not just from our son, making Joe wonder what it was about him that charged people up.

Once Joe had received a letter that began:

Dear Mr. Castleman,

You think you are GOD'S GIFT don't you? While I am just a LOSER!! But I am writing my own novel, and you'd better watch your ass, Castleman, for your [sic] in this book, too. And your character doesn't live to see how it ends. . . .

Joe had called the police in on that letter—I'd urged him to—
and when the two Weathermill patrolmen arrived that night, he'd
felt some embarrassment, for the more he considered it, the less
he could believe that someone would actually kill a novelist. A
nonfiction writer maybe, though even that seemed to defy credi-
bility. What was the point of killing a writer? Politicians, actors,
former Beatles: those he could in some way understand, for they
had tangible power in the world and could actually *do* things,
but *a novelist?*

Joe feared the psychotic ones, and had mild contempt for the
legions of readers who conducted online discussion forums about
his writing, who painstakingly sought out everything he'd ever
published, who needed to find new ways to keep him close to
them. When they confronted him in person, he hung back shyly,
a little bit frightened and irritated by the intrusion, but flattered,
always flattered, his eyes taking on a certain wet shine of vanity.

But when the fan was young and beautiful, he'd lift his head
and frankly stare into her eyes, leaning forward slightly, stepping
inside the outer edge of the circle of perfume she invariably cast.
It was the most obvious thing in the world, the way he moved
toward pretty women, wanting them so much, speaking in a low
voice that tenderized the warm skin of their necks. In the beginning, all those decades ago, I would often look away when this
happened, would go get another glass of reception wine, chat with
the provost if we were at a college, or Joe's introducer, or the pub-
licist; I'd turn my back on the seduction that was taking place only
a few yards away from me. Then, sometimes, I fought him, I chas-
tised him, and he told me I was making things up, or else he caved
in and apologized, saying that he knew how weak he was, and he
hated it. But as time passed and his behavior didn't change, I simply turned away again whenever it happened. I drank from my little plastic glass; I swooped a celery stick through a pool of dip,
knowing that behind me, my husband was becoming acquainted
with a young, beautiful girl, a faithful reader.

She might be saying to him, "You know the part in *Overtime* that begins with the daughter washing her hair? That is the most beautiful description of female adolescence I've ever read. How do you *know* such things, Mr. Castleman?" And he would shrug and thank her. Sometimes, days later, through means I never really knew, they would find each other again.

The charming young woman who faced him in the lobby of Helsinki's Inter-Continental Hotel was probably a brainy Finnish girl from a provincial background who wanted to hold a Helsinki laureate's hand for just a moment too long, and she was still smiling at him as he walked away from her and over to the elevator.

"Lucky you, they love you everywhere," I whispered as one of the bellmen inserted a key in a lock on a panel, and the glass cage rose with the lovely, cushioned swoosh that could only be found in European lifts.

"I don't think that woman loves me," Joe whispered back. "You're exaggerating."

"Oh, I would put a little money on it," I said.

"*Someone* has to love me," he said. "As far as I can tell, the job is currently unoccupied."

The bellman, standing by, gave no indication that he understood this cryptic marital sparring. The elevator rose and rose with its hum of cable and hint of fjord, letting us off at the silent, pristine VIP floor. In the distance, a maid scurried off. A wide oak door was swung open, and we were invited into the Presidential Suite. Enormous windows overlooked the cobblestones and the trees below.

"Hot," the bellman said proudly in one of the bathrooms, yanking a brass tap in the veined-marble sink. "Cold," he said, turning the other one.

There was a formal dining room in the suite as well as two bedrooms, a living room, a small library, and a sauna. The master bedroom held an enormous white bed with tall posts, and two thick robes were laid across it. Dazed from the effects of air travel and a surfeit of attention, and by all the splendor, Joe pulled off his clothes piece by piece and shrugged into one of the robes.

"I don't know what we're supposed to do next," he told me.

"You know what we do? We sleep."

He nodded, sat on the bed, testing the give of the mattress, and then he yawned ostentatiously. "Are you sure it's a good idea?" he asked me. "Shouldn't we wait until the evening? Shouldn't we force ourselves to stay awake so that we can start to get on their timetable? Anyway, I don't think I could sleep," he said. "You know I never do."

"Today you will," I said. "I bet you're more tired than you've ever been in your life."

"That's true," he admitted.

So we stripped and crawled under the deep white waves of blankets. We ignored each other's body; we were indifferent, like we'd usually been in recent years, except my indifference was mixed with hostility, which Joe tried not to notice right now. Loveless, we lay together. Elsewhere in the suite, hidden doors were opened and closed by meek and ghostly maids. Fruit was silently polished and arranged in baskets, and the ends of toilet paper rolls were fashioned into origami. Then eventually the distant collection of sounds stopped, and Joe and I lay in silence, our skin a perfect temperature against high-thread-count sheets. Joe appeared small beside me in the bed; bits of white chest hair frothed up over the edge of the blanket, and his nipples were exposed, those vestigial disks. He was frail and exhausted but contented, and uncharacteristically, for the first time in a very long while, he slept. We both did.

Voices awakened us eventually, an angel choir pulling us slowly from the unnatural sleep of travelers, and when we opened our eyes it was already late morning of the next day, and we were shocked to find our bright hotel bedroom filled with strangers, young girls dressed in white and carrying candles, singing their hearts out, all of it in Finnish. This was a Helsinki Prize rite of passage, someone at dinner later explained to us, a shameless copy of a similar Swedish display put on for winners of the Nobel prize, and while we lay there, dopey and sandy-eyed from sleep, photographers appeared at the edges of the room to document the spectacle.

As they did, the candle-holders stepped back and the plate-carriers stepped forward, girls bearing fruit and cheese and sugar-dusted pastries. And then they, too, stepped back, and forward came two girls carrying huge cups of coffee—bowls, they were, the kind that kittens lap at—and then the food and drink and candles were placed on silver trays at the foot of our bed.

"How long is this going to go on?" Joe whispered to me, but I shushed him and smiled at the girls, and he knew enough to follow my example.

On cue, all the pretty girls joined hands, raised their delicate arms, and sang to us in voices that would have stirred the most frozen heart that ever beat. I didn't know what the words meant; presumably they had something to do with the glory of the day and the greatness of the celebration, though I supposed that just as easily, for their own fun, they might have been singing:

> "*Fuck you, Joe Castleman,*
> *the overrated writer we despise*
> *Fuck you, American upstart,*
> *who hath come and claimed our prize . . .*"

* * *

Once upon a time there had been another hotel room, a very different one, in New York City. It was small and wretched, and no angel-girls sang to us in the morning. This was forty-five years earlier, but even after all this time I could visualize its shape and smell and its vague, implied filth. Joe and I had headed there first on the bus as we fled Northampton together, and then on a New York City subway train with its yellow woven seats and concave wall ads for Dreft laundry detergent and Chiclets. I was nineteen, hanging by a strap. In the middle of my forehead was the ludicrous purple goose egg that had been left when Joe's wife, Carol, had flung the walnut at me two days earlier. As I held on to the subway strap like an ordinary commuter, I saw Joe watching me, taking in the lump on the forehead and also the hollow of my underarm, that scooped-out place inside my creased yellow dress. I'd only brought a weekend's worth of clothes with me; the rest would be sent down in a steamer trunk from Smith later. Here I was on the subway, which I'd almost never been on in my life, though I knew every stop on the crosstown bus, which I used to ride with friends after school most days.

I was terrified to call my parents and confess to them what I'd done, though I assumed that the college would have the privilege of doing just that. They were right here in this city, and though it was possible that I might actually run into them, it didn't seem likely. They never went on the subway, or had reason to visit the part of the city where Joe was taking me. Their route was predictable and short, involving Park, Madison, and Lexington Avenues, and not much else. Of course I could have used their help, for Joe and I had very little money, but I somehow knew that I shouldn't take their money now. This part of my life had nothing to do with them, and I didn't want to bring them into it, at least not yet. I was with Joe now, and so I acted like a good sport, the willing undergraduate who'd thrust myself out the gates of Smith College and gone off to New York with my professor, though I suspected the mood wouldn't last.

And it didn't, of course. When Joe and I walked into the small, greenish lobby of the Waverly Arms, where the night clerk sat behind a barred window, I was appalled at what I found there, and I stood in pinched, schoolmarm silence while Joe signed the register. Room 402 was worse than the lobby; it too was greenish and had a window with so many dead flies trapped between the panes that they seemed to have been intentionally pressed there by a naturalist. The room gave off intimations of its unsavory history, convincing you that a particular type of soup had once been cooked there on a hotplate (Scotch broth), and that another time, someone had lain in a stupor of illness on the concave mattress of the bed.

"This is disgusting," I said, sitting on the edge of that bed and starting to cry.

Joe had thought I would be able to overlook the hotel's essential decrepitude because it was located in Greenwich Village. He'd hoped I would rise to the siren song of the Village, to the sounds of men dreamily practicing the horn, or just the way the people looked, dressing with a kind of defiant, jobless freedom. He'd hoped I would glance around and say: *This is what I want.* But it was impossible to take a Smith girl with no experience of the world except what had occurred in bed with you, and change her into something she'd never been, and didn't seem to want to become.

"Is *this* what I've wound up with?" I asked melodramatically as I cried. "A terrible, ugly little room with dead flies?"

"No, no, it's just temporary, Joanie," Joe said, but he too was worried that we'd made some kind of irrevocably bad choice.

Really, though, it hadn't been much of a choice; after she'd flung the walnut, Carol Castleman had thrown her husband out of their house, and he understood that even if he didn't resign from the English department at Smith he would be dismissed. So now he was ruined academically and financially. But as for me, when I walked out of Northrop House, it was with a strange combination of disgrace and power. I'd told Joe how my friend Laura Sonnengard and other girls had lined up in their nightgowns to say good-bye to me like orphans in a Shirley Temple movie, and that they were tearful and deeply impressed, knowing that I was going off to a life that was likely to be more compelling than theirs, at least in the short run.

"You say it's only temporary, but *life* is temporary," I said to him. "So you're not really making me feel any better." I knew I was pathetic, sitting there on the hotel bed with my lump and my insistently girlish clothes.

"It's not my job to make you feel better," he told me. "And don't give me your freshman-year philosophy. If you don't want to be here, then please go. Get back on that bus and go back up to

Smith. I'm sure they'll take you back; they'd be too scared of the legal end not to: the oversexed Jewish professor who raped the lovely young debutante."

"I am not a debutante," I said. "And screw you, Joe. You never raped me. I made up my own mind. I knew what I wanted to do."

This seemed to startle him. "You did?" he said, sitting down next to me. "I thought it was all me, kissing you in my office, setting things in motion."

"No, I felt it that first day of class," I said. "When you walked into Seelye Hall and you were such a mess, and your wife had just had a baby, and you read aloud from 'The Dead.' Every girl in that class wanted to have some kind of relationship with you."

"Oh," he said, pleased. "I didn't know that."

"Well, it's true."

"I love you, Joanie, you know," he told me, and I thought that maybe he actually did.

This conversation calmed me for a while, and soon I agreed to go out with him into the spring night, into the chatter and drifting music of the Village. Joe took me to supper at the Grand Ticino, where I ate a bowl of *spaghetti al burro*, the only dish I ever ordered back then in Italian restaurants, much to his irritation, and Joe ate brains. The hour was late but the place was still packed, which was so different from Northampton, where restaurants closed early. Joe talked about nights spent on Bancroft Road, pacing the rooms of his depressing house, fetching Carol the A&D ointment, watching her slick the rancid orange jelly onto the baby's bottom.

"I am so glad to be away from there," he said as he ate his plate of brains. "I thought I would die in that house. So thank you. Thank you for rescuing me from a life like that, even if it was unexpected."

"Ah, don't mention it," I said, and he held my hand across the table.

"You've got butter on your lips," Joe told me. "They're shining; I think you must be a saint. Saint Joan."

Soon we began to talk of other things, until, toward the end of dinner, he admitted that he didn't only feel relief at having left Carol and Fanny; he also felt a kind of sorrow. He spoke in a breaking voice of holding his baby girl and touching the soft place on her head, the fontanel, where the bones hadn't yet joined fully.

"I'll help you," I said automatically.

"You can't help me."

I couldn't understand the loss a young father felt, he insisted. But, weirdly, I seemed to be able to. Both of us had conjured up the image of the abandoned baby, the little girl he had named after the literary Fanny Price. In a few weeks, Joe would write his wife a calm and repentant letter; actually, he would outline the general ideas he wanted to convey, and I would put them into words. The letter would be moving and earnest but not overly sentimental, and in it he'd sketch out the beginnings of an alimony and child support plan that he'd discussed with his lawyer friend Ned, and he'd request that he be allowed to visit the baby every month, inhaling her with the urgency of a father who no longer lives at home.

I did help him, in my own, limited way. I stayed with him for weeks in the Waverly Arms, and we relied on sex to cut a swath through the days that kept appearing before us. I washed my underpants and hose in the little stained sink in our room, and when they dried they were stiff from the brown bar of soap I'd used. The toilet in the hall had a weak flushing mechanism, and other tenants left urine and toilet paper in the bowl, a glutinous puddle that reminded me of the egg-drop soup we ate in China-town. Sometimes Joe and I walked the streets for hours, stopping to sit and kiss on the stoops of buildings as we'd seen others do.

Mostly, though, we stayed in, and I knew that we'd eventually turn on each other if we were trapped inside that tiny room all day. He wasn't about to leave, though; he was a writer, or he was going to be one, and he needed to be there to write. He had some savings that would go toward supporting Carol and the baby, at least for a while. I didn't have the same fever to write that he did. At Smith he'd encouraged me, but now that we were in New York, we talked only of *his* writing, and I didn't mind. I didn't think I had too much to say, and even if I had, Elaine Mozell had assured me of the futility of saying it. Joe was the one who would work on short stories, while I'd go out and make some money, supplementing the small income I had from my grandmother. So I made a few telephone calls, using the skein of connections I'd made growing up in the city, remembering that Candy Mullington from Brearley's mother was head of personnel at the publishing house Bower & Leeds. Mrs. Mullington agreed to see me, and I was given a job as the assistant to an editor, Hal Wellman. Joe was thrilled; he loved that I had something useful to do and that I would actually be working *in publishing,* that I'd be around books all day, and editors, and potential contacts for him for the future, when he had a novel to sell.

Bower & Leeds was located on the ninth floor of a medium-sized limestone building on Madison Avenue and Forty-sixth Street, and I took the train up to Grand Central every morning, while Joe slept in. He admitted that he liked waking up just long enough to see me pull off my nightgown. Every day he noticed that I looked exactly the same as I had the day before; time hid itself from you, or at least gravity did.

The world in which I now spent my days was mysterious to Joe. He was grateful that he didn't have to be there, too, but he wished he could invade it anyway, to watch me as I sat in my cubicle and answered the telephone for the cordial, overworked, and red-faced Mr. Wellman.

"What's he like?" Joe asked.

"Mr. Wellman? Oh, he's a prince. He talks to me about everyone there, actually lets me in on things. He treats me as if I'm more than an assistant, and he lets me handle the slush pile."

"Lucky you," said Joe.

"There's nothing wrong with the slush pile," I said, "except for its quality. Anyway, *someone* has to read it."

At night, I brought home bagfuls of manuscripts. Together we sat in our hotel bed and amused ourselves over how bad they were.

"Listen to this," I would say to him. "It's a novel called *Courage, Be My Guide*. And it opens like this: 'Chester Mackey had been looking in pool rooms and gin mills for happiness, until one day he realized it damn sure couldn't be bought.' "

The ludicrous writing fortified both of us; it was a yardstick by which to measure ourselves. We read other people's sad attempts, and we acted as though we were both far beyond them, although the ghost of Joe's story "No Milk on Sunday" still hovered. But that story must have been an aberration. Why else would he feel so confident that the slush pile at B & L was filled with such unmitigated shit? He could separate the good from the bad; he understood the difference. His own work would grow, would get better with time. He had been very young when he wrote that story; he didn't really know what he was doing then, and now he was starting to.

One night we went to a party at the home of Joe's old friend Harry Jacklin and his wife, Maria, who lived in a walk-up on Grove Street. When we arrived, people lined the stairway, a powerful blast of reefer smoke drifting down. Joe led me protectively through the crowds, saying hello to old friends from Columbia and from the brief period of his life that he'd spent in New York with Carol. People were surprised to see him there, and of course even more surprised to see me with him, I could tell, and he had to quickly explain the situation, trying to make it all seem arch and humorous ("I traded up," he said to someone, or, "I got myself a newer model. Runs more smoothly. Doesn't throw things"). It became clear that no one had particularly liked Carol, though they hadn't had the courage to tell him before, and felt great relief that now the truth could come out.

Joe ached for a drink of some kind: something clear and powerful to set him right. Soon he was drinking vodka and pulling on a joint, handed to him by a thin black homosexual named Digby, a dancer who'd been asked to join Martha Graham's troupe, someone whispered. With the eerie strains of theremin music on the record player, Digby was holding court in one corner of the apartment, sitting on the radiator surrounded by young white women and talking about Negro rights. The women looked up at Digby with worshipful, half-shut eyes, as though he were Paul Robeson at a communist rally. What did these girls know of Negro rights? Not much more than I did, I imagined. They were strictly Sarah Lawrence or Bennington types; I could picture them dancing in togas in a field of flowers, and suddenly I wished I was dancing with them, feeling the mush of earth underfoot, having no attachment to a man, no terrible bed to sleep in, just being part of a chain of girls in a field. These thoughts were the result of the reefer stirring things up in me, I thought, and then I was even more certain, because within fifteen minutes I was doing an interpretive dance to an Yma Sumac record in the hall-way, and from across the room I saw Joe watch me with pride and admiration that together resembled ownership, though of course I'd asked for it, I'd wanted it, putting myself directly in the line of his vision up in the landscape of Smith College.

Later, when the party settled down with quieter music and the dancing stopped, a few of the men went out onto the fire escape to talk, and Joe grabbed me to go with them. Lyle Samuelson, who taught linguistics at City College, lined up a row of spent beer bottles on the windowsill and knocked the first one against the second, which sent the third one down, though none of them broke, just rolled.

"Look, remember Ike's domino theory?" Samuelson said. "There goes Cambodia, and Thailand, and, whoops, what the hell, there goes Japan." Then he called out into the room, to no one in particular, "We need some more beers here!"

Distantly, a woman's voice called back, "Coming right up!"

I didn't know these men, and though I was happy just to lean against Joe and listen to them talk—for their voices were deep and knowledgeable, even if what they said wasn't, particularly—

suddenly another one of them appeared and I realized he was someone from B & L: Bob Lovejoy, a baby-faced editor who never talked to any of the assistants, never said hello, always looked uncommonly busy and imperious although he had only been out of college himself a couple of years.

Lovejoy turned suddenly, and though it wouldn't have occurred to me that he'd know who I was, he said in a flat, odd voice, " 'Joan, Joan, the piper's son, stole two pigs and away she run.' " Then he added, "Why'd you steal those pigs, Joan?"

The other men laughed vaguely, Joe included, though it wasn't witty. What I felt primarily was the hostility in Bob Lovejoy, inexplicably directed toward me. What was I doing here, he was wondering, when I was only some editorial assistant? What was a pencil-sharpener, a paper-filer, a reader of the slush pile doing here on this fire escape with the men?

"She didn't steal anything," Joe said. "She's completely scrupulous, this girl. I trust her with my life. And anyway, Lovejoy, she's extremely quick. A very fine writer of the short story."

"Well, that's wonderful," said Bob Lovejoy. "We need more lady writers. Though I hate to admit there are a few pretty good ones out there these days."

He hated to admit it, and he was happy to admit he hated it. Lovejoy dutifully mentioned a few women whose work was taken seriously: an imposing, political playwright with the face of a sea turtle, a poet prone to sudden fits of self-promotion that involved giving impromptu readings of her own work at other people's book parties, and a novelist who cataloged small-town goings-on with tattletale vigor. The novelist had the creepy demeanor of one of the children from "The Turn of the Screw," and seemed to be a future suicide if there ever was one.

If I'd tried, I could have rattled off my own roll call of important women writers: Mary McCarthy always came to mind right away, with her extraordinary prose, her architectural cheekbones, her hair pulled back off an extra-long, Mannerist neck, and her various, public connections to high-wattage men. That last part seemed to be essential; without those connections she would have been too free, too exotic, less compelling. I knew that she was impressive and beautiful and scary; it would be difficult for a man to find a way to mock her, and so I assumed that few did.

Instead, they admired her. They thought she was one of a kind; they were either silent in her presence or nervously chatty and needing to rise to the occasion. It was as though she existed in order to defy all expectations and to deflect the arrows of the men who were shaken by the simple fact that she did exist. And, oh God, was she tough. She would have to be, taking on politics and art, chewing on them like twisty bits of rawhide. She and one or two other, lesser female literary lights had a demeanor that lit a fire beneath their brilliance and gave it style, allowing them to slip through the swinging doors that were clearly etched with the word MEN.

But what happened to the talented women who lacked sharp cheekbones or an ease in the universe? The ones who had no attachments to powerful men?

"Women writers—even if they don't necessarily take the world by storm, they certainly make life a little brighter," Samuelson was saying. "At least, the tolerable ones do, anyway."

"Have you ever noticed," said Lovejoy slowly, as though introducing a theory he'd been quietly cultivating for some time, "that a surprisingly high number of them are mad as hatters?"

"We drive them to it," said Joe. "That must be the reason."

"Yeah, we push them to the brink," said Lovejoy cheerfully. "Wouldn't you say so, Joan?"

They all looked toward me expectantly, as though I spoke for all women and their potential for mental illness. "I have no idea," I said.

"I've come across a few of that kind in my day," said Samuelson. "Boy, they give you a run for your money." The men all nodded and laughed easily, Joe included, though when he saw me looking at him he sobered quickly.

"You're not one of them, are you?" Lovejoy said to me mildly.

He leaned forward, reached out and then very, very lightly stroked the soft skin of my forearm with his fingers. I jerked back quickly.

"*Don't,*" I said.

Lovejoy removed his hand. "Sorry," he said, and then he shrugged at Joe. "It was just irresistible."

"Like women themselves," said Lyle Samuelson.

"Like women themselves," repeated Lovejoy.

"Hey, Bob," said Joe in a vague and muzzled voice. "Did you see the sign? 'No touching.' " I knew, then, that Joe had been made aware for the first time what it might feel like to sit outnumbered among the mutterings of men. It was as though he'd been given a rare glimpse into what a woman felt and thought. He had opinions, of course, the typical ones of the day concerning communism and race relations and Dien Bien Phu, but when it came to the landscape of women, he was at a loss to say much of anything.

The men kept chuckling and nodding together, while I sat uncomfortably among them. Bob Lovejoy had touched my arm and I'd felt pillaged, interfered with, but hadn't known how to respond aggressively. Men touched women, unbidden, and the women murmured "Don't," or shouted it out, or pulled away, and either the men stopped what they were doing or didn't stop; it was the way of the world. I was here with Joe, and I couldn't just get up and leave. I leaned against the railing of the fire escape and peered down miserably over the quiet street. Joe looped an arm around my bare shoulder, which was cold, in need of covering.

"Listen, you," he whispered into the whorl of an ear that poked out from under my hair. "Let's get out of here."

And I was grateful, too grateful, as though he were saving me, and we extricated ourselves and left the party, walking together through the Village after midnight, leaning into each other once in a while to kiss, as if in mutual apology, stopping beneath a streetlamp at Sheridan Square, where a newsstand was still open, the final edition of the *Herald* pinned up like laundry. Below us a passing subway train sent up a blast of warm air. We smelled urine, and peanuts, as though a circus train were rushing by beneath us, and we wished we could get on.

One Sunday morning upon awakening, Joe told me he had to begin writing a novel. "No offense, Joanie," he said, pulling himself from the bed surprisingly early, "but I have to get up. I'm going to start writing a book. No more stories. They'll get me nowhere."

He sat in boxer shorts at the writing desk with his little Royal typewriter in front of him, and he smoked and drank some Coke from a glass that until a few minutes earlier had held our toothbrushes. The walnuts were gone; since the incident with Carol, he'd lost his taste for them, and he never did regain it. I stayed in bed, enjoying the novelty for a while of watching him write, but finally I got bored and said I had to go out.

It was my parents' apartment I went to, the first time I'd been there since I'd left Smith. I was scared, but decided I was bigger than they were. I had Joe on my side. As I'd assumed, they had in fact been appalled when Smith informed them that I'd dropped out; an irate typed letter addressed to me on my father's letterhead had arrived at the hotel after they'd tracked me down. The letter called me "a disappointment," and it was signed "From your mother and father," with no mention, or even whiff, of love. Which is why it was odd that I was choosing to go there now. But the Waverly Arms was so depressing, and Joe, in his new, determined, novelist mode, was drawing up into himself like a fetus. Laura Sonnengard and the rest of my friends were off at college; right now they were studying, smooching with boyfriends, getting dressed in pristine sweaters and sensible shoes. I needed to get away from the grime of the room for a while and the silent, heavy presence of Joe. Reflexively, I thought I needed my parents, despite everything, and so I went there.

Ray, the day doorman at my parents' building, didn't know of my disgrace, for he tipped his hat and asked me how it felt to be a "coed," and Gus the elevator man pulled the brass lever as we rode slowly upward and he told me about his son, off at New Jersey Technical College, where he was studying refrigeration systems. Then I was right there in the vestibule outside the apartment I'd grown up in, with the umbrella stand and the wicker chair that had never been blessed with the pressure of a human posterior. I let myself in and stood in the front hall, calling out tentatively, "Hello? Hello?"

My mother, in an aqua satin robe, appeared, and when she saw it was me she burst out crying—a surprisingly unrestrained bleat that made me want to run. I couldn't comfort her; what could I possibly say? So we sat down in the pale living room with its low white couches and pastels of New York streets in the rain, and I watched her cry for a while. Finally she blew her nose in a handkerchief and then looked at me sharply.

"Your father is out playing golf with the Dorlings. We know that this isn't the end of the world," she told me.

"Good," I said.

"But when the college told us this man was a Jew—"

"They *told* you that?"

"Yes," said my mother. "We asked them. He's a Jew, and he's married, and somehow he's convinced you that this is love." Now she stood up from her couch and came over to mine; each of the couches was long and sleek, an individual ocean liner. "Believe me, Joan, I know how it is, they're very persuasive," she went on. "There was a man here once, a Mr. Milton Fish; he came to talk to your father about investing in his company. Something about textiles. I'll never forget what he wore—it was a striped suit—and by the end of the evening your poor father was practically eating out of this Mr. Milton Fish's hand, practically signing an enormous check to him that basically would have bankrupted our family forever. It was only when I called your father into the bedroom and gave him a talking-to that he came around. That he saw he was under this salesman's spell. Which is exactly what's happening with you and your professor. The powers of persuasion.

They speak well, they pride themselves on their history of 'education,' as they like to say, and they know how to use words with plenty of syllables, and they're dark and mysterious, so that you feel as though you've entered a Gypsy den, and how much more thrilling *that* must feel than being with the kind of boys you're used to, like Alec Meers, or the Bexleys' son, am I right?"

Her words were so rapid and wild that I began to blink like someone under a strobe light.

"Am I right?" my mother was saying. "You *have* been with other boys, Joan, no? I mean, have you been with them in a carnal way, as man and woman? Because if you have, then probably you're choosing your professor for his skills in that department. They aren't afraid of sex, not them! They want to do it constantly, even when the woman has her menses, and they—"

"Mother, are you completely off the wall?" I leaped up. "I came here because I was lonely and Joe was working," I told her. "He's Jewish, yes, and so what if he wants sex all the time; I do too." She blinked several times in response to this. "But he's a talented writer, okay? A *good* writer, and he's going to become famous and won't it make a difference how you feel about him then?"

"Not one iota," said my mother, her jaw as tight as the curls on her head that had been plastered there very recently; I could still smell the carnation odor of beauty parlor, could conjure the metal combs floating like specimens in blue water.

It was as though, having read Joe's poor story in *Caryatid*, I needed to defend his honor more fervently than ever; if I didn't, who would? His wife, Carol, hated him, and Fanny might soon be taught to hate him, too. His fledgling attempts at fiction weren't anything to write home about, and yet here I was: shouting compliments about Joe through the mayonnaise-colored living room of my childhood and hoping I would start to believe them. He *was* talented, wasn't he? He looked talented, anyway; he was brooding and unpredictable and bridling with sensations I didn't understand, sensations that I dubbed *male*. Male and solid and influential, the emotions of men at war, or men hunched around the smoking powwow of a poker game. I would tell everyone he was talented, and then he would rise to the occasion.

"So you won't meet him?" I asked my mother.

"Oh, really, what do you think, Joan?" she said, and it was true that the prospect of a sit-down with Joe and my parents was horrible no matter how you looked at it. He would see two skeletons clutching highballs; they would see a fast-talking garment salesman with a penis as big as a loaf of challah. No, they could never meet.

But of course they did meet, much later on, when everything had settled down, or had gotten all charged up, depending on how you looked at it, and Joe's place in the world was unshakable. They actually wanted to know him then, for the only famous writer they'd ever met was Thornton Wilder, who as a favor to a friend in the 1940s had spoken at my father's club, giving an eight-minute ramble about the state of the American theater, and then fled.

But for now, before his success, Joe was still the Jewish rapist, and I was still the girl who improbably loved him. I left my parents' apartment, walking down Park Avenue, which now looked as empty and charmless as my parents' living room. I was sprung; that I knew. But if I was truly going to be on my own with Joe, then what I'd said to my mother simply had to come true. Joe needed to be talented; he needed to be brilliant. It would cancel out his Jewishness, the unsavory scraps of his adultery, the crappy room he'd rented for us, and all the other flaws and disappointments that surrounded him.

Maybe he really was a talented writer. Maybe I couldn't see it, because I wasn't talented enough myself. But he'd told me I was; that was partly why he took me to New York with him. It wasn't only about going to bed with me; he could have had that with many other girls, who would have happily simpered and opened their legs. He just *had* to be talented; it would pick us up by our bootstraps, it would satisfy Joe once and for all and let him feel at ease beside me, at ease among other men; it would also make a point, pleasing my mother and my father, even if my mother insisted she wouldn't feel "one iota" different. *Iota;* what a strange word, I thought as I walked over to Lexington and climbed on the train, heading back downtown. No one ever said "two iotas," it was always one. Language only *felt* infinite; instead, everyone swam through surprisingly narrow channels when they spoke or wrote.

Iotas were dancing inside me, along with other things: my mother's words, so vulgar and crabbed; my grandiose dreams of greatness for Joe. He would be a writer; the hopes I had for him were like the hopes men had for themselves: to conquer, to crush and astound. I didn't particularly want to do any of that myself; it didn't even occur to me that I could. I kept thinking of Elaine Mozell, and how she'd tried to make her way among the men. Elaine with her drink held loosely in her hand, and her slightly sloppy lipstick. I didn't want to play in the same field as the men; it would never be comfortable, and I couldn't compete. My world wasn't big enough, wide enough, dramatic enough, and my subjects were few. I knew my limits.

By the time I got back to the Waverly Arms, a sort of miracle had occurred. It was as though Joe had been intuiting my new catalog of hopes for him, for when I let myself into the room, he stood and waved two masses of papers at me.

"What's this?" I asked, knowing full well.

"The first twenty-one pages of *The Walnut.*"

"I see. *The Walnut,*" I said. "So I guess it's a novel about someone working in a walnut factory? A gritty look at the world of walnut laborers?"

Joe laughed. "Oh, yeah. It's going to stand the walnut-packing industry on its *head,*" he said. He pulled me down onto the bed and lifted my hand, guiding it slowly, lowering it onto his pages. "You," he said. "Read."

Chapter Four

SO THEN HE was king. It happened quickly, the way these things do: one minute you're tugging a sheet of paper from your typewriter and pulling at the skin of your lips and muttering *I hate myself, I hate myself,* then the next minute there's a royal bugler at your door unscrolling a proclamation that makes your ascendance official.

And yes, he ascended, a straight shot upward, no qualms, no second thoughts, none of those late-night fears that sometimes terrorize young writers: What if everything's different now? What if *we're* different?

Joe wanted everything to be different, and so did I. Filth was boring, and so was a diet of egg foo yung. A man needed to have something to grab on to, something that made him feel fine about himself, or else every failure that had ever struck him in his lifetime would come creeping back, all the math tests, the ejaculations that didn't wait for their cue, and the halfhearted reprimands of a gentle, depressed shoe-salesman father whose face could barely be remembered after the assault of time. An unsold novel was just one more failure.

But an enormously successful novel was a thing of beauty,

and Joe and I jumped and slapped each other's back and dove into the bed and out into the street and talked of nothing else but the book, and him, and the reviews, and "the future," that nebulous hallway. In the winter of 1958 we moved from our room at the Waverly Arms into a real apartment on Charles Street off Greenwich Avenue with its own bathroom and high ceilings and wide-beamed floors, the kind of place where a successful young writer should live.

Writers need light. They always tell you this, as though they're parched, as though they're *plants*, as though the page they're working on would look completely different with a southern exposure. Writers need light, and the place on Charles Street was flooded; we had light, we had heat, we had a continuous drip of money for the first time since we'd been together. We clung and drank and collected new friends at every book party and reading and dinner we were invited to. My doubts about having left Smith disappeared. *We were having fun.* Mostly, the quality of our life had changed so greatly because of what he had been given. Sometimes I thought of it as a crown, at other times a key: a way inside the vast world of broad-shouldered writers. And in this world, the men feasted and drank until all hours, though once in a while they were summoned to stand up on stages and speak.

Joe loved this part best of all. While I watched, beaming nervously, nodding, he leaped up onto every stage, clutching the trim first novel that had gotten him there. Whenever he gave readings in those early days, he often repeated what he'd said at a reading the night before, having plotted and planned his entire set of remarks down to the jokes, the casual, off-the-cuff type of patter, and even the ritual sipping of water.

One night in New York City during that first year, Joe was appearing somewhere, I think it was the Ninety-second Street Y, though I'm not positive; the grand auditoriums have all come together in my memory by now as one enormous chamber with thousands of rows. I wore a blue velvet dress—that part I'm sure of—and no makeup, my hair pulled back in a ribbon. It was one of Joe's first readings and I was sick with overstimulation, retching into a toilet in the women's rest room, and was then so embarrassed about it that I didn't come out of the stall for a while. I just knelt on the floor, listening as two women stood at the sinks and talked about Joe.

"*The Walnut* is my favorite book this year. And I hear he's an awfully good reader," one said. "My friend Elise heard him read last week."

"Oh yes," said the other, "and he's very attractive. I just want to eat him up like a dish of ice cream."

"But you can't. He's taken," said the first one.

"So?" said the second, and they both began laughing.

At which point I forced myself to emerge from the stall, letting the door swing wide as if I were a gunslinger in a Western, bursting into a saloon. But the women paid no attention to me. I wasn't a threat, with my pale cloth coat and anemic good looks. I had the appearance of someone who's already landed the man she wants; they were two women still leisurely searching and enjoying themselves.

One woman was dark, with a sheet of black hair and olive skin. The other was fair and freckled, with improbably large breasts. I could imagine her nipples like twin pale snouts, poking into Joe's delighted face.

Which woman would he choose? It seemed important that I be able to tell, that I know what he would like, so that in the future I could block him, distract him, keep him from his ideal.

Foolishly, I spoke to these women. "You know," I said, "I'm so glad you both enjoy Joe's work."

"Pardon?" said one.

"Oh my God," said the other one quietly, under her breath.

"Wait, Joseph Castleman is your *husband*?" said the dark one.

"Yes," I said.

"He's wonderful," said the light one. "You must be really proud of him."

"Yes," I said, washing my hands. The water splattered out boiling hot, but I didn't even pull my hands away. It was as though I wanted to poach my hands right there in front of these two young women.

"Is he writing something new?" dark asked.

"Yes," I said. "A second novel."

"That's great," said light. "We're really looking forward to hearing him read tonight."

Then they were gone, and the bathroom door hadn't even shut all the way before I could hear their whispering and laughter. I knew what I was up against, that women would fling themselves at him like lemmings who had a love-wish instead of a death-wish. Adorable lemmings batting their eyelashes and trying to open his pants with their sharp little claws. I knew it, because in a way I had been one of them, and before me there had certainly been others. I just assumed, though, based on no evidence whatsoever, that Joe had learned by now to refuse the other lemmings, to gently pull their claws from his shirt, and that he would continue to refuse them as time went on, because now he had me, and I was different.

Onstage, Joe read the first chapter of *The Walnut*, in which Michael Denbold, a literature instructor at a small women's college in Connecticut, meets Susan Lowe, his most promising student; so begins an intense sexual relationship with her, during which he ultimately abandons his wife, Deirdre, an unhinged ceramicist, and their new baby boy. His novel was splayed open on the sloped surface, and he drank glasses of water throughout the evening because the novelty of giving readings excited him so much that his mouth dried out and his speech was filled with spitless ticking sounds, and he needed to drink and drink like a baby goat.

The audience ate him up, just like those girls had wanted to. The young men longed to be like him, and went home with a new resolve to work on their own novels; and the women, for the most part, wished they could have some piece of him, the edge of a sleeve, the tip of a finger, the thick feathering of an eyebrow, something that could be theirs for good. They admired him, wished he would hunch over a typewriter in *their* apartment, smoke a cigarette in *their* bed, spread himself across them so easily and casually, the way he did across me.

I sat in the front row, holding his briefcase that had carried his book and notes, listening to the words with pride, flinching slightly when he read a line I didn't love, and stirring pleasurably in my chair when he read one I did. *This is his briefcase,* I wanted to announce to the people sitting around me, especially the young women from the bathroom, to whom I also wanted to add, *Fuck you both, with your cinched waists and your batting eyes.* After he'd been introduced, Joe sprang forward and bounded up the steps onto the stage, as eager and harried as he'd been the first day of class at Smith, but now possessing some new kind of *fizz* that would have been inappropriate if he hadn't just become so famous.

Later, at the reception, I watched as the two dark and light women flanked him, saw his eyes dart from side to side, saw how his hand cradled his drink, and his back arched slightly and stretched. Hal Wellman, my boss and now Joe's editor, was standing beside me, watching me look at Joe, and in a kind voice he said, "Don't worry about that."

I turned to him. "No?"

"No," said Hal. He was tired, a big, stooped, ruddy man who had to catch a train at Grand Central soon. "Look, he's feeling pretty full of himself. Anybody would."

We stood together watching Joe and the women, saw the light one pull out a copy of *The Walnut* and ask him to sign it. The dark one offered up a pen, and then Joe said something that was apparently so hilarious that the dark one opened her mouth and basically shrieked, and the light one clapped her hands to her face.

"But still," I said to Hal. "It's not a pretty sight."

"No," he said. "It's not. So you know what, Joan? Let's get you a big glass of wine."

Throughout the rest of the reception, Hal stayed beside me.

We drank together, watching Joe and providing a mildly ironic commentary, and then finally Hal looked at his watch and announced he had a train to catch.

Over the next few decades Joe followed him to three different publishing houses, until Hal's death from a cerebral hemorrhage in his office, his head down on a pile of unread manuscripts. But for as many years as I needed him, Hal had stayed with me at those cocktail parties, protecting me from something vague and threatening that was always in the room.

That night at the Y, after the reading and the reception and the small dinner afterward at a French restaurant in the neighborhood, Joe and I came home to our Village apartment loopy and a little sickish. There was garlic on our breath and a pickling dose of wine that audibly sloshed around inside us when we moved, and so we fell onto the bed, side by side, not touching.

"You know what?" he said. "I'm a famous person."

"That you are."

"I don't *feel* famous," he went on. "I just feel like myself. It's really no different from teaching English to a bunch of silly girls. When you walk into a room, everyone looks at you. Big deal."

"I wasn't a silly girl."

"No, you weren't, not at all," he said, and I heard the indulgence in his voice. He lay on his back, stuffed and drunk and taking the pulse of his fame, listening for its sprightly gallop. I thought about the two women at the reading, their darkness and light, their interest in him, and his interest in return.

"What's the matter?" he asked me.

"Nothing," I said, and this was the same answer I would continue to give over the years, with notable, occasional exceptions when I accused him of betrayals and cried. Mostly, "nothing" became my mantra. Nothing was wrong, nothing at all. Or at least, if anything was wrong, I'd asked for it. I'd *asked* for him and all his problems. I'd demanded him, and here he was, mine. His divorce had come through when *The Walnut* was still in page proofs, and we'd gotten married shortly before its publication.

That fall, when *Life* magazine did a feature on today's bumper crop of new writers, Joe was the one they favored with an entire page. Amid photos of Khrushchev, and Ike and Mamie, and rural Southern children picking peaches, and teenaged couples locked in some ephemeral dance craze, there was a picture of Joe walking down the street with a cigarette in his hand, his face screwed into an expression suggesting deep thought. There, too, was Joe at the White Horse Tavern, talking to some other writer who was seen only from behind.

The Walnut had been written in the kind of first-novel, foaming fever that never repeats itself, no matter how hard a writer tries to re-create the recipe, the sleepless jangle, the effluvium of words. When the novel was finally done, we'd celebrated at the Grand Ticino, and the next day I bound the pages up in a thick rubber band and brought them to work with me at Bower & Leeds, where, mumbling and blushing, I placed the manuscript on Hal Wellman's desk, telling him he really ought to take a look at it, but not saying anything more.

That night, I saw Hal carry the manuscript home with him. I imagined it tucked under his arm as he boarded the commuter train to Rye, pictured him unsnapping the rubber band and leaning back against his seat to read. Then, later, I saw him in the living room of his Tudor house, stationed in an easy chair with a drink in his hand. I saw his children hanging on to him, trying to pull him down onto the floor for a ride, but he would resist them. The lure of *The Walnut* was just too strong, the siren song of this undiscovered writer. A *virgin.*

Virgin writers have a sheen to them, a layer of something that comes off on your fingers when you touch it, like powder from a moth's wing. A virgin writer still has a chance to surprise you, to club you over the head with his brute brilliance. He can become anything you need him to be. Joe was a very good specimen, with a clear, clean-lined book that had plenty of hubris and thoughtfulness behind it. And he was handsome and rumpled, with eyes that looked tired all the time; journalists sometimes commented on that, and he would tell them about not sleeping. Tired and sad and wise. *Wise:* I've always hated that word; it's so overused, as though weary, successful people somehow have secret access to larger truths.

Hal Wellman seemed to think this was the case with Joe. Hal read the manuscript of *The Walnut* that first night at home, and he said he just had to read on, he had to stay with it, he couldn't stop, because it was just too mesmerizing. Apparently he laughed out loud in a series of harsh barks, and Mrs. Wellman came in from the kitchen because she feared her husband was choking.

So Hal, not knowing that the author was the man I lived with, offered to buy the book for $2,500. I confessed to where I had gotten the manuscript, but Hal didn't mind; he published the novel the following fall. I could say here that I was surprised that it all worked out so well, but actually I wasn't. I knew the novel was good in a confessional, artful way. I'd been reading the slush pile, after all; I'd been reading *Courage, Be My Guide* and *Mrs. Dingle's Secret,* but I'd also been reading the books that we actually published at Bower & Leeds, and while some of them were terrific—"powerful and riveting," we editorial assistants routinely wrote as part of the flap copy—many were dull and just waiting to be dumped into remainder bins. There were World War II and Korean War stories, and there were gentle meditations by women on the nature of love. There were children's books with their soothing nursery cadences, and glossy books of photographs of Morocco and other exotic locales, meant to be placed on someone's coffee table beside a bowl of mints. But *The Walnut* was different.

Soon the book appeared in print, lightly edited by Hal, and then Joe was famous and found himself stepping onto stages and drinking glasses of water behind various lecterns. I was given a raise at work and the promise of being made an editor one day soon myself, but despite that promise, Joe began to urge me to quit.

"Leave," he said after his book went into a fourth printing.

"What do you want to stay there for? Your salary's tiny, and there's no prestige."

And mostly I didn't want to stay in that office where men were kings and women were geishas (except for one powerful woman editor named Edith Tansley, who looked like a hawk and terrified everyone, man and woman). The men often gathered together in some editor's office; I could hear their laughter and sense the force field of their pleasure at being together in a contained space. They were kinder to me now; they had to be, for I had been the finder of *The Walnut*. There was a sort of respect granted me that hadn't been given to an editorial assistant before, though it was still suffused with a mirth that I didn't understand.

"Morning, Joan," Bob Lovejoy would say with a wink. "Tell me, how's the wunderkind doing?"

"Joe's fine."

"Send him my regards. Tell him we're all waiting for his next one. And don't wear him out, okay?"

Finally I did quit; though some of the other assistants made me a party and said they'd miss me, I was relieved to be away from there. I would stay closer to home now, closer to him, where we could share our joy, our boundless excitement and self-love. Carol had never been a part of anything that was important to Joe; she didn't even read his work, he'd complained, insisting that fiction wasn't "up her alley."

"Nothing was up that alley of hers, actually," he'd said. "I think it was a bowling alley. But you, you're different, thank God."

I was the wife. I liked the role at first, assessed the power it contained, which for some reason many people don't see, but it's there. Here's a tip: If you want access to someone important, one of the best ways is to ingratiate yourself to his wife. At night in bed, before sleep, the wife might idly speak well of you to her husband. Soon you will find yourself invited into the important man's home. He might ignore you, standing in a corner with his fleet of admirers, telling stories in a self-assured voice, but at least you're there, inside the same room he's in, having made your way past some invisible velvet rope.

Joe often liked to boast to people that I was the central nervous system of this marriage. "Without Joan," he would say grandly, when we were out with a group of friends and everyone had been drinking, "I'd be nothing. A shriveled-up little shrimp in a shrimp cocktail."

"Oh, please," I'd say. "He's crazy; ignore him, everyone."

"No, no, she keeps me in line, this girl," he'd go on. "She keeps the world at bay. She is my discipline, my cat-o'-nine-tails, my better half. Truly, I don't think people appreciate their wives half as much as they ought to."

The implication was that *he* truly appreciated me, and he did seem to, back then. After all, he was the only writer I knew who wanted his wife around so much of the time. The other male writers Joe came to know—the circle of confident men that sought him out and lured him in, the way they did with any new male literary animal—were forever shrugging off the women in their midst.

Lev Bresner, at the beginning a haunted young immigrant whose English was still shaky but whose autobiographical short stories of life in the death camps had begun appearing with regularity in magazines, had a young wife he'd brought over from Europe, a tiny woman named Tosha with black hair piled in a bun. She was sexy in a malnourished way; you felt that if you took her to bed, first you would have to give her a hot meal.

Tosha appeared at events with Lev only infrequently, when the occasion required that men show up with women. There they were, the Bresners, at dinner parties and cocktail parties. But she never came to his readings, which freed Lev up afterward to go out to a bar and drink and argue with other men.

If Tosha was there, she would forever be pulling the edge of his sleeve, saying, "Lev, Lev. Can we please go home now?"

Why do women so often want to *go* and men want to stay? If you leave, then you can preserve yourself better. But if you stay, then essentially you're saying: I'm immortal, I don't need to sleep or rest or eat or take a breath. I can stay all night at this little bar with these people, talking and talking and swallowing so many beers that my stomach bloats and my breath becomes a hot, unbearable blast, and I never have to imagine that this wonderful, stunning time will ever come to an end.

Joe wanted me beside him. He needed me there with him before a reading, and during it, and after it was over. Much later, in an article on Joe, the critic Nathaniel Bone wrote:

> Often, during this early, fertile period of Castleman's career, his second wife, Joan, was by his side.
>
> "She was an extremely quiet person," remembers Lev Bresner. "Her reticence had a certain mysteriousness about it, but her presence was itself a kind of tonic. He was nervous, and she was very, very soothing."
>
> Another writer, unnamed, remarks that Castleman didn't want to be away from his wife very often, except "when he was on the prowl."

Reading this now, I still bristle at the image of young Joe on the prowl, lurking in corners and hunting down women, or even not having to hunt at all and simply letting them come to him, but of course it's all true, and I think I always knew that that would be part of the bargain, right from the beginning in his office at Smith, when he clanged his knees against mine.

His divorce had been surprisingly uncomplicated; because Joe had little to give Carol—almost no money, no property, for even the house on Bancroft Road was a rental from the college—there was nothing major she could stick him with. Out of cruelty she might have tried to force him to support her and Fanny in high style, but that wasn't her way. Instead, she froze him out entirely. Her own family in Sausalito, California, had money; they would support the abandoned Carol and her child. She didn't take money from Joe; she just took the baby. And Joe, for all his love of this baby, for all his sighs and soliloquies about fatherhood and about the soft spot on a baby's head, let Fanny go.

At first he balked. He wanted a schedule for visitation, he wanted it in writing, he wanted to be a *father*. His unhappiness was obviously a source of pleasure for Carol; she called our number in New York and taunted him, said that Fanny was changing greatly every day, that it was like one of those science films children are shown in school, in which the growth of a flower is miraculously speeded up, that she had begun to look just like *him*, that she was precocious, that she was amazing, that she, Carol, would teach the baby to forget all about the father who'd helped create her.

"Don't be such a bitch about this, Carol," I heard him say. "You're going to screw her up for life."

To which I'm almost certain Carol responded, "No, Joe, you've already done that."

So he stopped fighting with her. He backed away, relinquishing the last traces of the failed marriage. With Fanny whisked off to Sausalito, it was more difficult to see her anyway, though once, years later, he did visit during a book tour. On another occasion we packed up a box of toys and shipped it to California, but we never heard back. For a while Joe sent letters, and while some were answered by Carol, tersely, most were ignored, and after a while Joe lost interest. His sighs about Fanny came less frequently. She became a ghost, joining Joe's dead in that gallery of faraway, mourned souls: the fat, possessive mother, the melancholy father.

As far as he could see it, the collapse of his first marriage was still basically Carol's fault. His guilt was of a mild variety. As he told me, Carol had stopped having sex with him after Fanny was born, even months later, when her episiotomy stitches had healed and there was no medical reason for her continued refusal.

"I'm afraid you're going to rip me open," she'd confided to him in bed.

"That's delusional," he'd said, but before he'd even entered her—when he was positioning himself on top of her, both of them enduring the silent arrangement of body parts, his testicles grazing her skin—she'd pushed him off, weeping.

"I couldn't possibly have hurt you," he said. "I didn't even have a *chance* to. What's the matter?"

But Carol could do nothing but cry, and then, probably to her eternal relief, the baby joined in the chorus, rendering sex impossible for the night. *Whew*, thought Carol. *Fuck*, thought Joe, and he lay awake in a stew, wondering what it was about him that no longer appealed to her, and why women did this sort of thing, changing the terms, harboring inexplicable aversions. That was what her reaction was: an aversion. She didn't want to touch any part of him, and she didn't want him wrapped around her, marinating her in his smell, raising a topography of beard-burn on her cheeks, causing her to rise up from the protective crouch she'd been in since Fanny was born.

He didn't want to leave things be, to let her retreat, to simply engage in a pantomime of a typical academic marriage. "For God's sake, Carol," he'd told her. "Nothing's going to happen to you."

But still she refused, telling him she wasn't ready to be touched, she already had enough human needs to deal with, what with nursing the baby every few hours. And when finally he insisted, she howled in pain as though he were stabbing her with a pitchfork, and he felt like a rapist, a murderer. So he didn't try again after that night, and then time passed and he turned away from her and toward me, and I didn't refuse him; I had no stitches that could be loosened, no fear, no hesitation.

Our wedding took place at City Hall. We'd invited only my college friend Laura and Mary Croy, another editorial assistant from Bower & Leeds, and Joe's recent friend Lev Bresner, and the poet Harry Jacklin. Carol was gone from his thoughts, and so, I suspected, was their baby. He wanted another baby now, a parallel one whom he could learn to appreciate and love.

Pregnancy would be misery at first, he'd warned. But he was

wrong. There was no real misery, only a swollenness and dis-equilibrium tempered by fantasy: Who would this baby be? Boy or girl? Rocket scientist? I heaved and squeezed in the maternity ward of the now-defunct Flower Fifth Avenue Hospital, having chosen so-called natural childbirth over the far more inviting twi-light sleep. *Fuck you, Dr. Lamaze,* I thought as I huffed, imagining a suave and lean Frenchman in a tailored suit chain-smoking Gauloises. Joe himself was off in the cafeteria eating and reading. When he was brought in to see Susannah for the first time, I remember that he had a small slash of ketchup on his chin, and the *Times* rolled up under his arm.

But he loved our baby profoundly; he loved all of our babies in the same way I knew he'd once loved Fanny. I ignored the rapid burnout of his love for that firstborn; I pretended it was an aber-ration. We lay Susannah on our bed when she was an infant and sang her long love songs together, alternating verses, cracking each other up with what we hoped were witty rhymes. It was as though we were ensuring that the baby would never come between us, would never damage the marriage or the sex or the tenderness.

Joe liked to hold his children by the ankles and turn them upside down, or else lift one up onto his shoulders and stride down the street with him or her gripping his hair. It frightened me how carefree and loose he seemed with them; I was afraid they would fall off and die, their heads cracking open on the side-walk. He wanted them on his shoulders; I wanted them on my breast.

Whenever I was nursing, I felt as if there was nothing else in the world I needed to be doing. It didn't matter to me in those moments that I had no career of my own, no standing in the world. I was a nursing mother, and that was all I had to be. At first Joe liked the sight, was excited by it and moved, too, but as the months passed he would make remarks like "I hope you're not planning on doing this forever." Or, "I could be wrong, but I thought Dr. Spock said it's a good idea to stop nursing them before they start graduate school. It gets in the way of their classes." And so I did stop, sooner than I might have otherwise.

Later on, when the babies turned into toddlers, Joe felt some relief from anxiety. Nights were for sleeping through now. Also, Joe felt he was able to imprint them a little. Sometimes he had Susannah perform party tricks when friends came over for the evening.

"Now, Susie," he would say when she wandered into the living room at two years of age. The room was filled with smoke and writers and writers' wives. "Go bring me the most overrated book on the shelf."

And she would dutifully march over and pull down *The Naked and the Dead*, and everyone would roar.

But he wasn't done. "And why, Susie, is this the most overrated book on the shelf?"

"'Cause he's fulla hot air," she would say, and everyone would laugh again, though of course there was more to come.

"Oh ho, Susie Q, so he's full of hot air, Mr. Norman Mailer?" said Joe. "Why don't you show me a book that you find absolutely brilliant?"

And she would return to the shelf and look around for the familiar bright red spine, look and look until it leaped into her vision, and then she yanked on it hard with her fat, small hands and whipped it loose from the tightly packed shelf. Turning to face the room she would thrust out a copy of *The Walnut*, and the increasing laughter made her cheeks flush. She knew she was doing something winning, and that it helped her gain her father's love, although she had no idea of exactly what it was she was doing.

I wanted to protect her from him, to rush across the room and scoop her up and tell Joe not to use her this way, that it would only lead to unhappiness. But I would have seemed insane, like an overinvolved mother, someone who wanted to smash the delicate love between father and daughter. And so I just smiled and nodded from the side of the living room. Joe gave Susannah a kiss on her silky, fruity-clean head and dismissed her from her duties.

"Where are all the *good* fathers?" Susannah once complained to me when she was a teenager. "The TV fathers, the ones who go to work and then come home, and they're *there* for you, you know what I mean?"

We were sitting and braiding lanyards together at the time; this was something we often did back then. It was tedious and soothing all at once, the long, slippery strands twining together, formed into bracelets she could give to her friends or her sister and brother, or even to me and Joe. He would wear a bracelet for a few hours with a certain smirking pride, the bright colors shimmering on his hairy wrist, but even then she would understand the irony involved, the fact that Joe got a *kick* out of being seen wearing her bracelet. Sometimes it seemed as though he liked being a father more than actually being this particular father to this particular girl and her siblings.

"I don't know, honey," I'd said to her, ashamed that I hadn't given her the kind of father she wanted. I'd only occasionally seen such a man myself: a gentle father who was strong, too, not a monster and not a weakling with asthma and a button-down cardigan. Where *were* the good fathers of that generation? They existed, of course, but many of them were off somewhere else, having a drink or a smoke or playing pool or listening to jazz. They were restless, they owned the world, and they were probably out in it, looking around.

We hired a live-in baby-sitter named Melinda to help us when the kids were small and we were so busy, a young girl who took classes at the American Academy of Dramatic Arts and comported herself with a certain surprised and poised air, as though the world were Schwab's Drugstore and you never knew when you might be discovered.

Joe was drawn to Melinda, but I didn't know that for a while, managed somehow not to know the extent of it at first. But within weeks of her appearance in our house, he was most certainly making love to her up in the attic, where he knew I hated to go because of the mouse problem. Mice left their tiny hard little feces as calling cards on the floor, yet the old attic bed that was covered with sheets and quilts managed to stay droppings-free, or at least neither he nor Melinda seemed to mind the thought of mice scampering and crapping all around them, so taken were they with each other.

But it would be some time before I would realize all of this; mostly, when Melinda was in our house, novels got written. Though everything was chaotic, life seemed to be in balance. The children were loud and disorganized and project-oriented. One of the girls would hang on my leg, another would drag out a bag of flour and demand we make papier-mâché. There was Susannah with her lanyards, and Alice with a volleyball, and David in a dark room with a battery and two pieces of copper wire. I wanted to be with them as much as I could, but there was never enough time.

Once in a while Joe would suddenly turn to me and say, "Come."

"Come where?"

"Hunting and gathering."

This meant that he wanted to find some ideas for a story or a novel, and he needed me there with him. So I would kiss the children and reluctantly say good-bye. "Do you have to go?" they would cry. "Do you have to?"

"Yes, we have to!" Joe would shout back. And then he would grab me and we would head out into the Village night, as though ideas might be embedded, micalike, in the sidewalk. "They'll be fine," he'd say, waving a hand vaguely back toward our house.

"I know they will," I'd say. "But still."

" 'But still,' " he'd tell me. "You want that written on your headstone? Come on."

And he was right; the children would be fine without us, just the way they were during the day when we were unavailable. Usually, we stopped in at the White Horse, which inevitably gave Joe a dose of nerve, for he was always recognized there and he would engage in free-floating conversations about other writers, other books, or the buildup in Vietnam. We went to Folk City and to jazz clubs, and we listened to female poets standing at microphones, their multiple bracelets jangling like loose change as they read their quivering poems to an attentive audience.

One night Joe told me that he wanted his second novel to contain a scene with a prostitute in it.

"Prostitutes are boring," I said. "They're all the same. They've got those same terrible backgrounds: the lecherous father, the dirt road, the nowhere life."

"They're not boring if they're done right," he said, and I realized that he wanted to go visit a prostitute for research, and he wanted my permission. He wouldn't have sex with her, he would just ask her questions, trying to understand what it meant to be a woman who did what she did. The prostitute would need to be conveyed realistically, otherwise that section of the new novel, Joe explained, would feel pulpy and lurid. "You can come with me, Joan," he said. "In fact, I wish you would."

And so I went, wearing a powder blue cloth coat and carrying my little purse. We climbed the stairs of a small apartment building downtown near the Hudson River; the breezes brought in fresh shipments of garbage-stink. One of Joe's friends, a dissipated writer he knew from the White Horse, had arranged the visit. The prostitute's name was Brenda, and her hair was swirled into a blond beehive and she wore Capri pants and a man's shirt. Her face was rough and thick with makeup. She sat on an armchair and said, "What is it you want to know?" Her toenails, in their sandals, were painted milk white.

"So how did you get your start, Brenda?" Joe asked her, trying for familiarity.

Brenda paused, lighting a cigarette. "My sister Anita was in the business," she said, "and she always had cash to buy clothes with and whatnot. Our mother never had spending money, and she used to sew us these homemade dresses with big puffy sleeves that I hated. I wanted something more, and Anita had it.

She'd come home with these dresses and strappy shoes, and all I wanted was clothes like that. She told me to follow her lead, and I did. I didn't like it at first, all those fellows with hair growing on their back, some of them smelling like garlic or whatnot, but after a while I began to make lists in my head when I was lying there. I would make lists of all the things I had to do later, and of all the things I wanted to buy myself: the dresses, and the shoes, the stockings. And pretty soon the guy would make that little *sound*, and I would know he was finished and I could get up and go about my business and whatnot."

"What about pregnancy?" I suddenly asked, imagining the sperm of these garlicky men starting their mindless swim upstream. Joe nodded to me gratefully when I asked this, because the question would never have occurred to him.

"Well, I've had three accidents," Brenda said, "and each time I had it dealt with, you know? One of the other girls knows a doctor in Jersey City, and that's where everyone goes. First time I bled so much Dr. Tom got scared it wouldn't stop, and he wanted me to go to an emergency room and say I had done it to myself with a coat hanger, but I refused to leave, and thank God the bleeding stopped on its own."

As she spoke, Joe was scrawling notes in a little pocket spiral notebook. He was like a reporter, never trusting that a novelist could remember all he needed to when the time came to put everything down on paper, never trusting that the gelatin of art could contain and suspend it all. So he had notes about everything people said, jottings about styles of dress and moles that speckled people's cheeks, and about an interesting argument we'd once heard blooming between a man and a woman in a Chinese restaurant.

Brenda eventually appeared as Wanda, the fragile prostitute in *Overtime*, Joe's second novel. He had gone back to see her after that first meeting, and I had declined to go with him then. Maybe I knew that he wanted to go to bed with her that night, something that he would have furiously denied. I pictured Joe and that sexy but mangy woman, her head craned backward in a position that wouldn't destroy her beehive. Her toes, painted that peculiar, shellacked shade of white, wouldn't splay out the way people's toes did in orgasm, for there would be no orgasm, not with one of these customers, not ever. Joe was doing research, he'd tell himself as he tucked in his shirt afterward and hurried down the stairs, past the hamburgers spitting on the stoves in other apartments, past the half-heard voices, and even though Brenda had been depressed and forgettable, the experience would have given him an odd kind of charge.

These men, who have so much, need so much to sustain themselves. They are all appetite, it sometimes seems, all wide mouth and roaring stomach. Joe prowled around, just like Nathaniel Bone the critic said; I knew this, and I also knew that other people knew it, too, and that they assumed I *didn't* know it. Our friends would look at me with a kind of pity, thinking I was innocent and trusting. But really, it gave me more power to know something like this and yet do nothing about it. What could I do, anyway? We had some fights: I accused and he denied and then we dropped it and went on.

I accompanied him whenever he asked. I posed questions to the people we met, and he took notes. We did this repeatedly over the years, not just with Brenda the prostitute but also with a fisherman at the seaport, and a vacuum-cleaner salesman, who later appeared as the character Mike Bick in *I Hardly Knew You*, that not-entirely-successful short novel from the mid-seventies. We paid for child care all over the place, though when Susannah turned thirteen she was put in charge of the others.

Lev Bresner's wife, Tosha, that tiny woman with the number stamped on her arm and the black-olive eyes of a Chihuahua, could not imagine how I allowed myself to "join in," as she put it. All she wanted, she said, was to be left alone, to be allowed to go off somewhere with her women friends, to shop at a department store and have lunch with them and sit down with her shopping bags all around her and laugh.

"The *men*!" she said. "No offense, but how can you stand them, Joan? They just talk and talk and never shut themselves up."

This was true; they talked day and night, as though inside them an endless scroll of paper were unraveling out through the mouth. They were so arrogant! So certain of themselves, even when they were wrong. Why couldn't women be that way? (A few years later, of course, when feminism became such a force, the women would talk and talk in voices louder than the men's, smoking furiously, gathering in living rooms and comparing notes on the satisfactions of the handheld vibrator and the horror of housework, and much more.)

I could have been like Joe if I'd wanted to. I could have swaggered around; I could have been hostile, lyrical, filled with ideas, a show-off, a buzzing neon sign. I could have been the female version of him, and therefore not lovable but repellent. Or else I could have dazzled with my erudition and charisma and connection to a potent man. But I wasn't Mary McCarthy or Lillian Hellman. I didn't want the attention; it made me skittish and unsure. What a relief it was to see the spotlight tilt its cone toward Joe.

"What about your own writing?" a few people sometimes asked me kindly, the ones who knew that once upon a time I'd written a few decent undergraduate stories, and that in fact Joe and I had met in his classroom.

"Oh, I don't write anymore," I'd say.

"Joan is extremely busy," Joe would add, "baby-sitting for my ego." There would be laughter, after which Joe would lightly mention the charity that occupied some of my time. It was a refugee organization called RSA, and I'd gotten involved with it in the late 1970s. Someone, usually one of the other wives, would persist in asking if she could read anything I'd written in college, and I'd say no, no, nothing I'd done had been given a chance to mature, all of it would be completely mortifying to me if I looked at it now.

The things I used to write were nothing like the writing of these men. The men's prose spread out on the page, sprawled leisurely like someone having a bath and a shave and then yawning, arms outstretched. Male novelists made up words in their fiction: "phallomaterialism"; "ero-tectonics." They wrote about themselves, not even bothering to change autobiographical details. What would be the point? They weren't afraid to have alter egos; they weren't afraid to have *egos*. They owned the world, remember, and everything in it.

I didn't own the world; no one had offered it to me. I didn't want to be a "lady writer," a word-painter in watercolors, or on the other hand a crazy woman, a ball-breaker, a handful. I didn't want to be Elaine Mozell, the one who had warned me a long time ago. She'd been loud and lonely, and she'd faded from view.

I had no idea who could love a show-off woman writer. What sort of man would stay with her and not be threatened by her excesses, her rage, her spirit, her skill? Who was he, this phantom, unthreatened husband who was still attractive and strong himself? Maybe he lived under a rock somewhere, sliding out once in a while to celebrate the big ideas of his brilliant wife, before returning to the shadows.

His big ideas, of course, carried us far. Once, in the mid-sixties, I went to Vietnam with him. A cluster of writers and reporters would be traveling to Saigon for an informational tour of the region and Joe was among those invited. Most of the writers had been sent by newspapers and magazines. This was back in a time when your editor would say with a shrug, "Sure, why not, go ahead, write a long piece; use as many words as you need." War had never been a subject of great fluency for Joe. Wars existed on the outskirts of his fiction, both Korea and World War II and, later, Vietnam, though the men in his novels personally never made it past training camp. One of them, Michael Denbold in *The Walnut*, shot himself accidentally in the foot, just like Joe had done. Joe's characters were both frightened and excited by guns. They hated and were thrilled by the dreadful, heavy feel of them in their arms; it made their hearts race and left them helpless, the same way, later on, they would love and be frightened by the feel of their babies in their arms.

Just as Joe was uncomfortable during his brief stint in the army during the Korean War, he also wasn't entirely comfortable in the fictional fields of war. He read everything on it that he could, all hawkish and leftist views, and went to antiwar meetings and demonstrations, where once he was pushed to the ground and trampled on, and though some of his characters worried openly about how we would ever extricate ourselves from Southeast Asia, they never became obsessed with it.

Like everyone we knew, we did what we could to protest the war. We signed, and we worked, and we brought our children with us to storefront offices to make calls and type letters. We used mimeographs, the purple ink getting all over us, the place smelling like a schoolroom, and we headed down to D.C. in a long, fossilized traffic jam of cars. The children cried in the back-seat, and we pushed them on the Mall in strollers while they begged for juice, their faces blazing with heat, and Joe was among the writers who stood up and screamed into screechy, inadequate mikes.

But back then, Vietnam still felt fresh to us, a new, terrible subject to learn about, with a crash course in geography required, and Joe needed me with him, so I went. Our kids stayed behind with the boisterous, arty, menagerielike family of one of Alice's friends, who simply absorbed them into their household without seeming to notice, and off Joe and I went on an Air France flight. "They'll be fine," Joe said, a father's refrain, based on nothing except the intolerance of the possibility of disaster, and then there we were, standing on an airstrip in Bangkok during our stopover. I wore a kerchief on my head and wraparound sunglasses, a look favored by wives of that era.

There were a few other women along, and all of us gathered together except for one, a journalist who had cast her lot with the men, standing in a clutch of them and speaking in an animated fashion, though I couldn't hear her words over the stuttering choppers and cargo planes and delivery trucks that wove through the airstrip. Her name was Lee, and she was a serious, clever writer who seemed unconcerned about her minority status in this male world.

It was as though there were a box I kept under a bed and pulled out only once in a while, and in this box were crammed Mary McCarthy and Lillian Hellman and Carson McCullers and now Lee the journalist. If I opened the lid, their heads would pop out like jack-in-the-box clowns on springs, mocking me, reminding me that they *existed,* that women could occasionally become important writers with formidable careers, and that maybe I could have done it if I'd tried. But instead I was standing with the wives, the kerchief-wearers, all of us holding ourselves in a way we'd grown accustomed to, arms folded, purses slung over shoulders, eyes flicking left and right to keep watch over our husbands.

I shouldn't be here! I wanted to cry. *I'm not like the rest of them!* I wanted to be beside this woman Lee, to feel a confidence in the middle of this hectic and alien place. But somehow the men and the famous woman journalist were on one side, and all the other women were on the other side. The wives and I stood talking and clutching our kerchiefs so they weren't ripped from our heads in the wind. Lee wore nothing on her head; her hair was black and loose.

A while later we were off to Saigon, landing in the midst of smoggy honky-tonk central, with street carts selling watches and cigarettes and firecrackers in cheerfully colored paper wrappers that reminded me of taffy for sale on the Atlantic City boardwalk. Cyclos drove past with their solitary passengers riding through the spoiled streets past restaurants of all ethnicities. I imagined unclean, tiny kitchens in the back with blackened pots on stoves, and ancient Vietnamese women ladling some sort of generic, clouded broth. It was February, hot, mosquito-addled, my nylons sucking against my legs. A bus was supposed to have met us on the street, but it hadn't come yet, and so all the Americans clustered together, quickly overcome by little children who wanted money or who cheerfully offered to supply the men among us with "extra-discount fucks." Joe looked uneasily amused as he shooed them away, but they kept returning, pulling on the men's sleeves and trouser legs.

The next day our junket of journalists went out in helicopters over the trees and leafy fields to the west of the city, and as I sat with Joe and Lee and her husband, Raymond—also a journalist, though unknown—the four of us in pith helmets and head-phones and sunglasses, I felt that the helicopter was no more than just another cyclo carrying the privileged above the mess. Small airplanes continually dove and dropped their bombs into the greenery and then lifted again, and Joe and Lee and Raymond took notes in their pads, discussing the Viet Cong in knowing voices, though really all of us were just tourists, letting ourselves absorb everything we needed to know in order to go back to the States seeming knowledgeable.

We toured a refugee camp in Cam Chau, one that was considered temporary, and the filth there was head-breaking. A few pigs wandered around, scavenging for anything edible in the piles of garbage and waste. A woman was enduring childbirth inside her hut, screaming nonstop; the medic taking care of her kept asking the rest of us for sterilized water, please, please, he said, but there was none. The conversation went on and on, like dialogue in an absurdist drama:

"Water! Water! Sterile water!"

"No, we have no water."

"Water! Water! Sterile water!"

"No, we have no water."

There was almost no water whatsoever for this camp of two thousand people. In the doorway, a child stood watching mildly. The laboring woman continued screaming the same words over and over, and finally I asked one of the tour leaders for a translation.

"She say she want to die, because she is in so much pain she feel like a dog," he explained. "She say please shoot her like a dog."

Because no one told me not to, I went over and held the woman's hand. Her eyes swiveled to mine, and I held her hand. Together we squeezed hands as her baby crowned. "Crowning," what a crazy word, I thought as the skull came through the widening space with its flat black hair painted onto the head, the webbing of infinitesimal veins showing, and then the shoulders being turned and eased out by the medic, and then the mother holding her own baby's hand. He had crowned, but he was no king; he'd have to live in the rathole of Cam Chau forever. No one found sterilized water. Someone did bring a small plastic container of nondairy creamer, though, and the mother tilted back her head and drank it. The baby was attached to her breast and he drank, too, and though I wanted to stay, wanted to help if I possibly could, the men said we had to go, it was time to leave for the Marine Press Base, where we were all promised a four-star dinner.

The rest of the tour of Vietnam was a carousel of cheerful propaganda; on a nuclear carrier we were assured that they only hit military targets in the north, nothing more, but all of us were narrow-eyed and unconvinced.

"I hope you've been taking it all in," Joe said on our last night, as we sat in a dining room drinking martinis from big frozen glasses whose shape reminded me of the inverted, shellacked straw hats of the cyclo drivers.

"I've been trying," I said, looking out at the moon-bright Saigon night, the fronds shuffling together, and listening to a phonograph elsewhere on the base that was playing the swooning pop song "Town Without Pity." All the American writers huddled together at this final dinner, eating everything that was put before us, the bloody steaks, the twice-baked potatoes, some of the group already turning experiences into sentences, and sentences into paragraphs.

"Joan and I are a team," Joe was saying to the other people at our table. "She's my eyes and ears. Without her I would be nowhere."

"You're a lucky man," said Raymond, the chinless husband of glamorous Lee the journalist.

"I found him in an alley," I explained gamely. "He was all bent out of shape. Down and out." Joe always liked when I said such things.

"Yeah, she picked me up and dusted me off," he put in, "and made me into what I am today."

"*I* didn't make Lee into anything," said Raymond. "She emerged from her mother's womb fully formed. A pencil behind her tiny little ear."

Was that true? Could a woman writer simply appear in the world, unconcerned about her stature, or whether she'd be laughed at or ignored? This one could. I watched Lee drink her martini; the glass was so large that she looked like a cat lapping from a bowl. She had never once asked me anything about myself or really spoken to me at all the entire time we were in Vietnam. She was one of those women who has little interest in other women, and whose light is entirely directed toward men. She didn't like me, and so I decided: *Fine.* I would dislike her intensely in return.

Later, in bed at the hotel, under a slow fan in the stirred heat, I dreamed about the mother and her baby in the hut in Cam Chau, wondering how they were possibly managing, where they were, where they would go. I saw the baby's head growing and becoming covered with hair; I watched the bones join at the place where the head was still soft and unfinished. Then I saw the mother and baby hiding in the trees, exploding in gunfire, and I saw their hut burned to the ground. And in the free-flowing logic of dreams, the mother suddenly transformed into Lee the journalist. She was drinking nondairy creamer, which inexplicably turned into napalm—Incinder gel, they called it here—as she tipped her head back to swallow.

* * *

Joe and I went to many other cities together over the decades: Rome, for he had won the Prix de Rome and we got to spend a year with our children in a palazzo, fully funded; London, because the English loved him and wanted him on their chat shows; and Paris, because his publisher there had deep pockets; and Jerusalem, for its famous book fair. There was also Tokyo, though Joe's novels were a source of puzzlement there, the translations awkward (*Overtime* became, loosely, *When a Man Cannot Go Home Yet but Must Be at the Office After the Others Have Left*), and Joe himself was considered exotic. We went everywhere together, racking up mileage well before mileage counted for anything. We were globe-trotters, we were international; wherever Joseph Castleman's novels appeared in translation, we went there, dropping the children with this friend or that if we weren't able to take them along. I felt sick about leaving them, and missed them badly. We'd call home from wherever we were, and the sounds of anarchy would come through the phone, making me want to return at once. Susannah would complain, Alice would cry, begging us to come home immediately, and David would say he'd just read in a book that the world was coming to an end in five years, and was that true? Someone would drop the telephone, and there would be sounds of shouting for a while.

"They'll be fine," Joe would remind me, and of course he was right. When we returned they were the same as we'd left them, though maybe a little more melancholy. "It lets them know that their parents have a *life*," he'd said. "So many kids have parents who don't go anywhere, don't do anything. At least they know their parents are in the world. I think that counts for a lot." Year after year we traveled; he gave readings, he picked up awards, he made appearances, city after city after city.

And then finally we arrived here in Helsinki. At night the shining, quiet city sometimes possesses the atmosphere of a fraternity: young men, out for the evening, drink too much and knock into strangers on the sidewalk. Couples sit in cafes, eating sublime triangular Karelian pastries and drinking, and once in a while they slide off the chairs and onto the floor, where an unimpressed waiter lifts them up by the armpits and replaces them in their seats.

So it was no great surprise that when Joe Castleman came to Finland, he soon found himself afloat in a pond of alcohol. The reporters who came to the hotel to interview him all said yes when Joe perfunctorily offered them a drink from the enormous stocked bar in the suite, and then he had to join them. When he went to a television station to be on a morning news show, the greenroom featured a lineup of flavored vodkas. The second day, after we'd recovered from jet lag, his schedule was intense, non-stop, requiring Joe to traverse Helsinki and the surrounding regions, sometimes to show himself to the Finns, other times so they could show themselves to him. Wine was served at a small college in Jarvenpaa, where he appeared onstage before five hundred amazingly well-read students ("Tell me, Mr. Castleman, how you would compare the themes in the work of Mr. Günter Grass and Mr. Gabriel García Márquez."). And there was a constant flow of vodka and gin at the luncheon held in an enormous sunlit room in the hypermodern Helsinki Public Library with its Möbius strip design and unusually placed pinpoints of light.

After the library lunch was over, Joe and I were taken on a tour of the rare books archives, and all of us in the party were fairly sloshed as we made our way through the stacks, led by a tiny elf of a woman who suddenly turned and recited from *Kalevala*, Finland's famous nineteenth-century epic poem, which the Finns say served as the model for Longfellow's *Hiawatha*. Finland, like all small countries, has its stories, its anecdotes, its pride, and it carries them openly. For without the connection to Longfellow, without the fresh fish and Sibelius and Saarinen, there is the anxiety that Finland might crack off from Scandinavia forever, falling into the sea of forgotten things. Beautiful Finland might be *lost*. Like Atlantis. Like me without Joe, or so I always used to think. He took my arm now, but I pulled slightly away.

"You okay?" he asked.

"I don't know," I said. He looked at me for a moment but didn't pursue it.

Only later, walking back through the lobby of the Inter-Continental Hotel after lunch, having been driven there by our cool, square-headed driver, Joe said to me, "Whatever's been pissing you off so much on this trip, could it wait until we're back in New York?"

"I don't think so," I said.

"Oh, no? I thought you were looking forward to coming here."

"I was."

"And?"

"What do you think?" I said. "It's a bit *much*. And really, Joe, this shouldn't surprise you. But it's not just that. It's everything."

"Oh. Wonderful. Delighted to hear that, Joan. *Everything.* So now I know that it isn't possible for me to set things right. I'd have to take on the entire world. While we're here in Finland I'd have to look back through our entire history together and come up with all the things that piss you off. All the hot spots in the Castleman marriage."

"Something like that," I said.

And then a voice called, *"Joe."*

Together we turned. There on a couch in the lobby sat Nathaniel Bone, the literary critic who'd been an intermittent presence in our lives for a long time. He was around forty, still skinny as an adolescent with a long drift of brown hair and pink-rimmed eyeglasses that were hamster-effeminate. I hadn't heard that he was coming to Helsinki, though I shouldn't have been surprised, because he'd turned up at various places over the years. I have never trusted Nathaniel Bone, not since the first time I met him at our house in Weathermill, about ten years ago.

He had driven up from the city that day in hopes of ingratiating himself to Joe and being given the honor of calling himself Joseph Castleman's authorized biographer. Both an unauthorized and an authorized biographer, of course, would be allowed to sit for hours with their subject, if that subject was still alive and willing, or else sit for hours in an attic working open the drawers of an old warped bureau and pawing through ancient letters and diaries, if the subject was dead. But an authorized biographer is in pig heaven. He is happy, he gloats, he rolls around leisurely, because, unlike his unsanctioned colleague, he can show his conclusions to the world instead of coyly hinting, suggesting, flirting about his findings and then not following through with proof.

Nathaniel Bone, who'd been writing to Joe since college, had been certain that he would have no trouble charming Joe in person, since he'd apparently charmed everyone else from the moment he was born, not unlike Joe himself. Bone came from a wealthy family in California, with two psychiatrists for parents and college at Yale, where he charmed the chairman of the English department and was permitted to write an "experimental" honors thesis combining elements of history, biography, and fiction. It was this thesis that had landed him various magazine assignments after Yale. Bone did literary profiles and book reviews, commentary on different topics from both high and low culture, the kind of pieces in which he somehow managed to mention the names Jacques Lacan and George Jetson in the course of a single paragraph.

It helped that he was good-looking in a lesser-rock-star way, though I always thought he was spineless as a sea horse, slouching whenever he entered a room. His hair was kept long and scrupulously washed. A notable thing about him was that though he did in fact charm people in positions of power, no one else particularly liked him. He had no time for ordinary people, and they had no time for him. He sucked up without subtlety to everyone he wanted something from. I could tell this right away as soon as he came to our house that day.

But another notable detail about Nathaniel Bone was that he was the first person I ever met who seemed to understand the importance of sucking up to the wife. He actually seemed to realize that if the wife of an important man did not like him, then he was *fucked*. And so that first day, ten years ago, when Bone was a younger man in his early thirties, and he drove upstate to meet Joe and formally discuss his proposal to be Joe's authorized biographer, he brought me a little gift.

"Oh, wait, Mrs. Castleman," Nathaniel Bone had said, standing in the kitchen. I'd just let him in and we were waiting for Joe to come downstairs; as it would turn out, we would wait quite a while. After he became famous, Joe seemed to like to keep people waiting. "I almost forgot." (Yeah, *right*.) "This is for you." And Bone retrieved from his back pocket a beautiful, hand-tinted postcard of some young women onstage at a Smith College skit-night performance in 1927. *Northrop House Follies*, read the caption.

"Northrop!" I said. "I lived there."

"I know," he said, smiling.

The postcard was in fact the kind of thing I might have bought for myself if I'd seen it in a bin at a flea market. It was a clever gift, but immediately I didn't like him, felt him to be an obscure threat, and was uneasy that he was inside our house, standing in the kitchen in his jeans and snakeskin boots and casually drinking the iced sun tea I'd poured him.

Joe had had young men around him since his first book came out; they flitted and swirled and did a dance around him, although along with their excitement the men were jealous, secretly hoping to unseat Joe. Most of these young men were writing their own novels: long, rambling, "ambitious" books that weighed as much as full-term infants. Nathaniel Bone, as it would turn out, had been trying to write a novel for two years, but wasn't succeeding. His book, he himself had realized, was too wordy. "Too full of ideas," a friend had told him, and this was the kind of criticism that Bone could live with. "You should definitely do a book," the friend went on, "but make it nonfiction." So it was a short leap to bring Nathaniel Bone to the doorstep of Joseph Castleman, to whom he'd been writing since college. That first letter had been addressed to Joe care of his publisher, then forwarded, back when Bone was a sophomore at Yale:

Dear Mr. Castleman,

A few of us were sitting around the lounge at Silliman last night playing Essences, the game in which you have to guess a famous person based on certain impressionistic clues, such as: What animal is this person? And I had you in mind, Mr. Castleman, using the following clues:

What animal is this person? *A panther.*
What gem? *Opal.*
Which Beatle? *John, obviously.*
What musical instrument? *A bassoon.*
What food? *A kasha knish, with hot sauce.*
What part of the body? *The brain.*
What household appliance? *An electric can opener.*

I'm not sure if any of these answers will make sense to you, but I am sending them ahead with my deepest admiration for your work, which I've loved ever since I read The Walnut *in high school.*

With best regards,
Nathaniel Bone
Box 2701
Yale Station

Joe wrote back, vaguely amused by the nerviness of this young guy, thanking him for recognizing "the indisputable truth, that deep within my soul, I am but a kasha knish." And that was supposed to be the end of it, except that Nathaniel Bone wrote to Joe again, this time not through the publisher but using the return address on Joe's envelope, sending him an undergraduate paper he'd written about Joe's short story "The Cigarette Tree," a critical interpretation that struck Joe as being more intelligent than most of the reviews he'd read about his work.

"Look at this," he'd said to me, and I'd read it too, agreeing with how smart it was, but feeling as if the real subject of the paper was not Joe's short story at all but Nathaniel Bone's intelligence.

And then, as the years passed, Bone continued to write from time to time, sending compliments and thoughts about a particular novel or story or essay of Joe's. Joe always responded with a short note of thanks. I guess I ought to have seen, back then, that Nathaniel Bone was grooming himself, aiming for some sort of special place within Joe's world, but it just didn't occur to me. I thought he was simply a reader, a fan, a distant, foppish worshiper. But he was surprisingly persistent and scrupulous, showing off to Joe with fragments of his knowledge, preening in front of Joe, dazzling him (or trying to) even as he himself was dazzled by Joe.

And all of it eventually led to the young man standing in his snakeskin boots in our kitchen roughly a decade after he'd first written that note from New Haven. He stood nervously by the refrigerator, playing with a fruit magnet, playing with his hair, trying to appear casual and confident in the home of his favorite writer, trying to impress his favorite writer's wife and cause her to turn to her husband late that night after Bone was gone and say something like:

"That boy. The one who came today?"

"Bone, you mean?" a sleepy Joe would reply, yawning.

"Yes."

"He's hardly a boy."

"I suppose not. There's something very engaging and intelligent about him."

Joe would nod. "Oh yes. Bone is bright, all right. Brilliant, probably."

"He brought me a gift, you know. A little Smith postcard from 1927."

"That was thoughtful. He's a serious person, I think. He might be pretty good."

Both of us would nod, picturing young Nathaniel Bone, wondering why our own son couldn't have turned out like him, imagining, in a way, that he *was* our son. The one we'd been meant to have, instead of the underachieving, angry, sometimes violent one we did have. And we'd both drift off together into a kind of placid, parental sleep, nurturing Joe's future biographer in our minds.

But this was a fantasy: Bone's, not ours. As much as he loved his fame, Joe didn't like to think about being the subject of a serious biography. That would mean he would have to take measure of his life, and reconcile himself to its eventual end. He was terrified of death. More immediately, he was terrified of *sleep*, death's dress rehearsal.

Other books about him had been written already: short, undistinguished volumes published by university presses, but nothing particularly insightful, nothing definitive, nothing with dirt in it, with juice. Bone's biography would certainly be interesting; it would be very clever and garner the author a good deal of attention.

Joe said no.

The two men had gone upstairs that day at the house, and they'd sat in the study and smoked cigars, then later on they'd gone out to Schuyler's General Store and bought Sno-Balls, and Bone had amiably eaten a pack of them, too, in a show of ritual solidarity—as though he liked them as well, as though *every* grown man did. They sat on the porch of Schuyler's and ate those spongy, sugary Sno-Balls together and Bone talked about why he was the right man for the job.

"Someone's going to do it, and it might as well be me" seemed to be the thrust of his argument. Lesser writers, according to Bone, would present Castleman as a one-dimensional figure: the mournful, fatherless little kid from Brooklyn who turned into a man of letters. But because Nathaniel had taken it upon himself to make a study of Castleman's work over all these years, he would be the only person able to infuse the biography with an authentic sense of who Joe was.

"Like that first letter I sent you a long time ago," Bone tried. "In which I told you about the game of Essences I played, remember? What kind of tree are you, et cetera? I would show your *essence* in the book. And your entire readership would finally understand who you really are."

It was that last comment, I think, that sealed it. No writer I've ever met wants to be understood in the way that he was suggesting.

Joe took a bite of the pink, chemical pastry in his hand; I imagined there was the barest sucking sound of the marshmallow against his teeth. He swallowed, and then said, "I think not."

A pause. "*You think not?*" Bone was shocked that he was being rejected; he didn't know what to do with this information. "There's an old joke," he tried. "Descartes walks into a bar. The bartender says, 'Do you want a drink, sir?' And Descartes says, 'I think not.' And then he disappears."

Joe nodded, tried to smile; he wasn't going to disappear, he'd still exist in the world even if he wasn't written up by Nathaniel Bone. But Bone had been *studying* the man; he'd been painstakingly writing him letters, publishing little essays on his work, and for what? To wind up sitting on the front porch of some dark, cluttered general store in a little town in upstate New York, eating pink marshmallow-and-coconut garbage and being told *no*?

There was wheedling and begging. There was flattery, and then a few pathetic threats. Bone seemed about to collapse into tears, as though astonished Joe had said no, when in fact very few people had said no to him in his life.

But still Joe continued to say no, repeating his answer in a good-natured way, as many times as he needed to, until finally Nathaniel Bone was made to see that Joe wasn't going to change his mind. Standing up, shaken, straightening himself out, brushing coconut flakes from his shirt front, Bone told Joe, "You know, the thing is, I'm sure I'll end up writing the book anyway."

Joe nodded. "You'll do whatever you have to," he said. "We all do."

Probably this lack of anxiety on Joe's part incensed Bone; why couldn't he get a rise out of Castleman? What did it take to register on the radar of the great novelist? Bone didn't know yet that the men who own the world don't get to do that by being magnanimous and overly interested in other people. They get to do it by taking care of themselves along the way. They stoke the fire of their own reputations, and sometimes other people come by, asking: *What's that you're doing there?*

Oh, stoking the fire of my reputation.

Can I help?

Certainly. Go get some wood.

Bone was furious, though he didn't show it. A few months later he did in fact receive a large contract from a major publishing house to write an unauthorized biography of Joe, and from that moment forward, there was an uneasiness between the two men, a wariness that never shifted. A pure dislike, actually. Bone was as ubiquitous as the moon, showing up in the audience over the years at readings and panel discussions and even at the Hay-on-Wye literary festival in Wales, where Joe made an appearance. There he was in one of the first few rows with his long hair and his distinctive eyeglasses.

And now, ten years after Nathaniel Bone had stood awkwardly in the kitchen of our house, here he was, slouched against a sofa cushion in the lobby of Helsinki's Inter-Continental Hotel, once again, as always, waiting for Joe. We stood for a moment, taken aback, and looked at him.

"Oh God," I whispered to Joe, who sighed. Suddenly, after the tense talk between us, there was a brief moment of solidarity.

"Again with the showing up," Joe said. "Well, I suppose it wouldn't have made any sense if he'd skipped this one, would it?"

"No," I said. "Go to him. You have to."

"Hello, Nathaniel," Joe said, approaching with false pleasure. The men shook hands, and then Nathaniel kissed me on the cheek, and we all stood back for a "well, well" moment, after which Joe simply nodded, muttered vaguely, said, "Good to see you," and turned away.

This is the prerogative of the famous. Joe walked off without thinking he'd been rude to Bone. His thoughts were already else-where: on the prize he'd be receiving tomorrow night at the Opera House, and the banquet that would follow, and the swoon of attention that is everyone's dream throughout life, though most of us never achieve it, never even come close, and we feel a surge of giddiness when we so much as glimpse our own grainy image on a closed-circuit video screen in a Duane Reade drug-store. *That's me up there,* we think with a sad puff of pride.

I started to follow Joe out of the lobby with a quick smile to Bone, but then I remembered that Joe had invited Irwin Clay and the people from the publishing house to come by our suite for drinks and hors d'oeuvres. I didn't really want to be there, making small talk about Joe and the award and the various events of the week, so instead I turned and left the hotel. I was armed with a street map and so I took a walk along Mannerheim, where the shops advertised the usual assortment of delicate fabrics and Nokia cell phones as small and flat as throat lozenges. It was late afternoon and the sky had already dropped into darkness, a preparation for the sunless winter. As I walked along, someone fell into step beside me. It was Nathaniel Bone again; he'd appar-ently followed me out of the hotel.

"Joan," he said, clearly desperate. "Hello! Can I maybe buy you a drink? We're in Finland," he added. "Don't say no."

As though the fact that we'd both come to this strange, northerly country might affect my decision. Oddly, I think it did. I imagined him wandering the Helsinki streets later that night, drunk and blinking, or sitting in a bar having no one to talk to, or no one who would talk to him. The Finnish language wasn't pen-etrable to outsiders; it was a complex collection of aural hiero-glyphics, with the stress on every first syllable, and a deep, mooing quality infusing most conversations. *I am here at the end of the world, and you are here at the end of the world,* the people seemed to be saying. *So let us drink.*

Because no one else would drink with Nathaniel Bone, I told him I would.

Chapter Five

OKAY, SO that wasn't why I went for a drink with him. I went because it gave me a private pleasure to sit with someone Joe wouldn't want me to sit with. Even though I said nothing of substance, nothing controversial, it still gave me pleasure. We sat in a landmark Helsinki restaurant called the Golden Onion; above our heads, a slanted window looked out over the Uspenski Cathedral.

"The onion dome," Bone pointed out, but I was getting a little weary of all things Finnish: the domes, the planar architectural triumphs of Saarinen and Aalto, the smoked fish and clusters of hard little cloudberries, the Longfellow cadences of *Kalevala*. We drank vodka tonics together and talked stiffly of the trip, the various tourist sites we'd each been to, the array of people we'd met here, and how different the Finns seemed to be from every other group in Scandinavia.

"They got a bit of an inferiority complex, living under the shadow of the Soviets for so long," Bone said. "That's why they had to establish the Helsinki Prize in the first place. To give their country a boost, a little jolt of self-esteem. I think it's worked pretty well, actually. Everyone here gets so excited each year when the winner comes to town, and for a few days there's all this international focus on Finland. Everyone's really thrilled to have Joe as their man. Myself included, I have to admit. Look, you might think I've got a whopping case of spite and envy, but I don't, really. I don't hold anything against him. He's a great writer. He deserves what he gets."

"Oh yes," I said. "He does."

"I wish I could quote you, Joan," said Bone wistfully. "It would make my day."

"Well, you can't."

"I know, I know," he said, "but even if I could, the inflection wouldn't be there on the page. The way you said 'He does.' The way it makes you sound."

"How does it make me sound?"

"You know. Jealous," he said, and he tossed a nut into his mouth.

In the yellowing darkness of the Golden Onion, with murmuring all around us, Nathaniel Bone and I sat with our drinks and our plates of some sort of damp, savory, rolled pancakes in front of us. He looked stranger and more sinuous than when I'd seen him last. He was middle-aged now; soon he'd be finishing the book he'd been working on intermittently for ten years, while in that same period of time Joe had published four novels.

I felt sorry for Nathaniel Bone as we sat drinking in the Golden Onion. He'd been chasing Joe for a long time, and too many years had passed and here we all were, the three of us, much older, ragged, not nearly as compelling or attractive as we used to be. Who would read Nathaniel Bone's book when it finally came out? Maybe very few people would, although his advance ten years ago had been big, the kind of money that gets written up in media columns to show that someone has hit the jackpot in the mostly money-hemorrhaging enterprise of publishing. Because Bone's biography of Joe was taking him much longer than he'd thought it would, enough time had elapsed to create a literary sea change.

These days Joe was a leftover from another era, still important but rapidly on his way out. Sales of his last two novels had been extremely disappointing. Big writers today were different. In addition to the usual new crop of swaggering young men, there were many more women out there. This wasn't 1956, when I'd taken his fiction class.

The biggest woman of all was named Valerian Qaanaaq. She was a novelist who was a member of the Inuit tribe of Labrador. She was young and beautiful, with black hair, green eyes, and sharp, bright teeth. She claimed to have grown up in an igloo made of sod and snow, though already there was a backlash against her, a bitter muttering that she was a charlatan who used her looks and unusual ethnicity to get so far, that she'd only spent a few months in that igloo, and the rest of the time in an apartment with a satellite dish on the roof. She'd gone to St. Hilda's College, Oxford, after leaving home, and her first novel appeared when she was twenty-three. It was called *Whaleskin* and was about a woman whaler and the young member of Parliament who becomes obsessed with her. The novel was as long as the Bible, filled with arch, erudite, bawdy scenes, flights that took the reader from Labrador and into 10 Downing Street. The book was pan-ethnic, risky, maddening, and extraordinarily popular in the States and in Europe. Back when I was young, Valerian Qaanaaq didn't exist, but now her novel was beloved. More than 1.5 million copies of the hardback edition had been sold. The back of the book featured a glossary of words in the Inuit-Inupik language.

She was a recent phenomenon and there were a few others in this vein: women who were writing and publishing in ways that struck me as masculine. I tried to ignore their work, for its very existence made me unhappy. Better to stay among the dinosaurs like Joe and Lev and the others. Better to be miserable and feel cheated than to welcome this new breed that I didn't understand and for whom I had no affection.

Bone was leaning forward across the small table, his breath a warm, fermented current, saying to me, "Listen, we could talk a little bit while we're both here in Helsinki. You could tell me things. We could meet up again, and you'd tell me the things you want people to know."

"And what do you think those things are?" I asked.

"I won't put words in your mouth," he said. "It wouldn't be right. But I know you have things to say, Joan. People have been saying that for years."

"What people?"

"An old friend of my parents, in particular," Bone said mildly.

"Oh? Who are you talking about?"

"A woman I knew when I was growing up in California," he began, and from the way he drummed his fingers and pinched at his shirt front, I knew he was uncomfortable. "She lived a few blocks away with her husband," he went on. "He was some kind of failed artist, the type who paints driftwood. She was a shrink, like both of my parents, except she was definitely *out there* at the time, into all kinds of alternative therapy. But I liked her. She was one of those women from the sixties with those long, dangling earrings and flowered muumuus and nutty theories about everything. She had a daughter, too. Older than me, and really dark and smart. My older brother knew her. She wrote poetry for the high school literary magazine."

"Okay," I said, ungrounded in the story, bewildered by it. "Go on."

"The woman—the therapist—had been married once before," he said. "And it had ended badly; her first husband had left her and the baby, but she'd moved on, making a new life for herself and starting a career. The first husband became famous," he continued lightly. "A novelist."

"Oh shit," I said. "Not this." Quickly, Bone looked away from me, as though he was apologetic, embarrassed about his sordid errand here. I felt equally embarrassed and found out. "Okay," I said finally, holding up a hand. "I get it, Nathaniel. I get what you're doing here. The suspenseful narrative. The dragging-out of the story. The big surprise ending. Well, all right, I'm surprised."

"I'm sorry," he said. "Do you want me to stop now? Am I out of line?"

But I shook my head; he knew that of course I would want to hear the story of what had happened to these people, the abandoned, crazy first wife, Carol, and the baby, Fanny, who had disappeared into the baked depths of California.

"Carol was smart and sort of wounded, and she said a lot of things over the years to my parents," Bone said. "She told them all about her first husband, and how, though she used to hate him, she'd stopped. Hatred didn't last, she said, unless you made a real effort, keeping at it, rubbing two sticks together or something. Instead of hating him, she was always kind of *amused* by his success, because she'd never thought he was particularly talented. But then again, she'd always add, what did *she* know?"

I watched Bone as he talked. He was both embarrassed and stimulated; there was nothing particularly sadistic in his demeanor. He was just excited, like a literary detective who has found an important manuscript in the bottom of a drawer and is quietly savoring it and stroking it.

Joe and I hadn't had reason to speak often of Carol or Fanny for many years. They'd faded away like characters in a novel that has become unfashionable, and once in a while I would ask Joe about them, usually about Fanny, who would be forty-five years old by now. (That baby, forty-five!) Joe would shake his head and ask me not to bring the matter up, for it made him feel too bad. We knew where they were, and roughly *what* they were, but not much more. It was as though they were permanently installed in California, the mother a therapist, the daughter a lawyer. Facts were known, had been gathered over the decades, and, in recent years, with the help of the Internet. Face-to-face contact wasn't wanted either by them or Joe. For a long time he'd tried to see Fanny, every few years, out of both curiosity and courtesy, but when she rebuffed him he was relieved.

He'd visited them once, back in the early sixties during a book tour, and he had come home from California feeling depressed, for his daughter didn't know who he was and didn't seem to want to know. She'd played in her sandbox in the yard in Sausalito while he'd crouched on the green wooden edge and tried to ask her questions about herself. She'd answered in monosyllables and then finally, in the way of small children, she grew too bored and simply began to sing.

The house Carol and Fanny lived in then was small but pretty, the rooms painted like the inside of a seashell. Everything had a pink glaze to it, Joe said, including Carol, and when he looked into her eyes he had no idea of who she was or how it was possible they'd ever been married. Out of context—taken from a cold climate and transplanted into a warm one—she seemed like another person entirely, and this baby they'd collaborated on appeared distant and unknowable. There was heartbreak there for Joe to feel, if he thought about it long enough, but he decided not to let himself. He'd left that seashell house and hurried home to us.

"Tell me about the daughter," I said to Bone now. "Fanny. She's a labor lawyer; we know that much."

"Went to law school at Pepperdine," he said. "Unmarried. Hardworking. Humorless, I think."

"Joe tried to stay in contact with Fanny at first, you know," I said, but there wasn't real conviction to this statement. "He was busy," I went on. "And Carol didn't want his money; it wasn't about child support. She wanted very little to do with him, and then he'd become a big deal, and time passed, and we had our own family. She just wanted to be done with him."

I stopped talking, dredging up the ancient image of Fanny the baby lying beside me on Joe and Carol's bed in Northampton. I'd told that baby: *I'm falling in love with your daddy. And I'd really like to go to bed with him.* And then I'd done exactly that, as though it had nothing to do with Fanny at all, or Carol, but only had to do with Joe and me, the two of us floating on a tiny island, our very own Bali Ha'i.

We were terrible. *I* was terrible. I'd charged ahead, distracting him from his wife and baby, although I hadn't been able to see any of it back then, but had only heard Joe talking bitterly about the ways in which his wife denied him love, kept herself from him. He needed sexual release, he needed relentless love, he needed a woman, but Carol wasn't that woman. I was. The wife and child receded, as though they were bit players and their moment was over. *Fanny and Carol exit, stage left. Carol lifts the baby's tiny hand and moves it back and forth in a gesture of farewell.*

"Look," I said to Bone, "I know it's a bad story. It doesn't make me look good, or Joe either. But there it is. All I could focus on at the time was that Carol didn't make him happy. And anyway, she seemed crazy."

"Yeah. Nuts," he said, smiling. "The *walnut,*" he clarified. "I've heard the whole story from her point of view. She never thought she was actually going to hurt you when she threw it. She thought she'd just shake you up a little. Because the thing was, it wasn't the first time."

"What do you mean?"

"There had been someone else, apparently. Back in New York, when they first got married," Bone said. "A philosophy student. And apparently he gave *her* one of the walnuts, too. He admitted everything to Carol when she confronted him."

"*Oh,*" I said, imagining a truckload of painted walnuts being distributed to different women before me and after me.

"By the time she found out about you, she was really fed up with his behavior," Nathaniel said.

I'd always thought Carol was off-kilter, but maybe she was just furious. *Sorry,* I wanted to say to her. *Sorry,* I wanted to say to Fanny. *Sorry for ruining your lives.*

"Carol always felt mortified that Joe actually wrote about how she threw the walnut at you. But at least, she felt, the book was well written. That always impressed her," said Nathaniel.

We were silent for a little while, and then he said, "I hope I'm not being too aggressive about this, Joan. I was a little apprehensive about mentioning it to Joe. But sitting here with you . . . I thought I could do it."

"It's all right," I told him; I was the one doing the comforting here.

"You know, of course, I've read Joe's early work," he said suddenly. "There's one story in particular that I dug up, 'No Milk on Sunday,' from that little literary magazine. I have to say, it's not so great."

"I know. Awful," I agreed, and we laughed a little.

"Carol was always amazed that he'd come so far," Nathaniel said. "She started saying that maybe Joe was able to find his voice only after he'd ditched her. Or," he added, "after he met you. That maybe you became his muse."

"I guess I did, in a way," I said.

"The blond shiksa entrancing the Jewish guy."

"That's me. Upholding the tradition."

We stirred our drinks and tried to laugh a little; we both finally let our gazes lift and looked up at the rectangle of light. We were dawdling together in some strange, new way, as though we were finally comfortable with each other when in fact we weren't. He pushed a silver bowl of pretzel sticks toward me and I ate some, and then he said, "You could really add something to my book, you know. You'd finally get to speak; it would be a real feminist moment for you."

"Oh, Nathaniel, come on, you have no use for feminism," I said.

"Yeah, but you do."

In his own way he was seductive, if only because he wasn't Joe. I was getting old, and Joe was getting old, and Bone was relatively young. And long after Joe and I were gone from the world, Nathaniel Bone would still be kicking around, getting another book contract, appearing at the Ninety-second Street Y on a panel called "Truth-Telling and the Biographer's Task." Why not give everything to him? He hungered for it; he knew it was there in me. He wanted the Joe Castleman story to make sense, to have the satisfying shape and closure of a novel.

"I won't rush you, Joan," said Bone. "You can take your time;

we can do it however you want. I could tape you, or just take notes. We'll both be here for one more day, right? There's the ceremony, and then the banquet, and you'll be completely overextended. I'll be somewhere up in the peanut gallery. The *walnut* gallery. We could meet the next morning, say around ten, in front of the Academic Bookstore. Joe wouldn't have to know. That place is enormous; these Finns read and read, don't they? What else do they have to do all winter other than drink, am I right? We could meet, and you could make up your mind about exactly what you want to say to me. How does that sound?" I shrugged; that was all I'd commit to. "I think you really do want to talk to me," he said. "I'm like a therapist in a way. People have often told me that."

"Yeah, but you're a *bad* therapist," I said. "The kind who gives away other people's secrets."

"True," said Nathaniel, smiling. "My parents are psychiatrists—maybe that's why I went bad. Kids of shrinks are completely fucked up from the start. We don't even have a chance."

"Poor, poor you," I said.

"I know you're only teasing, but if you actually knew what my life was like, you *would* feel sorry for me," he said. "You, Joan, you've got this marriage, this life, your kids and grandkids, a house, lots of friends. I don't have any of that. I've got my work. The Joe Castleman project. That's my life. That's my house. My kid. Too bad for me."

Then Bone abruptly paid the bill, trying to figure out how many *markka* to leave, how many *penniä*, holding each coin up to the light of the sloping window, peering at it through his little lenses to see what it was and how much it was worth, though soon the euro would sweep these specifics into irrelevance. I left him there in the restaurant frowning over a confusion of lightweight coins and flyaway paper money, and headed out into the dark evening in this Midwestern-sized city where I knew no one and no one knew me, and people banged absently into one another like bumper cars on a wide, polished surface.

* * *

With or without my participation, Bone's biography of Joe will certainly include some basic facts that many people already know. We were once potheads, briefly, in that embarrassing way of the far-too-old, but we never let that stop us. In the late 1960s we were into our thirties. Picture us, if you can bear it: There's Joe with a paisley scarf at his neck and striped bell-bottoms, his black hair hanging down in a long, girlish sheaf, his eyes clouded with smoke. He was always tilting back his head and applying dew-drops of Visine to those eyes back then, or else laughing over something not very funny at all. And me in my paper dress or maxi-skirt and granny glasses, holding a bouquet of wildflowers. My hair was long and parted in the middle. I believe I owned five different shawls, which I wore throughout this time of marching, screaming, revelry, and a complete absence of irony.

But what was more mortifying than how we looked was what we did. Using the durable excuse of "research," Joe explored the world of "swinging," a term that is itself mortifying. *Ou sont les "swingers" d'antan?* If they are still alive, they are subscribing to *Prevention* magazine and baby-sitting for their grandchildren and taking gingko biloba supplements to restore their memories of details they probably would do better to forget.

Research took bell-bottomed Joe into a Manhattan club somewhere in the West Fifties called Den of Iniquity, a place with a "clothes-check girl" and a coed steambath and a dark room where men and women lay down on plush surfaces and opened their robes to each other.

I went with him there once, because he asked me to. We were still living in the Village then, and the children were at home with a sitter, David watching *Star Trek* and the girls dressing their helpless hamsters in doll clothes, and we headed uptown in a taxi, already slightly stoned from the joint we'd quickly sucked on in our bathroom, a place the children never entered. The admission fee to Den of Iniquity was outrageously high, and Joe paid it and we entered, walking along the purple carpet as if into a bad-taste suburban home. Some of the patrons were young and beautiful, and they located one another quickly. The older, homelier types stood alone in their robes, the men as though they'd come here for a chaste steambath, the women with a certain chin-up bravery, pulling in the soft stomachs that had long ago disgorged a baby or two, and moving their heads ever so slightly to the rhythm of the San Francisco psychedelic background music that was piped in over the quadraphonic speakers all around us.

Joe and I were somewhere in the middle of these two groups: too old to be beautiful, and too young to be repulsive. We entered the room with its rubberized suction door that made the place seem like the interior of a refrigerator, and we sat down together in our robes on the couch whose consistency, I would realize years later, was that of one of Joe's Hostess Sno-Balls. We were high and laughing, but the ambience was mammogram-waiting-room as opposed to sexual cave.

Soon a young guy with a tall bong in hand arrived and all of us in the room gathered around him. We passed the bong in a circle, and I recall being vaguely disgusted by the shared spittle that is a main feature of any communal water pipe. I thought that if I was disgusted by the communal spittle of strangers, then I was certainly not going to have a big future in group sex. But the man quickly dropped his robe and tentatively placed a hand on my neck, and Joe watched as the man bent forward to kiss me, though I was a good ten years older than he was. The woman beside me eased closer, touching her mouth to my neck; she was dark-haired and pixielike, and could have been Audrey Hepburn's stunt double.

I can't say the night wasn't arousing; it was, in the animal way that anything damp and breathy and rhythmic invariably is. The couple, whose names were Don and Roz, were applying all their attention to me while Joe watched. The husband's hands were large, and his wife had an extremely small mouth, which kissed me in hunt-and-peck fashion, as though she kept remembering and forgetting and then remembering what she was doing here.

"Oh, you're so soft," she whispered like a child revealing a secret, and though it was incumbent upon me to say something in return, I couldn't. Joe was watching; I saw him leaning back against the furred wall, nodding his head slightly in stoned appreciation.

I wondered what my life might have been like with another woman—a life away from men and their caterwauling and continual need for affirmation, for stroking, as though within their minds they were always deep in the Den of Iniquity, always waiting with robe belt loosely tied, wanting a woman to pull it open and make them happy. Men and women drifted through the room; distantly through the smoke I could smell a malodorous breath of anxiety, behind which someone wondered if they would find pleasure tonight, if their robe would be opened by warm, new hands.

By the time Joe and I left, the sun was coming up. Later in the day, thinking about what had happened, I would be appalled, forever ending my brief moment of casual, bisexual sex, and my brief opportunity to imagine escaping from the man I'd attached myself to in an early fit of girlish optimism.

In addition to such stories, Bone's biography will certainly include what happened between Joe and Lev Bresner on December 20, 1973, inside the Bresners' long-halled Riverside Drive apartment. Joe was never violent before that night—never, not once. I think the truly self-absorbed find it difficult to lift themselves up out of their stupefaction and inflict pain. The arguments we usually had—about his career, money, the children, real estate, and even occasionally about women—were never violent but were often savage.

"I hate when you do this!" Alice screamed at us once when she was small and Joe and I were in the middle of a frenzied fight. "Can't you behave yourselves for a change?"

"Your father," I said carefully, breathing in controlled little sips, "has trouble behaving himself. That's exactly the problem."

Alice and Susannah wept and begged us not to fight, and

another time, during what seemed like a peaceful family dinner, Susannah handed Joe a piece of construction paper covered with doilies like a valentine, on which she'd written:

> If you and Mom/Stop you're Yelling
> Believe me, Dad, they'll be no telling
> How much I will love you.

Which made Joe burst into tears.

He stood up then and knelt down beside our older daughter's chair; he crushed her against him, made her milk glass fall over and spill, made her cry with confusion, and made Alice uncharacteristically chime in crying, too. "I love all you little ducklings," he said. "I never, ever want to hurt you. Sometimes I do stupid things. Big, stupid things. Ask your mother. I'm so sorry."

"I forgive you," Alice decided after a moment, and then Susannah seconded it, her voice trembling. David said nothing, but just kept eating as though nothing was happening around him.

I sat there thinking how easily Joe got off the hook, how smooth he was, how penitent. Across the table, five-year-old David watched everything with the same cool, critical eye, and I have to say I admired him for it.

No, Joe wasn't violent. Not until December 20, 1973, anyway. It was the night of the Chanukah party at the Bresners' apartment, an annual celebration in which the rooms were all infused with the smell of frying, and tiny Tosha Bresner stood in her beige kitchen, a spatula in one hand and an enormous skillet of potato pancakes in the other. She was like a one-woman assembly line, shredding potatoes and onions and forming them loosely with her red, long-ago-frostbitten hands, and then dropping them into spitting oil, only to remove them moments later when they achieved an exterior perfection, and a moist egginess inside that made all who ate them forget about anything terrible in their lives. The wives, biting into these potato pancakes, forgot about the infidelities of their husbands. And the husbands, in turn, forgot about the anxiety of the literary horse-race that otherwise coursed through their bodies, upsetting their metabolism.

"Tosha, can I help?" I asked her that night.

"Oh, Joan, you are so good," she said. "Here. Could you maybe carry these out? The men are *starving*. They are like animals! Oh, I hope I have enough!" She giggled wildly and somewhat inappropriately, handing me a platter.

In the living room, men and women stood around various homemade, strategically placed menorahs and watched the colored candles burn down to stubs, and drank beer and wine and talked over the scratch and thump of a Jefferson Airplane album. We would soon be leaving rock and roll forever, donating it to our children, its real owners, but we didn't yet know it. Soon we would be able to tolerate only the music we'd grown up with: big band, and jazz, and classical. Nothing else would be able to penetrate our aging skulls.

What were we talking about that night? It was the twenty-four-hour Nixon channel back then: all Nixon, all the time, the paranoid and fleshy basset face, the fallout from the Watergate break-in, the elaborate White House gavotte. The living room was divided into clusters, and from each of those clusters an occasional name was spat out like hot oil from Tosha Bresner's pan: *Haldeman. Ehrlichman.* For laughs, *Martha Mitchell,* with her mouth that wouldn't shut up. We despised these figures, and yet we followed their horrific antics with a certain feverishness. Here it was Chanukah, wintertime, only eight months before Nixon and poor bony, hesitant Pat would leave the White House lawn.

Men's ties were wide as roads then, and the hair of male writers and college professors was still slightly long, or else overly wide, formed into the topiary that became informally known as the Jewish Afro. (There were, for the record, no black people in the room. We had known some well in the sixties, during the civil rights movement, and later on there had been the occasional black writer who would appear in someone's living room, but

they drifted away from our world, or else had been cut loose.)
Wives wore dresses of indigo and maroon, and beaded necklaces
from Central America. Most of them worked now, having
grabbed jobs or graduate degrees as though there were a big game
of musical chairs taking place and they needed to be gainfully
employed before the music stopped.

Into this room I brought a new platter of potato pancakes.
"Food!" I announced, and people came from their separate
groups and ate, taking the latkes with their hands, happily burning their tongues. When Tosha finally ducked into the room, she
was greeted with applause and responded shyly, pinkening from
this brief moment of attention, which represented the smallest
fraction of the amount of attention her husband received in a single day. She looked *too* happy to me, so happy that she might
split, and she ran her hands up and down the sides of her dress,
murmuring to herself.

"You're a genius, Tosha," said a garrulous man named Bel-
stein, whose novels all followed the life of a character named
Felstein. He gave her a kiss on the top of her head, where the hair
was pulled into a dark, gleaming ball. Someone else handed her a
drink and she stayed for a while and drank, which was unusual
for this woman, who liked to scurry off into corners where she
would not be seen. She was like one of the endless series of hamsters that had lived in our children's rooms. When you tried to
pay attention to those animals, to touch them or show them
affection, they scrammed into one of the tube-tunnels that had
been installed in their cages. The kitchen was often Tosha Bresner's tunnel, but tonight she had emerged from its heat and its
damp surfaces, just in time for what would turn out to be the
famous fight between the two famous husbands.

It started, as these things seem to, out of virtually nothing. A
bit of casual talk, a string of political remarks, and some lightweight dismissal of an overrated nonfiction writer. "Did you see
that picture in the paper last week?" Joe asked. "His nostrils were
huge. I bet he keeps entire reams of paper up there."

"Who cares about his nostrils?" said Lev. "You are making fun of the man physically? You are saying his nose, it is too big?"

"Well, he's an arrogant ass," said Joe. "The nostrils make him look snobbish. As though he had them deliberately carved. *Enlarged.* To give him an aristocratic look. His books are so false, Lev, even you can see it."

"What do you mean, *even* me? Am I so dense I am handicapped from seeing the truth about a writer?"

"Yeah, this particular writer, I seem to recall you have a blind spot about," Joe went on. "You always defend him for some reason."

"He is my lover," Lev deadpanned, the back of his hand to his forehead, and the circle of writers and editors laughed. These men had no homosexual blood, oh no, not them. No homosexuality, no hemophilia, nothing rarefied about them whatsoever.

"He's not your lover," said Joe quickly. "He's your fucking brother in the Talmud."

There was quiet in the room. "*What?*" asked Lev. He was reassessing Joe, taking his measure; this happened once in a while between Lev and other writers; I'd witnessed it before, but had never seen it between him and Joe.

"Nothing," muttered Joe.

"No, tell me."

"All right. You know you tend to favor other Jews. You know you do," Joe went on. "It's a fact about you. I accept it. Look, this isn't some anti-Semitic *gotcha* moment, Lev, so don't try to turn it into one."

But Lev kept at him, trying to parse his words, and Joe rose up, uncoiled, and soon the men were shouting at each other, smearing each other's work. Joe was "full of *shit*," said Lev. "A pretender to the throne of Big *Fucking* American Writer."

And Lev, said Joe, was using his "concentration-camp childhood like a free pass into important places."

"Fuck you," said Lev.

"No, fuck *you*," said Joe.

And then Lev slugged him. Joe staggered but wasn't badly hurt; anyone could see that. This wasn't fatal. No teeth were loosened or lost, and no lip was split, spilling blood in a dramatic but benign way. (The lip, oh the lip, so melodramatic with its endless blood, but no one ever died of a broken lip.) Still, the blood flowed, and it frightened Joe after he brought his hand to his mouth and it came back brightly shining. He struck back, and the men fought each other sloppily, slapping, punching, kicking, calling each other names: *"You little shit," "You fraud," "You prick," "You asshole, you."*

And then Joe added, "You know what? I'd like to see you write *one* novel, Lev, just *one,* in which you aren't allowed to use the following keys on your typewriter: H-O-L-O-C-A-U-S-T."

As the other guests watched, fascinated and appalled, the two writers fell into one of the bedrooms together. It was the Bresners' younger daughter's room, with pink walls and a canopy bed, and Lev and Joe both ended up on that bed, landing on an oasis of pointy-footed, half-nude Barbie dolls. Thank God our own children had refused to come to this party, saying it was boring and there was no one their age to talk to. Everyone crowded into the doorway, nominally trying to break up the fight between the two men, but no one really wanted the fight to end.

Me, I was ashamed. I didn't want to watch; I wanted a cigarette and I wanted to go home. Tosha, however, was hysterical. "Joan, get them to stop!" she cried, clinging to me, and I hugged her, amazed that she was so invested in this cockfight.

"It will be over soon," I said, and it was, but not in the way I'd thought.

Joe apparently reached onto the little girl's bureau and grabbed the first thing he could find. It was a jump rope, and he wound it around Lev's skinny neck, pulling it tight for one second, but long enough to send a pileup of guests frantically onto that canopy bed, which promptly collapsed under the collective weight of all those fiction writers and poets and essayists.

I am positive Joe did not want to murder Lev; it seemed that the gesture was for show, was a burlesque of anger, a kind of performance piece enacted with the most absurd prop in the world: a little girl's jump rope. Still, somebody called the police, and Joe was taken away to the precinct, and I had to follow in a taxi, horrified. There were reporters, there was an exhausting night of talk, and meanwhile over in the ER at Columbia Presbyterian, Lev's neck was examined by a few nurses who had never heard of Lev Bresner and did not understand what they were dealing with here, the boiling drama of this event, the reverberations it would have, the way it would become known as a "brawl," a "feud," a seminal moment in the lives of the two big men.

Tosha had to be treated for hysteria. She screamed and keened in the emergency room, shouting, "Mama! Papa!" though I knew that her parents had been murdered in the concentration camp long ago. The ER staff took her condition more seriously than her husband's; I heard that there was talk of hospitalizing Tosha overnight for a psych evaluation, though finally she calmed down with a sedative, and they sent her home with Lev.

The story hung on for months: the bail I had to post, the court date for Joe, and then, finally, Lev's very public dropping of the charges. He'd been convinced by their mutual friends to "let it go." There had been soul-searching, agonizing over the whole pathetic, mortifying situation, and finally Lev decided not to pursue the case and the two men became friends again, apologizing to each other and embracing and weeping loudly, wiping their eyes and noses on each other's shirts, laughing at it all, writing their respective sides of the event for a high-circulation magazine, going out to dinner again with us wives in tow.

We followed them and followed them, all around New York City. Once, on a rooftop (I'm not sure what we were doing there; it was freezing and late but the men wanted a view of the city), Tosha Bresner turned to me and said, "Oh, Joan, we have been putting up with these men for a lifetime."

"Has it been all that bad for you?" I asked.

She paused, flustered. "Not all the time," she said quickly. "And for you?"

"No," I said. "Ups and downs." I looked out over the buildings and the occasional flumes of smoke, and the Hudson beyond, which, if you followed it north, would lead to our house, sitting silent and dark, waiting. I used to like being there, waking up in the morning to the creak and stir of the settling wood, and even to Joe with his arm flung over his head, his eyes still squeezed shut as he held on to whatever sleep he could get. I wasn't exactly lying to Tosha. I *wasn't* always unhappy; Joe and I had had good moments, especially early on. We'd danced together in our living room. We'd made love against a wall. We'd baked a huge pie together for a party. We'd walked everywhere, wrapped together. And later on, for a while, there was comfort, small exhalations of relief. All marriages have moments. Even Tosha and Lev's. Even ours.

But now she and I were sad and tired as we stood on that rooftop, and though she'd tried to tell me the extent of her suffering in that moment, I didn't really want to hear it. I couldn't know that to her this lifetime *was* unbearable, all she'd seen and all she was left with, scrambling after a famous, intense, and ambitious man, having to climb a metal ladder in the middle of the night to be with him on the roof of a building.

This was the early eighties, no later than that, because Tosha Bresner committed suicide in 1985. Even now, the fact of it shocks me. She was too frightened, too unstable, and images of her murdered parents and her sisters seemed to flood her more frequently, causing her to leave rooms, to excuse herself from parties, to take various pills for a depression and anxiety that could never be quelled, until finally she swallowed a whole bottle of Xanax one night while Lev was off giving the Carl Sandburg Lecture at the University of Chicago (Chicago, I'd heard, was the home of a woman Lev adored—a young divorcée who ran an elegant little bookstore on Clark Street with leather club chairs and free wine), and when he came home the next day in a splendid mood from that bounty of praise and vigorous lovemaking, he found his wife dead in their bed, her hands splayed open, as if she were asking, *What else was I supposed to do?* He called us, sobbing and hysterical, and we went there.

I mourned her for years, and I blamed Lev, though I see that this was unfair of me. After Tosha's funeral, sitting and taking off our clothes on our bed, back to back, I said to Joe, "He should have known better."

"What does that mean? Known better than to leave her to go to Chicago? He didn't know she would do what she did. How could he have known? My God, he's devastated."

"It's just the whole *thing*," I said. "She was so needy for so many years. What happened to her as a child—her whole family *murdered*. Her sisters, and her parents, and her grandparents, too. And then, later on, Lev's thing with women. How many women were there?"

"I have no idea," Joe said coldly.

"It was the last straw," I said.

"You can't really know what pushes someone over the brink. And you also don't know what they said between themselves," said Joe. "How they worked it out."

As though he and I had *ever* said something like that, had ever openly acknowledged that a man's need to be unfaithful to his wife was something to be protected and supported at all costs.

Bone's biography will certainly include some of Joe's women. The book will have to mention the way Joe sought women and was equally sought by them.

Most of Joe's women would never come forward to speak to a biographer, and they've never been identified before by anyone; they've preferred to press into their own memory books the time when they were younger and Joseph Castleman caught their eye.

Women such as Merry Cheslin, who Joe met on a porch outside a cottage at a famous summer writing conference called Butternut Peak during the summer of 1987.

It seems improbable to me that Joe never realized I knew about her, when in fact she practically walked around that summer wearing a sandwich board that read, I AM FUCKING THE GREAT JOE CASTLEMAN. PLEASE LOOK THROUGH THE BACK WINDOW OF BIRCHBARK COTTAGE AT MIDNIGHT TO SEE US GOING AT IT LIKE ANIMALS.

I minded, mostly, but in another way I *didn't* mind, because I thought she was pathetic, this Merry Cheslin who had the looks of a dark-haired Rapunzel. She was young, in her mid-twenties at the time, an aspiring novelist like half the participants at Butternut Peak. But she was standout good-looking; it had been the thing she'd probably always had going for her. Ever since she started school, Merry Cheslin's looks must have been the defining quality about her, the one detail that could be counted on each year. ("Oh, look, there's Merry at her locker, she got even prettier over the summer, if you can believe it.") Of course she ached to be a writer. Like so many women, she burned for it, all she wanted to do was to publish, and her whole life was leading toward the moment when she found an agent and a publisher and her first book appeared.

It might have happened, too, if she had been even a little talented. It might have happened if she'd figured out a way to make it happen. She was so directed that palpable ambition was released from her like kapok from a pillow, and after a while she didn't bother to keep it in, but just let everyone know: Merry Cheslin was going to be a famous writer. She'd be one of those writers you hear about, those elegant, dark-eyed women whose novels are set in Hawaii or in Tuscany, and for whom "the entire town is a character," or at least that's what they say in interviews.

"I keep a journal," she'd confided to Joe one day after his first workshop at Butternut Peak, and then she looked away quickly, as though she'd told him something crucial and furtive about herself, like *I was raped by my uncle as a child.*

I'm making this part up. There was no journal; at least not one that I knew about. (But if there *had* been, it would have been covered in some quilted material and had dried leaves inside it.) I actually don't know *what* she said to him; Merry Cheslin is one of the people I have never spoken to. I can't say what they talked about during intervals between the slapping of their bodies against each other in Birchbark Cottage at midnight, though I can imagine.

"I keep a journal," she said, and Joe, who always hated journals, who loathed the concept of "writing for the self," as opposed to writing for others to read (even that promiscuous journal-filler, Virginia Woolf, must have known that those pages would one day be read by others), had looked at her and said, "Oh, well, good for you. If you want to be a writer, you've simply got to keep writing. A journal is a pretty good start."

Merry Cheslin's fiction was horrible. This I actually do know, because though I was the wife, I got to look at the manuscripts he was going to deconstruct in his workshop, which would be held on Adirondack chairs in a field overlooking Butternut Peak. The good-smelling, mimeographed copies of the manuscripts sat on our old chipped dresser in the cottage they gave us that summer, which was called Peachtree. Joe was off on some porch drinking with other writers one evening. They were both male and female; the women tended to be soft-spoken and kind to students, while the men were an uneven lot—some powerful, others doglike and grateful to be there, for their novels were largely ignored by the reading public. Only here in the summer could they feel big.

While Joe sat on that porch, I took the stack of his student manuscripts onto our bed and began to read. There were a couple of Joe imitators in the pile, all men, mostly young, and a trembly, single-spacing woman, probably old, who had written, beneath the title of her 100 percent unpublishable story, "Copyright, Gloria Bismarck. First North American Serial Rights. Approximately 4,213 words." Which was enough to break your heart rather than have contempt for. I imagined that Gloria Bismarck was a widow who lived in some suburb, and whose highlight of life was her two weeks at Butternut Peak. She didn't even really exist in the eyes of most of the faculty writers, because she was old and sad and ridiculous, and had bulbous veins in her legs, and for the rest of her life no one might ever touch her body or read anything she'd written unless they'd been paid to do so.

Merry Cheslin, on the other hand, immediately captured the attention of the men on the Butternut faculty. Most of them lifted their heads from their manuscripts or their conversations or their Bloody Marys when she stepped onto the porch, their nostrils quivering, their mouths dropping slightly open, wanting something from this woman simply because of the sheer wall of her beauty, which was all she had that mattered. Her work was irredeemably bad. She wanted to be poetic and whispery yet dark; she wanted to be irresistible and troubled all at once. The short story that she submitted to Joe was a mawkish girlhood reminiscence called "That Firefly Summer."

Though she had no talent, still she thought a lot of herself, and still my husband took her to bed in the single room she'd booked in Birchbark, and pushed up her tight little strappy dress. What was I doing at the time? I was sitting in our own room, in Peachtree, stimulating my gums with a dental pick and thinking about how many days were left before Joe and I would be able to leave Vermont.

Wives are the sad sacks of any writers' conference. Wherever I went during those twelve days—when I stepped out of Peachtree and onto the gravel path, voices would call out to me in gaiety: "Morning, Joan!" or, "Hey there, Joan, are you and Joe going to the picnic in the grove?"

Everyone liked me because I was not only a wife, I was the alpha wife, the spouse of the alpha dog. The alpha dog who, everyone knew, was blithely cheating on me, fucking himself dizzy in Birchbark, separated from Peachtree only by Wildwood and Silverspruce and by the great wooden dining hall, with its summer-camp smells and fresh-out-of-the-dishwasher glasses that warmed my orange juice each morning to approximately the temperature of the bath I took each night.

In the dining hall I sat beside Joe and across the table from other wives and their writer husbands. The occasional husband was there accompanying his writer wife, but most tended to stay away from the conference, saying they couldn't take time off from their jobs. There were a few children underfoot, too, though by now ours were fully grown and off in their own lives. All of us in the dining hall behaved with a certain jollity that is required at writers' conferences, for without it, everyone might look around and actually realize what they've gotten themselves into—all the narcissism and unpleasantness let loose among the scrub pines.

"Do you want to go into town this afternoon?" one of the other wives asked me. She was a woman named Liana Thorne, who looked like one of those stick-insects that can change color at any given moment so as to be entirely unnoticeable. Her expression was full of hope. Her husband, Randall Thorne, used to be famous, though in recent years his novels had fallen into remainder bins everywhere, but he was friends with the director of the conference and was asked back every summer.

Later in the day, when our husbands were off teaching their workshops—when Merry Cheslin was sitting near Joe, her eyes locked into his, taking down notes on every single thing he said about "voice" and "the willing suspension of disbelief"—I climbed into Liana's beat-up Yugo with her and two other wives, Dusty Berkowitz and Janice Leidner, and we headed to town.

"Free at last, free at last," Dusty Berkowitz said as the car pulled through the stone gates of Butternut Peak. "Thank God Almighty, I'm free at last."

We all laughed a little, and then Janice said, "Even Dr. King didn't have to put up with what we do."

"No, but I hear Coretta did," I said.

"It's hard, being them," said Liana finally.

"Being *black*?" Dusty asked.

"No, being those men," Liana said. "Writers whom everyone

wants to listen to. The kind of men who other people decide hold the key to everything. Randall tells me that he tries so hard to please everyone, but he just can't do it."

Dream on, Randall, I thought, imagining the way that Liana's husband must certainly have envied Joe's currency in the world.

We arrived in town and uncollapsed ourselves getting out of the car; this, I thought, was the kind of car that most writers' money could buy: something squat and ugly and perhaps unsafe, with a faculty parking sticker slapped on the windshield. Although all four men had been known to be unfaithful, I believe only Joe participated in his affairs in such a vigorous way. We four wives looked at handmade scarves in a window of one of the local crafts shops, Vermont Country Artisans, admiring weave and texture and color, then soothed ourselves inside the store, fingering material, gathering our own sensual pleasure where we could. An eggplant-colored shawl had long, silken fibers that I ran my hands through as though they were hair.

Merry Cheslin's hair was darker than that. I put my face against the shawl, nuzzled it.

"Isn't that a beauty?" the young saleswoman said, trying to be helpful. "It's made by a local craftsperson. And she happens to be blind, which I think is really neat."

What did Merry Cheslin have to offer, besides long, frequently shampooed hair and bad fiction and a body that could be smoothed out onto a bed like this shawl, like a comforter, an offering? Joe needed that; it was blood plasma to him. *It's hard, being them,* Liana Thorne had said, and I never really tried to think what exactly was so hard, what it was these men lacked, what they needed, what we couldn't give them.

We gave them everything we had. All our possessions were theirs. Our children were theirs. Our lives belonged to them. Our weary, been-through-the-mill bodies were theirs, too, though more often than not they didn't want them anymore. My body wasn't bad; it still isn't, and yet while I lay my head against an eggplant-colored fabric in a crafts store, Joe was looking into the eyes of the woman he would be lying down with later in Birchbark.

And then, in the middle of Vermont Country Artisans, I burst into tears. The other wives, alarmed, hustled me out of the store and into the little vegetarian cafe next door, where they gathered around me in solidarity.

"I admire you, I really do," said Janice, after I'd admitted why I was crying. "We all see what Joe's up to, summer after summer, and yet you always seem as if you don't really care."

"We had no idea it upset you," Dusty Berkowitz murmured. "We thought you were somehow . . . completely above it. Like you knew everything but didn't give a shit. Like you were superior to the whole thing."

I blew my nose into a napkin made of brown pulpy paper and let the other women take care of me. Why had Merry Cheslin gotten to me? I wondered, when last summer that student of Joe's named Holly something hadn't bothered me one bit? Why did the author of "That Firefly Summer" cause me to weep openly in town in front of these women I hardly knew?

I'd never cried at great length before about one of Joe's affairs, or at least not in front of anyone but Joe. I'd maintained that I was never entirely threatened, because as far as I knew, most of the women he slept with weren't talented, and neither, of course, was Merry Cheslin.

But what if talent didn't matter at all, at least when it came to Joe's women? What if talent wasn't simply meaningless, but was actually a liability? Did he like her more because she was a bad writer? Did it make him feel safe sliding along the body of a woman who would never be a great challenge to him?

Yes, it did.

I believe he spent the entire twelve days at Butternut Peak engaged in an affair with Merry. He seemed happy during those days, agreeably doing his part during the skits that the young waiters sometimes put on at dinner. "It's time to play Butternut Peak *Jeopardy!*" the headwaiter, a rotund twenty-three-year-old fiction student exclaimed one night, while the rest of the serving staff hummed the perky game-show theme. "I'm your host, Aleksandr Solzhenitsyn Trebek," he said, to much genial laughter.

There were a series of "answers" put to three "contestants," a shy short-story writer named Lucy Bloodworth, Harry Jacklin, and Joe, who was coaxed from his seat, where he had just begun tucking into a dish of bread pudding.

The tone was jokey-literary, and the first Daily Double was directed at Joe. Part of a paragraph from a recent novel of his was going to be read aloud, and he would be asked to finish it.

"I quote," said the headwaiter, " 'Shirley Breen was not a covetous woman. No one had ever said of her, "There goes Shirley Breen, desirer of things she cannot have." In her life, there was only *one thing* she wanted that she had not been able to get.' " The headwaiter paused dramatically.

This was an easy one. The answer, in the form of a question, was: "What is . . . 'a shot glass that had been drunk from by Mae West.' " At least one-quarter of the dining hall could have shouted these words in unison. But Joe just sat there in front of all of them, scratching his head and looking embarrassed.

"Oh God," he finally said. "I'm royally screwed now. You've all learned my terrible secret."

"And what secret would that be?" asked the headwaiter.

I watched Joe with curiosity. "That I've got a bad case of Alzheimer's," he said. "Can't even remember my own writing a minute after I finish it. Somebody shoot me now."

In the vegetarian cafe with the three other wives, I wept and wept and they were a mass of heads and elbows, comforting me, or trying to. "I just feel so humiliated," I said, "getting up every morning and stepping outside the building, knowing what everyone else knows. Do you all think I'm ridiculous? A pathetic figure?"

"No! No!" they cried. "Not at all! Everyone admires you!" But who *were* these women? By default, they were my friends, my companions, these weary wives with their own careers that people tried hard to be interested in.

"How's the social work going, Liana?" a conference student asked her at a picnic one afternoon, though there was no answer that could have kept his eye from leaping away from her and onto the more desirable targets: famous novelists spitting watermelon seeds in that grove.

"How's the refugee work going, Joan?" an older, shy female poet named Jeannie asked me another time, for she'd heard about my occasional involvement with the relief organization. I told her just enough to be conversational, and no more, though she seemed disappointed, and truly wanted to hear. Joe had exaggerated my involvement with the charity over the years, trying to make me sound as though I was engaged in something in a way that would command quiet respect.

"I have *nothing*," I said to the wives, and they told me I was wrong, I had so much, I contributed to the world, I was a positive presence, they'd always thought I was "stylish and intelligent," to use Janice Leidner's words.

"It's like you have a whole other life going on inside you," said Dusty Berkowitz.

"We all do," I said.

"*I* don't," she said with her rolling, self-conscious laugh. "What you see is what you get."

Dusty Berkowitz, fifty-five, her chest freckled from sun exposure, her hair as red as a leprechaun's, no longer existed for her husband.

Janice Leidner still existed for her own husband, though only in outline: the idea of her, rather than the particulars.

Liana Thorne, deeply melancholy and bland, had a husband who longed to be part of the men's club and who continually elbowed his way in, to the exclusion of any other activities or interests.

And me, blond, thin, aging but preserved in the acidity of this long marriage. The marital juices kept me alive, kept me going. Joe and I swam in a jar together; I swam alone whenever he went off to kiss the tender parts of Merry Cheslin. Then, tired, he always swam back to me.

There he was at 3 A.M. that morning, slowly opening the door of our room in Peachtree and appearing with the hall light behind him.

"Joan?" he said. "You up?" He came into the room, bringing a draft of cigarette smoke with him, much of it absorbed into his hair, his sweater, the pores of his skin.

I lifted my head from the deep sleep I'd been in. "Yes," I always said, even when it wasn't really true. "I'm up."

He hoisted himself onto the bed beside me, that smoky, clouded man, too old for blue jeans even then but wearing them anyway, his eyes inflamed from the smoke that had filled the room he'd been in, that party with godly writers and lowly students coming together, and then the private party afterward, in Birchbark, when he climbed onto a bed identical to this one, with a woman who bore no resemblance to me whatsoever.

At three in the morning that summer, and the summers that preceded it and the summers that followed, we were together, a husband and wife united in the foggy middle of a Vermont night. Bats circled the pines all around our cottage and sometimes hung like change purses from the roof of our veranda, and the night bristled with forest-bright animal eyes, and the arrhythmic clicking of strange bugs that I hoped never to see, but which I'd simply agreed to live among for twelve days. He was with me; we slept together and we woke up together, day after day, which is a lot more than I can say for Merry Cheslin, who, after that summer, was never heard from as a writer, and who, in the Butternut Peak alumni newsletter, recently described herself this way:

> "I'm divorced," writes MERRY CHESLIN, "no kids, never published my novel (sigh . . .), but I'm happily working for a small educational software company in Providence, Rhode Island, which believe it or not actually gives me a chance to use some of the creative skills I learned all those summers ago in Vermont. . . ."

* * *

Merry Cheslin will appear in Bone's biography, at least in some
vaguely described way. So, too, will other women from Joe's visiting stints at universities, as well as occasional hangers-on and
New York publicists. There were beautiful young women in
gauzy blouses and cowboy boots, and stylish, recent college grad-
uates looking for jobs in publishing.

In addition to the women, Joe's "attempted strangulation" of
Lev will make it into the biography. And so will Joe's heart attack
and eventual valve replacement; this is a distinctly unsexy por-
tion, for instead of jump-rope weapons or awards or couplings
there is only a miserable scene in a restaurant called The Cracked
Crab in the winter of 1991. There we were, six male writers and
some wives, the men having achieved various footholds of success in their writing lives, their pitons dug deep into a rock wall,
hairlines receded or vanished or else the hair itself staying
resiliently wiry and Einstein-clownish.

Joe, in this group, still occupied the center. He wasn't the
loudest (that would have been Martin Benneker, with his roar
and flying hail of spittle) and he wasn't the richest (definitely
Ken Wooten, whose urbane and chiseled espionage novels had all
been turned into movies), nor was he the most intelligent, not by
far. (Lev had that role; he'd lunged for it.) Joe had a special, inde-
finable position among these men, a kind of quiet seniority. Joe
loved to talk, and once in a while he loved to cook thick, undif-
ferentiated stews that he could stand over for hours, pouring red
wine into the pot and tossing in some meat and bones and
the occasional handful of parsley. He loved to read and listen
to jazz and eat his Sno-Balls and drink at a tavern and play
pool.

We sat at a large, round table at The Cracked Crab that night.
The surface had been lined with white butcher's paper, and was
covered with crabs, as though we'd stumbled upon a colony of
them. There they were, a mess of claws and jointed legs doused

with a spray of Old Bay seasoning. Beer bottles, lifted and low-ered during animated talk, left their rings all over the paper.

As usual, the wives had somehow banded together from their separate seats, straining forward to talk, maybe discussing some new Chinese-language film, and the men were joshing and boasting in their usual way, and there was the incessant, almost soothing sound of crab cartilage being crushed or pulled, when suddenly, with a mouth full of food, Joe reared back in his chair and said, *"Shit."*

Then his chair slammed forward to the floor and his face smashed down onto the butcher paper, and all of us leaped forward.

"Are . . . you . . . choking?" boomed Maria Jacklin in a voice she'd learned from CPR class, and Joe made the slightest move-ment with his head that indicated no. His eyes were squeezed tight in pain, and his hands clasped his chest, and he seemed to stop breathing, and immediately the men were hoisting his body up onto the table, right into the middle of the crustacean bed, where they fell upon him the way they'd done long ago during the fight with Lev.

Lev Bresner, by now a widower for years and still sexually active, but more depressed than ever, took over, starting the tilt-ing of the head and the application of his lips to Joe's, and then the pounding of Joe's chest, and the next thing I knew, paramedics had pushed through the wooded back room of The Cracked Crab and had Joe on a stretcher with an oxygen mask over his face. Someone put an arm around me; I heard a mesh of voices, and I reached out toward Joe, but he was already being wheeled away.

Five months later, after a long, cranky recovery from what had actually been a fairly mild heart attack, Joe required surgery to replace one of his human valves with a pig's. He lay in our bed in Weathermill and read letters and novels, talking on the phone to various people around the world. Both of our daughters came and stayed at the house a couple of times, trying to cheer me up and be helpful to their dad. Even David telephoned, and though he didn't ask directly about Joe, I knew that was why he was calling.

I clung to Joe that year, extremely frightened. I forgot his flaws; they flew away as quickly as the taste of that meal. I have never eaten crab again. I fretted at his bedside, and I wished desperately for his recovery, and I got what I wished for.

On our final night in Finland, Joe and I walked up the wide marble steps of the Helsinki Opera House side by side, my arm in his, surrounded by the chatter of cameras, which weren't meant only for us. Anyone of prominence in Finland was here tonight, all the writers and artists and members of government, the people with curiously interesting names like Simo Ratia, Kaarlo Pietila, Hannes Vatanen. The names rang similarly, seductively, and the faces bore the same high color and fine bone structure. Everyone's teeth looked strong and even, too, as though one orthodontist serviced the entire country. Men and women filed into the Opera House in their bulky Nordic parkas; only after they had entered and stripped down to their evening dress could you see how prepared they were for an evening of high couture. Here was a high point, the annual release from a frozen, static state, the tiny crack in the ice that let in the world. And the crack in the ice, this year, was in the name of Joseph Castleman, a small, overweight man in a tuxedo walking beside me up a set of shallow steps and into the gilded light of the Helsinki Opera House.

I was seated in a box beside the President of Finland and his wife. While Joe was ushered backstage, I was formally introduced to the president, a man of my age named Mr. Timo Kristian with a stern face not unlike Finnish architecture. He wore one of those diagonal sashes fashioned of multicolored silk. His wife, Mrs. Karita Kristian, slightly younger, dressed in black, with a string of amethyst around her neck, sat frozen in place beside him. They had nothing to say to each other, or so it seemed, and they didn't even try to give the illusion of rapport. Presidents served for six years in Finland; this was the beginning of Kristian's fifth year in office, and both he and his wife looked very tired.

Finally Mrs. Kristian took it upon herself to speak to me. There we were, wife to wife. "So, Mrs. Castleman," she said in careful English, "you are enjoying your stay here in Helsinki?"

"Oh yes," I said.

"What are your impressions of the Finnish people?" she wanted to know, and I spoke a little about their quiet pride, their good eye, their elegant simplicity, all of which seemed to be the right responses, for she appeared pleased.

"And how about you, Mrs. Kristian?" I said. "What is your life like here in Helsinki?"

The president's wife was confused. I immediately realized that the question probably seemed insolent and strange. Or maybe she was just unused to such direct interest. "My life," she began uncertainly, and then she quickly looked around to see who might be listening. No one was. The president was talking to one of his cabinet members, a man with an enormous blond mustache. "My life," Karita Kristian went on in a quiet, controlled voice, "is so very unhappy."

I stared at her. Had I heard her right? Maybe she'd said her life was so very *happy* instead; how could I find out? Her face gave nothing away, but appeared as placid as it had been moments before. The lights dimmed just then and everyone in our box and in the entire audience grew silent. Mrs. Karita Kristian, the First Lady of Finland, turned to face forward as the heavy, scalloped curtains were pulled upward on the stage, revealing a small sea of men that included my husband. One or two women sat among them, their dresses providing the only bright bits of color.

Soon Joe was given a medal by the acting president of the Finnish Academy of Letters, Teuvo Halonen, the man who had first telephoned to inform us that Joe had won the prize. The gold disk hung on white silk, the disk engraved with a miniature copy of *Kalevala*, and a pair of hands holding it open, and even from all the way up here in the opera box I could make out the medal's winking light. Short selections from several of Joe's novels were read aloud by a film actress who flipped back her hair often as she read in a sonorous voice. And then finally Joe stood up.

"Good evening," he began, "and thank you for your kind welcome." He tipped his head in the direction of the Finnish Academy. "Members of the Finnish Academy, I would like to say that I am deeply grateful and moved." And then, slowly, he raised his head in the direction of the box. "President Kristian," he said. "Thank you for honoring me in your beautiful country." *Blah, blah, blah,* he went on. No, that's unfair of me, the words were reasonable, though mostly uninteresting. I listened hard. He hadn't let me see his speech beforehand; it was important to him that he wrote it himself and that no one else offered an opinion before he came to Finland. "I've felt, ever since I arrived here," he said, "what a tonic this land is after the harsh locus of resentment and plenty that is otherwise known as the United States. In these days since terrorism has accelerated its global pace . . ."

I was mortified that he was talking about terrorism; it was such an easy subject, an all-purpose, cheap one. All you had to do was invoke the specter of terrorism and everyone dutifully went somber on you. Lips pursed. People bowed their heads slightly. Couldn't he have come up with something more original? Joe went on in this vein, quoting Rilke and Saul Bellow and Baudelaire's *Les Fleurs du mal.* And his speech meandered predictably through the war against terrorism—through the windy caves of Afghanistan, and the Middle East—and wrapped itself around the world until it returned home again. He was almost done. Joe paused here, and then his eyes moved subtly over to me as he said, "I'd like to say a few words about my wife, Joan."

Everyone dutifully looked upward, their heads tilted toward me. "My wife, Joan," Joe repeated, "is truly my better half."

Don't, I thought. *Don't do this to me. I asked you not to.*

"She has made it possible for me to find the stillness inside myself—as well as the noise—to write my novels," he said. "Without her, I am certain I would not be standing up here tonight. I would instead be at home staring at a blank piece of paper with my mouth open in stupefaction."

There was indulgent laughter; of course he would have been up here anyway, the audience thought. Yet how admirable it was for the winner of the Helsinki Prize to be so generous toward his wife, to acknowledge her like this as he stood onstage to accept this award for a long, hard labor on the fiction chain gang. He'd been breaking rocks apart, and there I was, wiping his brow, offering him cool drinks. He'd been nearly prostrate from the heat and the strain of being a novelist, and yet I was always there, stripping away his soiled shirt, bringing him a clean one, helping him slip his arms into it, doing up the buttons myself, urging him on when he needed encouragement, lying beside him at night, telling him *you can do it*, even as his ankles were shackled together and he was exhausted and in tears. You can do it, we wives said, you can do it, and when they actually did do it, we were as happy as mothers whose babies have taken a first, shaky step, letting go of the furniture forever.

Those well-meaning Finns regarded me, those people who had given my husband a check worth $525,000. They gave us their *markka* and they smiled up at me, nodding and praising the charms and subtle skills of the wife.

Everyone knows how women soldier on, how women dream up blueprints, recipes, ideas for a better world, and then sometimes lose them on the way to the crib in the middle of the night, on the way to the Stop & Shop, or the bath. They lose them on the way to greasing the path on which their husband and children will ride serenely through life.

But it's their choice, Bone might say. They make a choice to be that kind of wife, that kind of mother. Nobody forces them anymore; that's all over now. We had a women's movement in America, we had Betty Friedan, and Gloria Steinem with her aviator glasses and frosted parentheses of hair. We're in a whole new world now. Women are *powerful*. Valerian Qaanaaq will probably be standing on this very stage in a couple of years, wearing traditional Inuit garb and reflecting upon her childhood in that notorious sod-and-snow igloo.

Some women don't make that choice, it's true. They live another life entirely: Lee, the journalist I met in Vietnam; Brenda the prostitute. Or else they work out some version involving elaborate child care or a husband who doesn't mind staying home all day with an infant. A husband who lactates, perhaps. Or maybe they don't even *want* babies, some of these women, and life opens out to them in an endless field of work. And once in a while the world responds in a big way, letting them in, giving them a key, a crown. It does happen, it does. But usually it doesn't.

You sound bitter, Bone would say.

That's because I am, I would tell him.

Everyone needs a wife; even *wives* need wives. Wives tend, they hover. Their ears are twin sensitive instruments, satellites picking up the slightest scrape of dissatisfaction. Wives bring broth, we bring paper clips, we bring ourselves and our pliant, warm bodies. We know just what to say to the men who for some reason have a great deal of trouble taking consistent care of themselves or anyone else.

"Listen," we say. "Everything will be okay."

And then, as if our lives depend on it, we make sure it is.

Chapter Six

DRUNK; Joe and I were drunk in a way that is allowed, even expected, following moments of great, preening triumph. You would have seen us in that Opera House at the banquet and thought, from the way he leaned in to whomever he was talking to, and tilted his head and slapped his knee, that we too were Finns. Drunken Finns, trying to forget the encroaching half-year of darkness; happy Finns; carefree Finns—*Huckleberry* Finns. Joe had received his award and given his remarks and we'd spent the evening at the banquet, circulating, being circulated around, meeting the luminaries of not only the Scandinavian countries but also the clusters of novelists, journalists, and publishers who'd been imported from London, Paris, Rome. The ceilings were high in the Opera House's atrium, where extremely long tables had been set up and draped in linen, and the acoustics amplified the excited, multilingual jabber. Toasts took place in many languages, without interpreters, and Joe and I smiled and raised our glasses along with everyone else, never really knowing what we were toasting, what we were signing on for, what we were gamely laughing at.

The president and his wife left early; someone mentioned in

passing that Kristian liked to watch Sky TV every night and then go right to sleep, and that he never deviated from this strict routine, not even once a year for the winner of the Helsinki Prize. I wanted to say to his wife, "Oh, couldn't you stay on without him?" but it was too late, they'd been swept away, back down those marble steps and perhaps into some waiting coach driven by reindeer.

Hours later, Joe and I finally left, too, in the company of two dozen agreeable publishers and writers and dignitaries who begged Joe not to end the evening just yet, but to let it go on and on a bit longer, this one special night that, like Passover, was different from all other Finnish nights. Passover, a holiday that few of these people would know a good deal about. ("Yes, yes, that is the one on which the *Yewish* people recline, no?") They were charming and lively, wanting to discuss American fiction and geopolitics with Joe, wanting to talk more about terrorism and anxiety about the future. In a fleet of limousines, we rode off to a very old, classic brasserie in the middle of the city; the management had been told we would be coming, and was prepared, for when we arrived the rooms were festooned with flowers and ornaments and brightly lit ice mountains on which crayfish lay, but none of us could eat much, for the banquet earlier had been an embarrassment of riches, with bricks of foie gras and individual game birds and a geometrical array of cheeses.

Some of the members of the Finnish Academy were now patiently teaching Joe the opening lines of *Kalevala* in both Finnish and English. Slurring, they looped their arms around one another and recited. Joe was in the middle of the crowd, beaming, impish, his voice louder than anyone's. He'd eaten too much tonight; I'd seen him shoveling in the solid blocks of trans fats and animal flesh with its scorched jackets of skin, and cheese upon cheese, followed by the best wines of the world, the bottles brought up from deep down inside some Nordic cellar. I'd watched him pack it in earlier, saw him with his mouth open so wide that I could view his dental history, the silver and the gold packed into the hollows, and the long, dark throat that led down toward his imperfect heart with its secondhand valve.

Our business was almost done, I thought as I tossed back another drink and watched him. Our entire transaction was nearly complete, the endless exchange of fluids, of vital information, the creation of children, the buying of cars, the taking of vacations, the winning of prizes in far-flung places. The winning of *this* prize. The effort of it all: God, what effort. Enough already, I should say to him. Enough of this. Let me go now, and not have to wake up beside your satisfied face every morning for the next decade, and your well-fed stomach that deprives you of the sight of your own penis, curled in wait.

"I'm going back to the hotel," I whispered to him. "I'm ready. I've had it for the night." He was telling a story to the entire table about growing up in Brooklyn; I heard the word "brisket" spoken, and then a translator gave an explanation to everyone in Finnish about what a brisket was, and I knew I really wanted to be out of there. I'd heard all of Joe's stories many times, the unadorned or embellished tales.

Joe turned. "You sure?" he asked, and I said yes, I was tired, the driver would take me, and Joe should stay, which of course he would. Everyone bade me a fervent good night, all these new friends I would never see again, the elegant men and women of this lovely, brave country. Brave, I thought, for being located so far from the rest of the world it partially emulated, away from horror, from easy thrills. Brave for knowing it would soon be put to sleep for an entire winter, only to be roused again, with the bears, when the earth's rotation brought it briefly into sunlight.

I slid across the backseat of the limousine and the driver started us toward the Inter-Continental Hotel. It was after 3 A.M., and we drove slowly past the harbor, where a boxy, aging Russian ocean liner—the *Constantin Simonov*, I read on its side—was docked beside a sleeker Norwegian one. I remember looking at the enormous ships, and listening politely as the driver told me some bit of waterfront history, but then I succumbed to my drunkenness, my head a punch bowl filled with various Finnish liquors. I lay down in the backseat with my feet up and thought about the pleasure of leaving a party alone. Often the Siamese-twinship of marriage keeps you waiting in rooms you'd rather vacate, but tonight I was out of there on my own. He was my other half and I wanted us divided.

"Are you really going to leave him?" a voice asked.

It was a woman speaking to me from inside the drunken punch bowl. I could see her without even bothering to open my eyes. She was someone I hadn't seen in over forty years: Elaine Mozell, the novelist who'd given that reading at Smith. She looked the same, her hair full, her face red. She *was* the same, a frozen ghost, and she was still drunk, but I was drunker.

"Yes," I said to her. "I am."

"Did you get what you want?" she asked.

"I'm not sure what it was she wanted," said someone else, who was quickly revealed to be my mother, hovering nearby. "That man was a *Jew*," she continued. "That was her first mistake."

My mother's hair still stank of the beauty parlor, even eighteen years after her death. In the afterlife, then, there were beauty parlors, with upright, lost souls sitting under inverted cones and staring at nothing, the thoughts blasted right out of their heads in the heat.

"She wanted to be by his side," another person said, and I saw that it was poor Tosha Bresner, the suicide. A small, scrawny woman, her hands still fashioning something out of wet potatoes and egg and onions, moving it from hand to hand.

"Who wouldn't? It was her chance to be with a big man. To prop him up," explained Elaine.

"No, that's not it at all," I said to the row of faces. "You don't get it at all."

"She could have done it differently" came a new voice, accented, commanding, and this belonged to the novelist Valerian Qaanaaq, dressed in full Inuit garb. "*I* did it, after all," she said.

"And I had absolutely no help. Do you think my family expected me to become a writer? Get real. Yet I did it anyway."

They waited, these wraiths; they floated in place, wanting to hear what I had to say for myself.

I had to think back to the early days, to an archival image of me at nineteen sitting in my carrel in the Smith College library, writing stories. Professor J. Castleman, M.A., had brought out that desire in me, had extracted it through the way he spoke about books, through the way he revered literature, revered James Joyce's small, perfect masterpiece, "The Dead."

"Well, I guess, a long time ago I did start thinking about becoming a writer," I admitted to them.

"So did you get to be one?" asked Elaine.

"*I* did," sang out Valerian Qaanaaq, as if anyone had asked her.

"I told you that they wouldn't let you in, didn't I?" Elaine Mozell said.

"You did. But maybe I was *weak*," I said.

"Oh no you weren't," said Tosha. "I admired you. You seemed so bold. I could never do half the things you did, or say the things you said. I was afraid, but you weren't."

"I was afraid, too," I told her.

"No, you were just realistic," said Elaine. "You knew you couldn't have what they have. You wanted their muscularity. You wanted to matter. To make sure your voice still kept chattering from beyond the grave. Chattering on and on in the hell that a certain kind of writer goes to when he leaves this world. The thing is: the minute he enters hell, he owns *that place*, too."

"He's a *Jew*," said my mother.

"A big fat novelist," said Elaine Mozell. "The man who took everything."

"He's my *boy*!" cried a new voice, and this, I saw, was Joe's mother. She circled above all the others in her flowered dress, huge and luminous, her face pink with pleasure. "That's all he is, a *boy*! Why are you giving him such a hard time? You should forgive him everything. After all, what other choice do you have?"

* * *

In the lobby of the hotel, two clerks stood at attention as though it were a reasonable hour of the day instead of the dead middle of the night. They nodded as I picked my way across the room's grand dimensions in my silvery gray evening gown and heels, and I tried to appear gracious and dignified and regal instead of simply drunk.

"Did you have a nice evening, Mrs. Castleman?" asked one of them. "We watched the proceedings on television."

"Very nice," I said. "Thank you. Good night now."

I stood for a moment digging into my little purse to find the key to the elevator. As I stood riffling through it, I thought about how I would go upstairs now and dip my fingertips into a small pot of face cream, and before a wall-sized mirror in one of the stunningly large bathrooms, I'd remove the makeup I'd scrupulously applied hours earlier. No one would be there to unzip me; no Joe with his hand on my nape, moving downward, the zipper sound itself like the distant cry of a woman heard beneath the strains of a zither.

No Joe. I would have to unzip myself from now on after we separated for good, learning to tip my elbow up at the proper angle, as I used to do, and then switch hands midzip, taking it all the way down to the tailbone, the bottom, and then stepping out.

Our hotel suite had been made up for the night, worked at, apparently, by an army of maids who had sent their arms whipping across the comforter on our bed, flattening it so that it was like sand blown across a desert. After I got undressed, I pulled back the comforter, ruining the effect, and fell immediately asleep.

At 5 A.M., I heard Joe's card in the door and the quiet, responding click that allowed him access. He stumbled in, his tuxedo askew, the cummerbund slung over his arm, as if he were a waiter carrying a napkin. He looked dopey and happy, his medal still around his neck. He came into the room and removed first his medal, then his shirt and undershirt.

"You up, Joan?" he asked.

"I'm up," I said, sliding to a sitting position against the headboard.

"I'm drunk," he said, unnecessarily. "And I ate too much, like a dog. They wouldn't stop feeding me, those Finns. God, I love the Finnish people; they are completely underrated. And that *Kalevala* is terrific! One of the members of Parliament—that fellow with the pointy red beard—kept reciting it, and everybody began crying like babies, myself included. My next book is going to have a Finn in it. Definitely."

"Joe, stop," I said. "You're just talking at me, and it's too much right now."

"Sorry," he said. "It's hard to turn it off, you know, to just shut it down." He shook his head. "I'm going to take a sauna."

And then he stripped off the rest of his clothes and went down the hall of the suite to the sauna. I heard the door open, and he was in. I followed him to the tiny room, peered through the dark square of glass and saw him lying down on the wood under a towel, already half dozing. I opened the door, entered the blaze in my nightgown, which immediately seemed to turn liquid.

"Joe."

He looked up at me with one eye open and said, "What, Joan? What is it?"

I breathed in, then out, and told him, "I have to say something. There's no good time to do it."

"So say it," he said, sitting up.

"Okay. When we get back to New York, I want a separation. I've thought it all through."

"Oh, I see," he said. "You wait until my body's heated to a million degrees to tell me this. You wait until there's nothing I can do, until I'm *fried*." He poured some more water, and it sizzled on the coals.

"Look, try to imagine my situation. I want another chance at life," I said. "I'm sixty-four years old. I'm almost a *senior*. I can go anywhere half price, and I want to go there alone. Please don't act furious, or heartbroken, or shocked, none of which you could possibly be. For once, try to be thoughtful, just try to listen."

"So that's my big congratulations," he said. "Well, you know what? Fuck that."

"Big congratulations? Why exactly should you be congratulated?" I asked. "Don't you get enough of that elsewhere?"

He paused. "I happened to introduce you to the world, remember," he said, but no, this wasn't true; I was the one who had taken him there, who had led him in. I saved the day for that young writer of "No Milk on Sunday."

"The thing is, I recently realized that I'm exhausted from you," I said.

"That's why you've been so bitchy," he said.

"It's amazing to me that I lasted this long," I told him. "Realistically, I should have been gone years ago." He was flushed red and damp. He put a hand to his head. I'd looked and looked at him for so long; I'd made a habit of it, a vocation, and I could stop looking now. "When we get home," I went on, "I'm going to see Ed Mandelman and start the process."

"You almost never used to complain about what we had," he said. "You used to be *content.*"

"A long time ago."

"Yeah, and you were thrilled," he said. "You told me how exciting it all was. To be a *part* of everything. Then you got old and all of a sudden nothing was acceptable. You became like all those old ladies in restaurants: *Send this back. I don't want it.* You know, it's this prize," he went on. "That's what did it, I think. That's what pushed you. The fact that when I die, someone might actually remember me and think about me for about two minutes, even though my son hates me, and my daughters think I've failed them, and my wife tells me she's done with me."

"Don't you ever wonder *why*?" I asked. "You think these things just happen to you, don't you—that you're this innocent bystander."

"No, I never said that."

"You kept the children at arm's length," I said. "Even now. Their father wins the Helsinki Prize, and you don't particularly want them there."

"Did it ever occur to you why I wouldn't want them to watch all this, or to *see* them watching this?"

"No," I said. "It hasn't."

"Well, maybe it should."

"You're completely mysterious to me, Joe," I said. "I never understand how you can do the things you do."

"I see," said Joe. He lay on his back and closed his eyes for a moment. "I'd like to remind you that no one forced you to accompany me through life, Joan," he added.

"Define *force*," I said. "You were who you were; you demanded things. And I had nothing, I was in awe of you. Basically, I was a pathetic person." He didn't try to refute this, and I added, for some reason, "I had a drink with Nathaniel Bone."

Joe stared, then he nodded. "I get it. He started working on you, is that it? What did he say? *Leave him, Joan. Have your own life. You can do better. He's a pig, that husband of yours, wouldn't give me his blessing, wouldn't authorize me to write his biography.*"

"He said nothing like that," I told him.

The heat of the sauna was everywhere on me now. I thought I'd faint, or melt, or decompose. Finally I sat down on the wooden bench across from Joe, the two of us red-faced and furious and unrelenting in this tiny room. I tossed water onto the pile of rocks and watched as a wall of steam sprang up between us.

"You," Joe had said to me that afternoon in the Waverly Arms in 1956. "Read."

He'd brought my hand down onto the pile of pages he'd written that day while I went off to my parents' apartment. I'd made the appropriate cooing sounds of enthusiasm and surprise, and then I'd sat on the bed to read the first twenty-one pages he'd frantically written of *The Walnut*. He actually sat across from me and watched me read to myself.

"Joe, you're making me nervous," I'd said. "Please stop." But I was just buying time, for already, three minutes into the thing, I was panicking.

Finally I kicked him out and he walked through the Village on his own, wandering along Bleecker Street, stopping in at a record store, where he stood in a booth and listened to Django Reinhardt. Eventually he couldn't take it anymore—he just had to know what I thought—and he came back to the hotel.

"Well?" he demanded, the moment he came into the room.

I had finished a while ago. The pages were already facedown, and I was smoking. I thought of the rejection letters he'd told me he'd received from literary magazines, even the teeny, inconsequential ones. "Try us again," they'd offered in a sprightly handwriting, as if he had all the time in the world to keep trying, as if someone might support him financially while he painstakingly tried and tried.

"Look," I said, and I was almost in tears. "You asked me to be honest, and I will," though later, when I thought about it, I realized that he hadn't, in fact, specifically *asked* me to be honest; that was my own assumption of what he wanted. I paused, then said, "I'm really, really sorry. But it just doesn't work for me." I squinted up my eyes and tilted my head, as though in sudden dental pain. "Somehow it never really comes alive," I added quietly. "I wanted it to more than anything, and I mean, my *God*, it's the story of the beginning of our relationship, so shouldn't it actually *resonate*? Shouldn't it make me feel all the emotions I've actually been feeling? Like the part where Susan goes to the apartment of Professor Mukherjee to feed his cat, and then she and Michael Denbold sleep together? I found myself thinking, *I have no idea of who these people are.* Because, well, no offense, Joe, you haven't made them real."

He slumped down beside me. "But what about 'No Milk on

Sunday'?" he said angrily. "That wasn't so different. You liked that story."

I cast my eyes down, plucked at the pilly blanket. "I was lying," I whispered. "I'm really sorry. I couldn't think what else to do."

"Oh, fuck this," said Joe. He stood up then, and said, "This isn't going to work."

"*What* isn't?"

"This whole thing, this relationship with you. This life. I can't do it, I just can't."

"Joe," I said, "just because I didn't like your novel doesn't mean—"

"Yes, it does!" he cried. "What am I supposed to do, be your little houseboy? Sit here and wash the clothes and cook a crown roast while you become a literary sensation?"

I seem to remember that at this point I began to cry. "Our relationship isn't about writing," I said. "We have other things, other ways in which—"

"Oh, just shut up, Joan," Joe said. "Just shut up. The more you speak, the worse it gets."

"Joe, listen to me," I said. "I left *college* for you. I know this is right. Think of what it feels like."

"I can't remember," he said petulantly.

He got himself a pack of cigarettes and smoked one after another, calming himself down. He didn't have to break it off with me tonight, he seemed to realize; he could still take more time to think, to figure it all out. Where was he going to go, back to Northampton to his angry wife, Carol, and their beet-red, crying baby and a college that no longer wanted him?

After a while he picked up the doomed pages, held them out to me, and said, "All right. I've been humbled. Show me what's wrong. I can take it."

"Really?"

"Really."

We sat together with the pages spread out before us, and I

pointed out the obvious gracelessness of certain lines, the missed opportunities of others. I found I was able to see everything with clarity, as though the bad passages had all been highlighted by some overly helpful undergraduate. I'd been the undergraduate, once, reading novels for my literature classes and seeing the thread of the text, the art and nuance and sly imposition of meaning. *What did the writer intend?* This was the question we always posed, though really it was pointless to ask this. No one could know; no one could see into the densely packed, squiggled brains of those nineteenth-century novelists we read. And even if we *could* know, it wouldn't matter, because the book became the body, the brain, the guts of the author. And the author himself— or, occasionally, *herself,* those bonneted Brontës, that arch social observer Austen—became the husk, the dried-out casing, no longer good for anything.

The books lasted if they were good enough. If they spoke loud enough. Who cared, finally, *who* had written them? I loved them as things, as jewel boxes, as jewels themselves. And I wanted to turn Joe's manuscript into something I could love, too, and so I started in carefully.

"Now if it were me," I said, "I would do it this way. You're *not* me, of course, so please feel free to ignore this," I continued, and I took a pencil to the pages and began gently crossing out words, replacing them with words that, the minute they appeared, were so obviously better, so obviously the antidote to his poor choices. I kept crossing words out until the page was simply one long blacked-out sheet. Then, after I'd finished, I retyped the new version on Joe's typewriter; God, I thought, even my *typing* was better than his. I sat there working like a pert executive secretary, the words arriving as though they were being dictated by a hidden boss. I simply wrote them as if I'd lived them; it was no different from writing the stories I'd done in Joe's class at Smith, and yet now the scenes lasted longer, the dialogue could be as charged as I wanted, I could be leisurely with description yet always economical, because I knew that less was more. Professor Castleman had told me. When I was finished I handed the manuscript to him in silence, but I was thrilled, suppressing my own happiness, my own pride and vanity, which seemed capable of spilling over if I wasn't careful.

Later that night, when we were both calmer, we went for a walk in the neighborhood, stopping in at a bright little Italian pastry shop to eat the squares of chestnut cake we both liked. "I'm very confused about everything in my life," he said. "If I can't write a decent novel, if I can't get it published, then I'm fucked, Joanie."

"You're not fucked."

"Yes, I am."

He told me about how he'd always wanted to be a writer, ever since he was a fatherless kid at the Brooklyn Public Library, escaping his apartment of overbearing women, crouching in the stacks reading novels. He was almost in tears now as he talked about this. He turned away, his mouth tight, trying to keep himself composed. "My father was there every day, and then suddenly he wasn't. And that was it."

Joe wanted my help now, he said. Would I do that for him? It would only be this one novel; he could tell me things about the world that he'd witnessed or learned or simply intuited, and I could write them down; his head and his life were stuffed with experiences.

"After this one book," he said, "it'll be your turn. You'll do a novel. You'll be amazing."

And it made sense to me; I could help him just this once, I could basically walk him through the entire book, and it wouldn't be so bad. I would give him a crash course in how to do it, and then he'd never need me again in quite the same way, and I could in fact go on to write my own novels, as he'd said. He would be a novelist, and he would be mine, and we could move from the Waverly Arms into someplace better.

Joe had piles of favorite novels back in the house he'd left in Northampton; he could quote from them with his eyes shut, those brilliant, heat-packing men like James Joyce, whose work made him lovesick each time he read it. But he wouldn't become part of that fraternity, those men who had been packaged into neat paperbacks, carried everywhere under the arms of college students and dreamy lovers of literature. All he had was the look, the attitude, the reverence and the desire to be a great writer, but that was meaningless without what he called "the goods." If he kept at it now, on his own, he'd spend his life publishing stories in *Caryatid* and the like, those tiny magazines printed on cheap paper in someone's basement. *Try us again! Try us again!* the rejection slips cried in mocking mouse-voices.

It would just be one book, *The Walnut.* And I would be its shaper, working every evening after I came home from Bower & Leeds. It was a noble act on my part, and it would rescue us. Neither of us wanted a life of lulling routine, of sleepy academia, of a husband and wife listening to the songs of *South Pacific* as we got dressed for a faculty party on a snowy night. That was a life he'd already lived, and which I'd seen up close. I could even write about it if I had to. First novels were always at least somewhat autobiographical, and this one would basically leave nothing out from Joe's first marriage, from the triangle we'd formed, Joe and me and the rejected Carol.

"Just this once," he repeated.

Just this once is meaningless. *The Walnut* was too big, and everything worked too beautifully, our life opening wide, Joe so happy and calm, together with Elaine Mozell's cautionary words. Back then, who needed to try and struggle to become a woman writer in this world that had little regard for women, except *extremely* occasionally when they were brilliant and beautiful and attached to important men like Mary McCarthy was, or, more often, when they seemed empty and blank, or when they smelled delicious and paraded before you in their scant and scalloped underthings? Women were dazzling, they were ownable, and when they became writers the things they wrote were ownable too: dead-on miniatures that often focused on a particular

THE WIFE / 199

corner of the world, but usually not the whole world itself. Men were the ones who owned the world; Joe could do that, too, and he would never be threatened, would never leave me, and I, too, would have an extraordinary time of it, seeing everything, going along for the ride. I was meek, I had no courage, I wasn't a pioneer. I was *shy.* I wanted things but was ashamed to want them. I was a girl, and I couldn't shake this feeling even as I had contempt for it. This was the 1950s, and then it was the sixties, and by this time Joe and I had ironed it all out; we had a rhythm going, a style, a way of life together.

The children got raised, mostly, with lots of help from sitters. I had to hand them off all the time, like all working mothers do, and it almost broke me apart. They would cry as a sitter carried them off, and they would reach out to me with desperate arms, as though they were being taken to the electric chair. We had as much baby-sitting help as we needed, though often Joe and I had to lock ourselves in the room while the kids pounded on the door and wanted something from us.

"Focus, Joanie," he would say. "We've got a long way to go here."

He gave me plots, and anecdotes, and he disciplined me, keeping me in that room with him. He lay across the bed and I sat at his typewriter. We threw ideas back and forth; he told me stories from training camp during the Korean War, and he told me stories about the household he'd grown up in, all the women surrounding him, his big, florid mother and his grandmother and his aunts, and sometimes I climbed onto the bed and lay across him, saying I was wiped out, overwhelmed, that I didn't know what it was like to be male, that I was out of my depth, but he always told me he would be my guide.

"And what am I supposed to be?" I asked.

"Well, let's call you my interpreter."

In the beginning, I always wrote slowly, just a page or two a day when I came home from Bower & Leeds. This made Joe irritable. "I know I don't have a right to complain," he'd begin.

"You're right about that," I'd say.

"But can't you try to grease the wheels, so to speak?" he asked.

" 'Grease the wheels'? What a cliché. Good thing you're not the one writing this," I said.

He'd stand behind me and rub my shoulders. After I really understood the direction a book was taking—after Joe and I had talked it through in bed at night and I'd sat thinking about how to solve some plot problem—it came faster and freer and I could pound out many pages in a row. I'd quit my job by now; all I did was write. My metabolism was pitched high, and I didn't need to stop and rest or even eat very often. Joe made us coffee and ran out for cigarettes, happily waiting around until I was done with a draft. Then I would hand it to him and he would ritually type out the final copy, sitting and pecking the whole thing out, making mostly insubstantial changes, but developing a familiarity between himself and the prose, getting to know it so it could feel like his.

The first book was dedicated to me. "To Joan, muse extraordinaire," he'd typed out himself, though as a joke I'd later substituted the words "To Joan, muse extraordinaire, with love from Joan," which he did not find funny at all. He ripped up the page like someone destroying evidence.

Months later, when one of the manuscripts was in production, I'd bow out completely, letting Joe go through the page proofs himself with a red pencil. He was happy doing that, the long pages spread out all around him, Mozart playing on the phonograph, and he was equally happy when Hal Wellman called to discuss flap copy for the book. Flap copy Joe could do. He was a perfectly good writer of the concise descriptive paragraph.

When the reviews came out in the early years, I rushed to read them first, then handed them over to him. We howled; we screamed in pleasure. Our friends were happy for Joe, though Laura Sonnengard seemed slightly confused. "You do help him with his work, right?" she asked.

"Oh, in some way, I suppose I do," I said. "I mean, I'm pretty supportive. Why?"

"It just seems so different from him," she said. "So *thoughtful*, no offense intended. You know I think Joe's terrific."

And our children, each in their own separate ways, had suspicions. The girls were quiet about it, mostly, though Alice was occasionally troubled.

"God, Mom, it's like you do most of Daddy's work for him," she'd once said when she was a teenager.

"I'm just editing, Alice," I replied lightly.

"Oh, don't bullshit me, Mom. You know better than that. My bullshit detector is going off. Whoop! Whoop! Whoop!"

She was old enough to have woken up a little bit from the dream of adolescent self-absorption and noticed a few of the events that were taking place around her, though also old enough to sustain only a dwindling interest in anything that did not directly concern her and her friends. "I think you actually do a lot of the heavy lifting, Mom," she went on, "and he just sits there clipping his toenails and eating those Sno-Balls."

My trilling laughter was excessive. "What a funny idea," I said to her. "I've basically propped your father up professionally. Why? Who would do such a thing?"

She looked at me and shrugged. "You would."

"And why would I do that?"

"I have no idea," she said.

"Well, it simply isn't true, miss," I said. "Your father is extremely talented."

Susannah, for her part, seemed as if she couldn't care less; she had little real interest in her father's novels, and whether or not they were actually written by twelve monkeys with MFA's from the Iowa Writers' Workshop. She stayed out of it, congratulating him when his books came out and rarely expressing interest in a particular novel. She didn't read them, I don't think, though she pretended to.

David, however, was intensely absorbed by fiction; so much so that, when he was young, a novel he'd read before bed would give him violent nightmares, and he'd wake up screaming and terrified. He never directly confronted me about Joe's work, though finally, it came out anyway, on the night of the book group at Lois Ackerman's house. The terrible, terrible night. I was sitting with the women blithely talking about Henry James and narrative strategy, while back at our house, David, who was staying with us because of his flooded apartment, walked quietly down the stairs to the living room, where Joe was sitting listening to jazz. Suddenly there was a steak knife at Joe's neck. Joe reared back.

"Don't move, you fat fuck," David said from behind him.

"David," said Joe, his voice a whisper, "what is it you want from me?"

"I want you to admit what you've done," David said.

This, out of nowhere. What had brought it on?

"What is it you think I've done?"

"*You* know."

"If I've been a less-than-perfect father, I apologize."

"What you've done to *Mom*," David broke in.

"Your mother is fine. She's at her book group."

"She's not fine," David insisted. "You've kept her your *slave* all these years."

"Oh, give me a break," Joe said. "I don't know what you mean. Your mother is content."

"She *thinks* she's content. You've obviously tricked her."

At which point Joe began to cry a little. "I love you, David," he said. "We used to go hiking, remember? Mount Cardigan, and that stream we found with hundreds of little fish, and you wanted us to count them?" David was unmoved. "I tell you what," Joe went on. "We'll call Mom right now at the book group and ask her to come home, okay?"

"Fine," said David.

And so they called me at Lois Ackerman's house, and though I didn't know anything yet, I was alarmed and roared home immediately. Soon I was back in our house, where Joe and David were now pacing the living room, regarding each other in mutual distrust, David still holding one of the steak knives, though no longer against Joe's neck. Joe was playing the good, slightly impotent father, a soft-bellied, easygoing man.

"Sweetheart, what's happened?" I asked David. He looked sickly and sweaty, this boy we'd once driven to Wesleyan with a station wagon full of things, the trunk and the extra-long sheets and the mini-refrigerator that he was supposed to stock with Coke and beer and peanut butter and other college-boy things, but which instead remained empty, its door swung open like a looted safe.

"Ask him," David said.

"He wants to kill me," Joe blurted out. "He held that knife to my throat."

"Give me the knife," I told my son. "It's a good steak knife. It belongs in the set." I was improvising. To my astonishment, he simply handed it to me. "Thank you," I said. "Can we all sit down now?"

So we all sat in the family room, beneath the row of Audubon prints, the birds staring blankly, and David said, "I've always known what a monster Dad is, with a big swinging dick. It's like he's turned you into his fucking handservant."

"I will not sit here and listen to this garbage," Joe said. "Because it's nonsense, okay? Absolute, raving nonsense." I didn't say a word. "Feel free to jump in at any time, Joan," he added.

"All right. It's nonsense," I said, and David watched me, his eyes narrow, wanting the truth, trusting that he could get it from me, and I nodded slightly and he seemed to relax a little. "Total nonsense. I'm not your father's handservant. I'm his wife. His partner. Just like any other couple." The words were ludicrous; they embarrassed me as I spoke them. But what was I supposed to do? Come clean? Make him feel justified? I couldn't do that; I had to be his mother. He was a grown man but he was still immature and fragile. He needed to be protected from his own fears. He wanted them negated.

"You don't write his books?" David said.

"No," I told him. "Of course not."

"I don't believe you," David said, but he seemed uncertain. He kept looking at me, wanting guidance.

"I can't make you believe me," I told him softly. "It's up to you what you believe." He looked as though he would cry. And then I took his head in my hands, that head filled with stylized comic-book imagery, all of it laid out in frames and dialogue balloons, and I pressed it against me, onto my shoulder, the edge of my breast, the wide swell that women use to comfort men and children alike. "I'm fine, David. Really," I said. "No one controls me."

David didn't understand that in the early years with Joe, everything was more than bearable. It was *fun*. The reviews excited me. I possessed a secret talent, and the secrecy added to the pleasure. Joe was expansive and loving to me, and because we stayed close together for the gestation of each novel, he truly felt that he was, in a sense, the actual, sole author. He must have found a way to believe it, because if he didn't, his life would have been excruciating. As it was, over time, there were nights when Joe would pace and smoke and fret, and he'd say to me, "I feel so bad about what we've entered into here," never naming it directly, always alluding, as though the house were bugged, and I would end up calming *him* down, which then made me forget that I was the one who needed the reassurance, not him.

We fell right into it; it happened fast and slow and after a while it didn't seem so strange, sitting in those rooms together all those years, me at the typewriter, him on the bed; then, later on, me at the Macintosh computer with its little smiling face, him on the Abdomenizer, desperately attempting to corrugate his softening abdomen.

But there were tiny cracks. He began to cheat in obvious ways; his abdomen was being corrugated not for me but for other women. His betrayals had started early, not long after his first book came out, and I both knew it and didn't know it, because when I thought of what I'd done for him, I felt there ought to have been some reciprocity.

But here is the partial list of Joe's women:

Our baby-sitter Melinda.
Brenda the prostitute.
Several women at readings Joe gave around the country.
Merry Cheslin.
Two publicists named, coincidentally, Jennifer.
The occasional letter-writer and ardent reader who came on
    a pilgrimage to meet him.
The young woman who worked at a grocery in Chinatown.
The film producer who made *Overtime* into the 1976 dud
    starring James Caan and Jacqueline Bisset.

I ignored it whenever I could. It never occurred to me to say, Okay, here's your part of the deal: *Control yourself.*

Control yourself. But they can't, these men, can they? Or *can* they, and we simply don't require them to? I tried to force him every few years, confronting him and making demands, and he'd be vague and apologetic or perhaps defiant, insisting I was making it all up, at which point I thought it was better to drop the whole matter. What if he *left*? I knew I didn't want that, so why harangue him since he seemed incapable of change?

"You should take a lover," my friend Laura suggested, for after her divorce she'd slept with a string of men and had enjoyed herself thoroughly until she contracted genital herpes from an urban planner. But I had no interest; Joe was more than I could take.

Most of the men I know from this generation have made love with women who weren't their wives; it was a requirement, at least back when they were young husbands. If you were a man, you worked so very hard, your neck bent in unnatural positions over a keyboard. So you needed the downtime, the recreation, the notion of women as Ping-Pong, poker, women as a dip in a stream. Sorry, wives, they'd say, but this is something you'll never understand, so we husbands can't even try and explain it. Just let us be. The long-term damage to the marriage will be insignificant compared with what it would be if we *did* control ourselves, and forced ourselves to keep our bursting needs under wraps.

He told me details for the novels, sexual stories of great interest, and we pretended that they were all fantasies from an imaginative and restless man. "What if," he said about a character, "the husband has an affair with the young woman at the grocery in Chinatown? The one who sells him star anise?"

"All right," I said. "Tell me."

So he told me why and how and what it might feel like to this character, this flawed male we were inventing, and then I *interpreted* for him without judgment, put it all into a storm of language that came from somewhere—who knew where: my history, my education, my central nervous system, the lobe of my brain that was wired for imagination?—all the while sitting stone-faced at his writing desk.

He sat on the bed and watched me type, nodding like someone listening to jazz as the clack-clacking went full tilt. He loved me so much and so continually. His gratitude could be intuited at all hours of the day, at least for a while. I was his other half, his better half, and there hasn't been a single day, all these years, when I haven't been reminded of this.

The walls in the Presidential Suite of the Helsinki Inter-Continental Hotel may be especially thick, but they aren't thick enough to have contained the argument Joe and I had inside those massive rooms. Other guests down below must have heard us fighting at dawn, though most likely none of them knew exactly what they were hearing, for our words were spoken in rapid, anguished English.

We were back in the bedroom now, out of the sauna, both of us still pink and overheated, him in a towel, me in my sopping nightgown.

"If you were this miserable with everything, miserable enough to leave," he said, "then you should have told me, 'I can't take it anymore.' And I would have done something."

"What?" I said. "What would you have done?"

"I don't know," Joe said. "But we're *married*. Doesn't that count? We have kids, and those sweet grandkids, and real estate, and Keoghs and IRA's and friends we've known forever, who are going to start dying on us one by one, and where will you be then? Where will you be, Joan? Living on your own in some apartment? Being brave? Is that what you want for yourself? Because I find it hard to believe it is." He was pleading, which was something I'd rarely seen him do over the years, and I was surprised. "Every marriage is just two people striking a bargain," he went on in a softer tone. "I traded, you traded. So maybe it wasn't even."

"No, it wasn't," I said. "It was the worst deal in the world, and I grabbed it. I should have done my own work, taken my time, waited awhile and watched things start to change in the world. But they haven't changed enough anyway. Everyone is still fascinated by the inner lives of men. *Women* are fascinated. Men win, hands down. They've got control. Look around. Turn on the TV; there they are in Congress, with their bad ties and their seaweed comb-overs—"

"Joan," said Joe, "I'm not a terrible person."

"No, you're not. You're an enormous baby, that's all you are."

He nodded. "I'm sure that's true." Then he shook his head and said in a small voice, "I just don't want to be alone at this point in my life. I can't even think about what that would be like."

But I knew he could take care of himself, even if that meant he fed himself forever on ham in a can and wheels of Brie and liquor-enriched stews, and the lunches his editor or agent or an awards committee treated him to. He didn't need my physical, corporeal presence, either, for there would still be young women skimming by who would approach his overstuffed body with awe. He needed me at the computer, me with my head bent, tapping away.

"No more of this, Joe," I found myself saying. "You'll get used to living with yourself. *I* did." Then, less angrily, I said, "You'll be okay."

He sat on the bed and lay back against the pillow, as if he was beginning to give in to the idea that I really would leave him when we returned home, that this wasn't just histrionics.

"So let me ask you this," he said finally. "What exactly did you say to Nathaniel Bone?"

"I said nothing to him that would freak you out," I assured him.

"Oh, good," he said. "To be honest, I thought you'd probably said something you couldn't take back."

We were quiet, and I wondered what good it was to leave Joe. Would it register with him at all? So he'd never publish another book; so what? He'd already published enough; Helsinki was honoring him now, saying, *You've done a good job; now you are free to fade away with aplomb.* Finally, maybe he understood that that would be the best option. Taking more accolades from the world would be too greedy. Even now, I realized, he was possibly a little embarrassed about himself. Perhaps that was what he'd meant when he asked me to think about why he hadn't really wanted Alice and Susannah to come to Finland. This prize was so big, too big, that he wouldn't have been able to meet their gaze. He would have been ashamed of himself.

Maybe he'd always been a little bit ashamed. But that had never changed things before, and probably it wouldn't change anything now. He wanted to keep going and going forever, with me beside him.

"You know, I think I have to tell Bone, actually," I said after a moment.

"What?" Joe said. "Joan, don't forget, I'm an old man here; I'm not your enemy. It's just *me.*"

I thought of Joe as a young, thin man with dark curls and fanning chest hair, and was again astonished at the change and bloat that had taken place, that I'd helped to take place. He'd gone soft

as a Sno-Ball and so had I, and we'd had a soft, good life together
and now it was almost done.

"Yeah, Bone should probably hear everything," I said to Joe,
and I stood up and walked into the dressing room with its hulk-
ing bureau. I'd get dressed, I decided, and go see Nathaniel, waking him up in his own hotel room and starting to talk to him
before he even understood what was happening.

I was taking a bra from the drawer when Joe's hand moved to
my shoulder and he turned me around to him.

"Come on, this is crazy," he said. "Don't make us go through
this. You know you're just putting on a show for me. And it's very
effective."

"Stop it," I said, pulling on my bra. My hands were shaking as
I closed the clasp. "Bone is staying on the sixth floor, he gave me
his room number, and I'm going to sit down and have a drink
with him and tell him to get his notepad out, and then I'm going
to give it to him because I don't want to be this person I *hate*. I'm
a good writer, Joe, really good. You know what? I even won the
Helsinki Prize!"

That was too much for him. As I moved to get past him again
he pushed me back against the dresser. The blond wood shuddered but didn't sway; everything in this room was built for royalty, for people who needed their furniture to be as thick as trees.
I pushed him back, not hard, pushing like a *girl*, I thought, using
both hands.

He fell against the bed and all of a sudden his shoulders rose
in a peculiar way and he clenched his jaw and said, "*Shit*, Joan."

Which was just like his heart attack at The Cracked Crab, the
same tight words, the same staccato. "Joe," I said now, "are you
okay?" He didn't respond. "Help!" I cried out into the room.
"Someone, help!" But my voice was tiny and the suite was a
fortress.

"Okay, now, okay," I said to him, to myself, terrified, and then
I called the front desk and heard the cooing European ring. I
shouted into the phone; the person who answered was calmly

confident, and I knew that paramedics would be rushing in momentarily, and that they would administer CPR to Joe, breathing their cold, snow-blown breath into him. But until then I had to do it, for he seemed to have stopped breathing, though I wasn't sure, was too frantic to think clearly, and I knelt over him the same way Lev Bresner had done once before in that seafood restaurant, applying hands and pressing hard, putting my mouth against his and wildly blowing.

In emergencies, men and women tilt each other's chins up, swipe a finger in to clear the airway, then hotly breathe, trying to remember the sequence laid out in the CPR manual, the code to crack. I couldn't remember anything I'd learned so long ago, and so I just pushed on him and breathed and breathed into him.

It was as if we were engaging in some alternate language, some strange ritual, like the way Eskimos say hello by rubbing noses, at least according to the legends of children. My own daughters used to do that with each other, standing with no space between them, tip of nose to tip of nose, heads moving from side to side, feeling the graze and touch, the thrill that accompanied the barest connection of separate bodies. After all these years, I crouched over Joe Castleman, his head tipped back, our mouths open upon each other, a husband and wife finally saying good-bye.

Chapter Seven

DYING IN A strange country is similar to being born: the confusion, the nonsensical language, the activity, the fuss, with the flickering light of the person in crisis as the centerpiece. They worked on him and worked on him, those indefatigable Finns, and though he didn't respond at all, I held his hand and told him insistently he was going to live. Someone pressed an oxygen mask over his face, and those dark eyes of his did a fade, and I tried to pull him back to me, to keep him, to hold him here.

Death was pronounced not in the hotel room but later, in a triage room at the nearby Loviso Hospital, where a young doctor, who appeared to me like a lesser character in an Ibsen play, removed the earpieces of his stethoscope, which trembled like fronds, and said, "Mrs. Castleman, I must say to you it is over."

I was stricken and shocked, and my voice cracked, and I sobbed against that man's narrow chest. He didn't try to stop me, but then after a very long time I simply stopped on my own. Joe was lying on the table with loops of wires still attached to him. He was Gulliver, passive, slumbering, inappropriate, huge, and it was an unbearable sight. Excruciating. A dead man is nothing; it's all gone from him, everything you've ever thought was his. Eventually, two nurses came in and quietly removed the wires; I could hear sucking sounds as the rubber cups were taken off. I sat on a hard chair beside Joe, terrified to touch him, for his body seemed so abraded now, with its Venn diagram of pink circles everywhere. For a few minutes we stayed awkward and resigned and pitifully lonely, side by side, the way we'd often been in the last years of our marriage.

The next day, after the paperwork of death had been finished, after I'd cried until my eyes could barely open, and then actually slept at night, pushed along by the tiny blue pills the doctor at the hospital had given me, I left Finland forever. Joe's body lay in a temporary, plain casket secured in the cargo hold, and I held a crushed, wet bloom of tissues in my hand. Several stunned representatives from the Finnish Academy had accompanied me to the Helsinki-Vantaa Airport, though I told them it wasn't necessary, for the delegation from Joe's publishing house and literary agency was there, too. Everyone seemed frightened to talk to me at length. Joe's agent, Irwin Clay, could barely meet my eyes. I was steered into a VIP room and it was arranged for me to board the plane early, so as not to confront the several reporters who were quietly collecting nearby. When I said good-bye to the people from the academy, Teuvo Halonen spontaneously cried, and had to be led away so he wouldn't upset me more.

Beside me on the plane was a mournful, slightly jowly woman from the academy named Mrs. Kirsti Salonen, whose job it was to accompany me back to New York, even though I said I would be all right. If I'd wanted company I could have sat with Irwin, but the academy had insisted on sending someone, and for some reason I was grateful. Mrs. Salonen patted my hand and whispered solicitous, parental comments to me. She spoke gently about how important it was to be good to myself and, as time passed, to let others do good things for me. Somewhere in there she spoke about God, too, and about how I should try to sleep.

"Mrs. Salonen, may I ask you something personal?" I suddenly said, and she nodded. "Are you married?"

"Oh yes," she said. "My husband and I just celebrated our twenty-seventh anniversary." She reached into her handbag and produced a photograph of a lanky man in a short-sleeved shirt with a pen clipped onto his pocket. "Erik is a chemical engineer," Mrs. Salonen went on. "A quiet man who likes things just so. We have a weekend house in Turku that we enjoy."

Will you be *my* wife? I wanted to ask her. Will you take care of me now, the way you certainly take care of Erik the chemical engineer?

I'd been a good wife, most of the time. Joe had been comfortable and safe and surrounded, always off somewhere talking, gesturing, doing unspeakable things with women, eating rich foods, drinking, reading, leaving books scattered around the house facedown, their spines broken from too much love. Late at night, or during the day, he told me stories of things that had happened to him, or ideas that had occurred to him, and I filed them away or took them out for reuse whenever the time came, and allowed an anecdote to be boiled and cooled and transformed into something recognizable but new. Something that would be mine, but would still always be partly his, too. It wasn't fair, of course; it had never been fair, right from the beginning. Fairness wasn't what I'd wanted.

Sleep, now: *that* was what I wanted. The flight home was long, and I tilted my seat back and thought about Joe as a child, attending his father's funeral. The moment his father had died, something might have collapsed in Joe and never been restored. Or maybe that was simply an excuse, for plenty of young boys without fathers grow up to write strong and urgent prose, often about loss. Joe could never do that; he didn't have the natural ability, and no one could ever have implanted it in him, like a microchip, a pig valve, a miracle.

Suddenly the brunette flight attendant appeared again, the same woman Joe and I had been served by on our way over, she of the booming bosom, who had leaned across him with her scented acreage of flesh and her basket of cookies and brought him briefly to attention. If she'd been there in the moments when he was dying, would she have saved him? He'd always been so directed toward women, yet so uninterested in them at the same time, a disparity that caused a kind of bored erection to lift, a pointless hot-air balloon, a need to possess a woman that was immediately followed by a need to be somewhere else, to be out in the world, walking around and thinking of simple things that men like Joe Castleman love: the taste of a barely cooked steak with a heap of fried onions, the mossy smell of an aged single-malt scotch, the perfect prose of a novella written by a genius in Dublin nearly a hundred years ago.

"Mrs. Castleman, I'm so sorry about your loss," the flight attendant said to me when she leaned over now with a tray of canapés, and I thanked her. Mrs. Kirsti Salonen and I chewed the soft dough in silence. Then dinner was placed in front of us, and we ate that, too, and drank wine and settled back into our seats for the ride.

Hours passed, and eventually we reached the time in any transatlantic flight when travelers fall into a kind of shallow sleep, eyes skittering beneath their lids, no dreams penetrating the endlessly rebreathed air above everyone's lowered or thrown-back head. Mrs. Salonen was now asleep beside me, her head leaning slightly too close, as though we were a couple, two lovers crossing the Atlantic. She would have been embarrassed if she saw how near to me she was; she would have drawn back and murmured apologies, but I would have seen for myself that even beneath a thick lacquer of formality, there was often a stirring toward love.

If Joe had lived, he would have been wide awake beside me. Bored and restless, his fingers moving on the thick, fleshy armrest. I would have been dozing and he would have been the sentinel, staying alert. I thought of how, that first day we'd met in his class at Smith, he'd read the end of "The Dead" aloud, a piece of writing so memorable that it briefly silenced everyone who read it or heard it. Who in the world could write like that? Neither of us could; neither of us could even try. We'd just shaken our heads, marveling. Then one day we'd talked, and stirred, and met in Professor H. Tanaka's bed, and started a life. It had swiftly carried us here, to the highest point, the lowest point, the end.

Now the lights were all off up and down the rows of the airplane, except for my own, which sent its yellow beam spreading down onto me and onto the edges of Mrs. Kirsti Salonen's hair. I was almost asleep when I suddenly became aware that someone was standing over me, saying something.

"*Joan.*"

I looked up and was startled to see Nathaniel Bone. His trip was over, too, and he was returning home.

"Nathaniel," I said. "I didn't know you were on the plane."

"Yeah, I'm way in the back. In steerage," he whispered. "I hope it's okay that I'm here. You probably want to be alone."

"It's okay," I said.

"Listen, my God, I'm so sorry about Joe. I was going to write you a condolence letter when I got home. I've already started composing it in my head. I'm stunned, Joan. Stunned."

"Thank you," I said. Beside me, my seatmate moved around and opened her eyes briefly.

I turned back to Nathaniel. "We can't talk here," I said. "Maybe we should go back to where you're sitting."

He nodded eagerly, and I stood up and followed him down the aisle, parting the ice blue Marimekko curtains that separated the first-class passengers in the nose of this Finnair plane from the larger group lying in repose in business class. They were, it seemed, actually all businessmen, their ties loosened and tossed to the side, their heads flung into profile, eyes shut, computers resting on tray tables, or clutched in laps like transitional objects. Then, onward through the next curtain we went, entering the bad-breath air of Economy, the long, enormous cabin with its pockets of darkness and light, entire families sitting four across, with bags of chips openmouthed, rustling, their bodies turning rotisserie-style under inadequate squares of blanket, the occasional baby howling and being dandled by an overworked mother singing a Finnish lullaby. The aisle itself was littered as though there had been a windstorm. I stepped on a newspaper, and then on a woman's shoe.

In the second-to-last row, Nathaniel's seatmate was asleep, leaning halfway onto the other seat, and because the seat across the aisle was taken, we stood together in the very rear of the plane, by the bathroom and the metal drinks cart.

"Who's meeting you at Kennedy?" he asked.

"My daughters."

I'd called Susannah and Alice from the hospital, and their voices, even from so far away, and with the accompaniment of that inevitable overseas hiss, had sounded so forlorn. Heart-broken. "Oh no, Mom," Susannah had said, sobbing. "Oh my God," said Alice. "*Dad.*"

I'd had to leave a message on David's answering machine with the news. (It was a miracle to me that he even owned an answer-ing machine.) I didn't like telling him this way, but I wanted him to learn it from me, instead of from somewhere else. He hadn't called back yet. I didn't know what his reaction would be, whether he would seem indifferent or glib or even, maybe, heartbroken, too. I really had no way to predict.

"You won't have to go back to Weathermill alone," Nathaniel was saying now. "That's good."

"I know," I said, imagining the way Alice would come in and commandeer the house, and Susannah would immediately make me a jar of preserved lemons that I would never use and which would become barnacled in the back of the pantry. But at least both daughters would be there at night, sleeping in the rooms they grew up in. Now grown women too big for their childhood beds, they would return, briefly leaving their own families to help their widowed mother find her way, and to help themselves through the bewilderment and clumsy sorrow brought on by the death of a parent.

At night, when I found myself unable to sleep, just like Joe I'd wander the house and pause outside their doors. I'd hear them breathing, and maybe it would calm me down a little. They were still my girls, my children, Joe's and mine, along with everything else we had: the huge flea market of things we'd assembled, gathered up, the astonishing array we'd amassed throughout the years, like any couple does.

"I came to the Academic Bookstore like I said I would," Nathaniel was telling me softly. "You didn't show, and I was surprised. Then I heard someone talking about Joe Castleman, saying he was *dead,* and I thought, *This can't be,* and I ran back to the hotel to ask the concierge if what I'd heard about Mr. Castleman was true, and he said it was. I couldn't believe it. I still can't."

Bone was both heartfelt and unconvincing, I thought, and I was reminded that Joe had never liked him, and that I didn't either. He was insinuating, he was always around, he was like a cat in a bookstore window, letting his tail slowly drape across all the books as he wandered by. Joe's instinct was sound when he'd decided not to give him anything all those years ago.

Now Bone was waiting to see what I would tell him. I wanted to tell him nothing. What Joe and I had done together was my business and not his. I didn't want to make a gift of this information; I didn't want to let him run with it. It was mine, and I'd do with it what I wanted, but not yet. Joe had just died and I was now alone, the slap of it stinging, the rest of life waiting.

Talent, I knew, didn't just disappear from the earth, didn't fly up into separate particles and evaporate. It had a long half-life; maybe I could use it eventually. I could use parts of what I'd seen and done and had with him, making something vicious or beautiful or loving or regretful out of it, and maybe even putting my name on it.

"What you were talking about the other day at the Golden Onion," I said to Nathaniel. "About Joe and me? About his writing, and how he hadn't seemed talented early on?"

Bone nodded, and his long hand jerked slightly, as though his impulse, like any journalist's, was to reach for his notepad. But he stopped himself and ran his hand through his hair instead.

"Yes," he said.

"Well, I wanted to say that what you implied isn't true."

"It's not?" His voice became suddenly flatter, and he looked hard at me.

"No," I said. "It's not. It would be great if it were," I went on. "If I could claim to have written like that." He kept looking at me, shaking his head. "I guess in a way I was sort of playing with you the other day," I said. "Sorry about that."

"Oh," he said, slouching down, turning into himself. "I see."

Then he shrugged, absorbing the disappointment all at once, starting to move on. For though he hadn't gotten what he'd hoped, he'd actually *been there* in Finland when Castleman died, and that was an extraordinary feat, he imagined. He would flesh out the final scenes for his manuscript based on the words of ancillary figures in the story: nurses' aides in strange, pie-crust-crimped hats, frightened maids at the hotel, the young Ibsen-character doctor, who may well have provided him with a physical description of Joe in his last moments: the slack mouth, the powerlessness of an old man with a fragile heart.

Nathaniel Bone would be all right, I saw; he'd go on and on, rarely at a loss, always being slipped information, treated specially, given access, allowed to roam the world. He didn't really need anything further from me now, after all, and yet here we were together, and for some reason I felt I ought to think of something else to say before I went back to my seat.

"Look," I told him, "I'll help you with the archives if you want. You can publish a couple of the letters, maybe."

"All right, great," he said, but his voice was neutral and he was probably already thinking about something else: about how odd and shocking this trip had been, or about resetting his watch back to New York time, or about a woman's long, warm back pressed up against him.

"And I'll tell you something else," I added.

All around us, people rearranged themselves in their seats like dogs in little beds, trying again and again for comfort. Another flight attendant, this one blond, opaque, unknowable, eased past us in the narrow space, carrying a tangle of headphones down the aisle. The airplane shuddered, bounced slightly, and then lifted itself higher above the world.

"Joe was a wonderful writer," I said. "And I will always miss him."

About the Author

MEG WOLITZER is the *New York Times* bestselling author of *The Female Persuasion*, *The Interestings*, *The Uncoupling*, *The Ten-Year Nap*, *The Position*, and other novels. Wolitzer lives in New York City.

THE WIFE

1. After attempting her first short story in the library stacks at Smith College, Joan, the protagonist of *The Wife*, imagines "what it [is] like to be a writer: Even with the eyes closed, you [can] see" (page 46). Explain how this observation could also be made of wives. What does Joan see even when other people think her eyes are closed?

2. In Chapter 2, Joan meets the writer Elaine Mozell, who warns Joan against trying to get the attention of the literary men's club. How might Joan's life have been different without Elaine's discouraging advice haunting her?

3. On a trip to Vietnam with Joe, Joan finds herself on an airstrip, in a segregated clump, with the wives. But Lee, the famous female journalist, chats with the men. Joan laments to herself "*I shouldn't be here!* I wanted to cry. *I'm not like the rest of them!*" (page 134) How is Joan different from the rest of the wives who appear throughout the novel? In what ways is she similar?

4. Joe's friend Harry Jacklin praises Joe's work, telling him, "You've got that extra gene, that sensitivity toward women" (page 25). Indeed, we discover that Joe's "sensitivity" is primarily thanks to his wife. How do you think Joan would have been received in the literary world if her name had been attached to the same material? Do you think she would have been as successful?

5. After Joe receives the call confirming he has won the Helsinki Prize, Joan envisions the days ahead, realizing that "I wasn't going to handle this well; it would inflame me with the worst kind of envy" (page 37). Discuss envy, regret, and loss with respect to Joan's choices regarding her writing career.

6. Over the years, many people come to admire Joan for her steely resolve in the face of blatant betrayal and infidelity. Is Joan, in fact, an admirable character? Why do you think Joan waits so long to decide to leave Joe?

7. There is a lot of talk from the women about "The Men." Specifically, Joan describes Joe as "one of those men who own the world" (page 10), and Elaine Mozell harbors contempt for the men who conspire to "keep the women's voices hushed and tiny" (page 53). What is your opinion of Joe and the men he represents? Consid-

ering that the reader sees him through the eyes of his wife, do you think he is presented fairly?

8. On being a wife, Joan admits: "I liked the role at first, assessed the power it contained, which for some reason many people don't see, but it's there" (page 119). Discuss the quiet power of wives, particularly during the late fifties, when Joan is initiated into wifehood. Do you think the power wives wield is more visible today?

9. Toward the end of the novel, Joan reveals the secret that she and Joe long shared about his career. Joan acknowledges that, among others, her "children, each in their own separate ways, had suspicions" (page 201). As a reader, are you surprised by Joan's revelation or does Joe's sudden merit as a writer seem suspect? What clues support your hunch?

10. At one point, their children, David and Alice, go so far as to confront both Joan and Joe about their secret. Do you think the children are convinced by Joan's staunch denial? If Joan were your mother, would you be disappointed or proud of her?

Look for more Simon & Schuster reading group guides online and download them for free at www.bookclubreader.com.

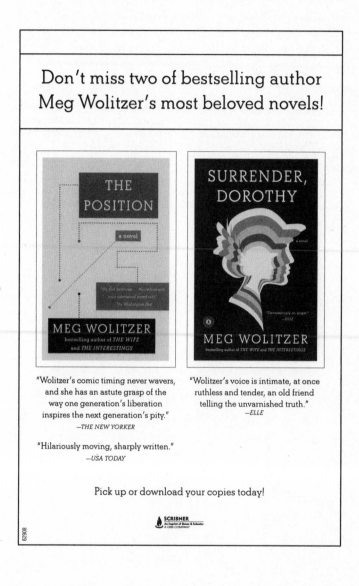